To my mother who instilled

Prologue

Hecton, West Riding of Yorkshire,

Saturday, 23rd March 1950. 6.42pm.

Detective Sergeant Douglas Blake slammed the phone down. *Talk about stupidity*. 'Robin.' he called as he struggled into his overcoat.

A puzzled Detective Constable looked up from his typewriter. 'Sarge?'

'Get your bloody coat. Now.' A single glance told Robin Mitchell to move, and fast. He'd never seen the Sergeant so animated. Overcoat in hand he poked his head around the office door. 'Magnus Yarney's out.' said DS Blake. 'The bastard's escaped from the general hospital toilets.'

The telephone began to ring. 'Fetch Mr Spencer whilst I take this.'

DC Mitchell hurried off. DS Blake took a deep breath and relaxed in an attempt to keep the tension out of his voice. The last time Yarney had been free God's voice told him to kill. He opened Christine Jones' throat to the spine. 'C.I.D. DS Blake.'

There was the muffled sound of a child crying. 'Please,' the voice was female, tremulous, faint. 'Don't hurt her.'

He looked at his watch. His heart sank. 'Hello, who's there?'

'Is that Sergeant Blake?' said the voice.

'Yes, I am. Who am I speaking to?'

'There's a man here. He's threatening to hurt my daughter.'

God no, he thought. *Not again*. 'Is his name Magnus?'

'Yes,' came the incredulous reply. 'You know him?'

He snatched up a pencil, hovered over his pad and waited. 'We've met,' he said, his voice stark. 'Now, quickly, the telephone number and your name and address.'

'Heckton 2469. Alice Collins, 27 Garden Lane, Littletown. My daughter's name is Deborah.' He jotted them down.

'Your husband?'

'Lionel, he's at Bill's, his brother's. He lives near to the Bookies on the S.Y.D. estate in Knottingley. I don't know the address.'

'Don't worry, we'll find him.' There was a clatter as Detective Inspector Ivan Spencer and DC Mitchell burst into the C.I.D. office. DS Blake put his finger to his lips and pointed to the earpiece holding it away from his head, allowing the others to listen. 'Can I talk to Magnus please, Mrs Collins?'

There were a few mumbled words before a familiar voice. 'Detective Sergeant Blake,' he said. His voice languid. The tone patronising. Anyone who didn't know him might assume that he was rational and lucid. They couldn't be more wrong. 'How nice to hear your voice again.'

'What game are you playing, Magnus?'

'Game, Sergeant?' There was a humourous edge to his voice. 'This is not a game. I just stepped out for a breath of fresh air. I will surrender, Sergeant, but only to you.'

'We have officers en route, Magnus.'

'I sincerely hope not, or have you forgotten Christine Jones.'

The threat implicit. He was more than capable of carrying it out. 'There's no need for that. I'll be there.'

Yarney exhaled slowly. 'You're wasting time, Sergeant. One hour. Or this beautiful little girl dies.'

The handset gently replaced cut off the anguish of the mother's scream and her daughter's whimper.

The three men straightened and stood back. 'Christ!' DI Spencer took a deep breath and blew out slowly as he looked out of the window gathering his thoughts. He turned to the others. His newest detective sergeant and constable. 'Right. Blake, take Mitchell and get to the hospital. Find out what happened then go to Garden Lane. I'll see you there. Mitchell, first caution these bloody half-wits. Keep a full record of everything they or anyone else says. Frightened people will want to justify their actions. Sometimes they tell the truth before they have time to think. Then find out who was where and when, and seal those toilets. No doubt there'll be someone from the prison coming down as well. And not a word about this phone call to anyone. Understood?'

Mitchell nodded. 'Yes sir.'

'Wait there until I contact you. If anyone wants to know where Sergeant Blake has disappeared to, you don't know. Blake, you two get off. I'll go and see the super. He will be delighted.'

Blake tapped his barometer as he passed: 28 and falling. More snow was forecast. Great!

The birthday card from the typists for Brian's eighth birthday two days ago still on his desk.

The uniformed officers at the rear of 27 suffered in silence hoping for a speedy conclusion as DS Blake drove slowly along Garden Lane. The information that he'd received from the hospital just something else to take into consideration. 27 looked serene. The front door was closed. The landing light was on as were those in the hallway, lounge and kitchen. All the downstairs curtains drawn. The kitchen blind down. Only the report of screams from 27 and the telephone calls from Mrs Collins and Magnus Yarney indicated there was anything amiss. He would surrender, but only to him. Now the man who twelve months ago claimed he was doing God's will is hearing God talking to him again. Urging him to kill.

Next week would be the first anniversary of Jones' murder. A sight he would remember to his dying day. Petite. Pretty. Naked. A gaping throat wound. A discarded overgrown ragdoll. Last time he gave no warning. What was he playing at? Blake parked and alighted. Turned his collar up. Pulled the brim of his trilby down and took those few icy steps. He nodded to the DI and cast an eye at the clouds as the first snowflakes, incongruous yet pretty against their surroundings began to fall. The street lights emphasised the gloom. He checked his watch. Twelve minutes. He was worried. 'More like January than spring,' he observed. He paused and stared at 27 again. 'Of all the twisted bastards to escape it has to be him. How are Mrs Collins and Deborah?'

With a grim smile DI Spencer looked over his left shoulder. 'I spoke with her not five minutes ago. She's terrified and pleading with him. He's still got the knife to the girl's throat.'

Blake glanced at the house the picture of Jones in his mind. It wasn't happening. Not again. 'I understand,' he said. 'Any news of her husband?'

'Traffic are fetching him from his brother's. The last I heard they were in Featherstone.'

'Good. Let's hope we can end this without anyone getting hurt before he gets here..'

'Agreed. What happened at the hospital?'

He snorted a laugh. 'The Super's got everyone running round in small circles. One of these days he's going to disappear up his own arse. The prison officer put Yarney in the toilet furthest from the window. Then went for a cig. Yarney did a Houdini. Gave him a five minute head start. According to the hospital Yarney's been having psychotic episodes. God is telling him to kill those who persecuted him. Probably means me.'

'Maybe, maybe not, but no unnecessary risks.' This was stupidity personified. 'They know his history and his present state of mind, yet they bloody well leave him unsupervised in a toilet with an insecure window. It beggars belief. Did you get the details?'

'The Warder's details, yes. Mitchell the rest. It leaves a nasty taste when this sort of thing happens,'

'True. No doubt the Home Office will do their own internal enquiry in due course.' DI Spencer shook his head. 'Barmy bastards!' He paused. 'We said last time that Yarney must have had an accomplice. Forensic agreed. And he couldn't have made it here this time without. That worries me. This must have been planned. But by who? Whoever it was, and the first thing tomorrow go to the prison and get a copy of

Yarney's visitor record, where the hell are they? Why didn't he make a clean getaway instead of taking hostages? Last time had nothing to do with the Collins's... And why here of all places, so close to where he murdered Jones? That'll be a year next week. I don't like it, Blake. Be bloody careful.'

'I will. Who else have we got?'

'Marksman en route from Huddersfield. With this coming down he might get here tomorrow. Valentine is freezing his nuts off ten yards to the left at 29,' he indicated with a nod. 'A couple of uniforms round the back, these two in front.'

'Fair enough,' Blake said glancing at the sky. They were lucky to have so many.

The DI pulled his overcoat tighter. 'There's an ambulance and a dog en route.'

Blake checked his watch again. Five minutes. Time was getting tight. 'Fine, I'll give them another two minutes then I'll go and have a chat with Magnus.'

The dog handler and ambulance arrived in convoy. The handler waited with the DI. His Alsatian looking as miserable as the weather.

Accompanied by the two uniformed officers and two blanket-carrying ambulance men they left their tracks. The tingling in his neck that was always present in moments of acute stress was running riot. Yarney had been completely off the radar. No previous convictions. No intelligence that he was mixed up in anything. Then he walked into Hecton nick almost twelve months ago dripping Christine Jones' blood on the floor. Put a craft knife on the counter and admitted her rape and murder. Jones had been an attractive eighteen year old convicted prostitute, but he couldn't think of anyone who deserved to die like that: Raped, and her throat opened to the spine. In his opinion Yarney should have hanged. That was no longer an option. Found unfit to plead. Now, thanks to some God almighty cock-up he'd managed to escape and taken two hostages. But why? Why abscond, take hostages and offer to surrender? More to the point he can't drive. How the Hell had he got here so fast? Just what was the bastard playing at?

DC Graeme Valentine stepped silently out of the shadows. 'Be careful, Douglas,' he said to his friend.

Blake nodded and placed his finger to his lips motioning the two officers either side of the doorway. Banged twice on the door with the edge of his fist. 'Magnus, this is Detective Sergeant Blake. You know me. You've had your fun. Now let Mrs Collins and Deborah go.'

'Are you on your own?' Magnus Yarney replied in a strong voice.

'I've got two ambulance men with me to take care of Mrs Collins and her daughter.'

'Get rid of them. Nobody's hurt. They're not needed.'

'Mrs Collins,' Blake was taking no chances. 'Has he hurt you?'

'No,' came the hesitant reply. 'We're all right.'

'Just a minute.' Blake glanced over his shoulder and nodded.

'We'll go back to the ambulance, Sergeant,' one of the ambulancemen said as they turned away, 'We'll wait there.'

'Ok,' he nodded. 'Leave me the blankets.' They passed them over. 'Right, they're going,' he called. 'There's just me.' He waved Valentine back into the shadows of 27. There was no point in upping the ante, putting Mrs Collins and her daughter at further risk. We didn't need a trigger.

Ten seconds later. A lifetime. Bolts withdrawn. A key turned. The door opened slowly, silently. Magnus Yarney standing two feet back from the threshold. Five eleven and thick set. A look of superiority. Yet his eyes were like a dead turbot. Evil personified. He liked to manipulate people. A small kitchen knife in his right hand. Mrs Collins and her distraught daughter now behind him. At least the threat of him cutting the girl's' throat had diminished. Neither wearing coats. They'd be freezing. Blake brushed the snow from the blankets. 'Here,' he said tossing the blankets to Mrs Collins. 'Put these round your shoulders.'

Yarney turned to his right. 'Ok,' he said cheerfully. For all the care in his persona he could have been in a children's playground with his daughter. 'I promised I wouldn't hurt you if Sergeant Blake came. You've got your blankets to keep you all nice and warm, you can go now.'

Blake was wary. Now was the time it could go completely tits up. 'All right Magnus, drop the knife and step back out of Mrs Collins' way.'

As if he were playing a game, Magnus Yarney held his right arm out to the side at shoulder level and slowly uncurled his fingers. The knife fell, four pairs of eyes following as it tumbled and clattered on the tiles in the hallway. He stepped to one side, and like a lazy copper on traffic duty nonchalantly waved them through.

Blake leaned forwards, his hands held out towards the distraught little girl, beckoned with his fingers and smiled. She couldn't have been any older than Brian. She looked terrified, poor kid. 'It's all right Deborah,' he said. 'You're all right now. He won't hurt you,' and breathed a sigh of relief as she and her mother took their first steps past Yarney, unseen, slid his right hand behind his back.

Valentine, back to the wall, slid a yard closer to the open doorway. The two uniformed officers followed suit. Ten yards behind, DI Spencer, the dog handler and Alsatian, and the ambulance men moved nearer.

Mrs Collins, her arm round her distraught daughter's shoulders guided her outside. As she passed the detective sergeant he stood. She said softly. 'He's got another knife tucked in his belt.'

The little girl was sobbing. Blake was struggling to hear. He turned his head to the right.

'What was that?' he said as the word KNIFE flashed into his brain. He spun round and raised his hands as Yarney, chef's knife in hand, lunged through the open doorway. Valentine diving towards Yarney in an attempt to intercept.

Blake felt the thud against his rib cage as the knife, driven deep between the ninth and tenth ribs, penetrated his heart. He felt no pain as he staggered backwards. Somewhere close-by a woman screamed. Puzzled, Blake looked at the knife hilt. Yarney was looking straight at him, a supercilious smirk on his face as Valentine tackled him to the ground. He didn't resist. The two uniformed Pc's cuffed him. Blake's knees buckled. His final thoughts of Dorothy standing in the kitchen doorway watching Brian ride his bike towards the garden gate. His vision began to blur as Graeme's face above him faded into blackness.

'I was only doing what the Lord commanded,' was the only thing that Yarney would say.

It'd been great. Mum and Dad had bought me a new bike. A proper bike: a Raleigh with a gleaming bright red frame, 3-speed sturmey-archer gears, chrome handlebars, a big black saddlebag and a dynamo for the lights. Grandad called it a real bobby-dazzler. It was a proper bike. The best bike in the street.

The weather was lousy. Mum said that I couldn't go out so I played with my new Meccano set instead. Dad had shown me how to make a racing car. So I tried. It wasn't easy and I was tired. I wasn't really bothered that I'd gone to bed before Dad came home. It happened often. Detective sergeants often had to work late as I would when I joined the police. I was still awake when I saw the blue flashing light shining on the ceiling through where the curtains were folded. That didn't bother me either. It was just Dad coming home. He sometimes put the blues on as he called them when he scrounged a lift. It was normal. His little joke. I didn't worry even though I didn't hear the door open, just Dad knocking because he'd forgotten his key, again. Mum was always telling him off for doing it. It was when I heard Mum crying and strange footsteps on the stairs I knew something was wrong. I'd never heard Mum cry before.

The policewoman, holding a handkerchief in the right hand, grabbed me at the top of the stairs.

'Why's Mum crying?'

'It's all right Brian,' she said and put her arm round my shoulders. 'Let's go down.'

'But what's the matter? Why is she crying?' There was no reply. I thought the policewoman was crying.

Mum was sitting on the settee wiping her eyes with a handkerchief. The Inspector standing facing her his cap in hand. Nobody was talking. He looked over his shoulder and nodded. The policewoman took her hand from my shoulder and I ran. Mum put her arms round me as the tears ran down her cheeks.

'Mum, what's the matter? Where's Dad? Why's the Inspector here?' Over her shoulder I could see my birthday cards on the mantlepiece. Smack in the middle was the one that Dad drew for me. He always drew one for my birthday. A pen sketch of a policeman with an arrow 'PC Brian' pointing to it. This year's with a villain in each hand and a bubble coming out of my mouth, 'You're nicked!'.

The tears came. I felt the warmth of Mum's tears as they trickled slowly down my cheek and mixed with mine. 'Brian, you've got to be brave. Dad's been badly hurt at work.'

I was confused and frightened. 'But, he's coming home.'

She loosened her arms and looked me in the eye. 'No Brian, he can't. He died.'

'No,' I shook my head. I didn't believe it. It wasn't possible. 'But he promised to make me a crane with my Meccano.'

Mum kissed me on the forehead. 'I'm sorry, I really am, Brian. He's not coming home.'

Mum said that my Dad was dead. My Dad dead? I wanted him back. My blood froze as fear took me in its icy grasp, and squeezed. ...

A Shropshire Lad

Into my heart an air that kills
From yon far country blows:
What are those blue remembered hills,
What spires, what farms are those?
That is the land of lost content,
I see it shining plain,
The happy highways where I went
And cannot come again.

A. E. Housman[1] - 1859-1936

1. https://poets.org/poet/e-housman

One

If I'm being honest my childhood came to an abrupt end the day my father was murdered.

And now, following twenty-three years of life: Bereavement. Fear. Love. Nurture. Nourishment. Education. The day had finally arrived. 10th June 1963. Within the hour I would be sworn as a police officer and follow in my father's footsteps. Along the way I had accumulated a stepfather – Joe. Identical triplet step-sisters. A half-brother. A black belt in karate. A degree in exercise physiology and anatomy, and, an attitude.

Wakefield is a small city. Administrative centre of the West Riding. Quarter Sessions Court House. Maximum security prison and, headquarters of the West Riding Police. Today was wet, umbrellas and vehicles vying for superiority. Progress was slow. Civic museum and Town Hall on the left. Police Station on the right. I glanced to my left at the four massive Doric columns fronting the building adjacent to the Town Hall and spotted the notice board. 'This is the Quarter Sessions building on the left, Joe,' I said. The wiper blades scything through the deluge. 'Next right, first left.'

'Thanks Brian,' he said. 'I see it.'

Sixty seconds later we joined the short queue of private cars disgorging their cargo of would-be police officers. I had to report to the Billiard Room at the bottom end of the Police HQ car park. 'Got everything?' said Joe as the rain relented.

That triggered a laugh. 'I hope so. One letter, one briefcase and two holdalls. Plus, uniform to collect inside.'

We shook hands and hugged. 'Keep your nose clean and we'll see you at the weekend.' As he let go he slid several folded bank notes into my breast pocket and smiled. 'Don't say a word. See you Friday.'

It was pointless arguing. I stood and raised my hand watching until my stepfather pulled his hand inside as the car disappeared between two large three-story red brick buildings.

I hadn't been a violent child, but after my father was murdered I was picked on at school by one of the older boys. "Your dad wasn't such a good copper was he? Getting himself stabbed? Go on cry-baby, cry." He'd said and prodded me hard in the chest. I thumped him twice on the nose. Mum had to see the Headmaster. We moved to Huddersfield to be near Gran Westmoreland.

Joe taught me karate. Helped me to deal with my fear and my anger. To understand that walking away from confrontation was not weakness. Not defeat.

I smiled, collected my luggage, a selection of butterflies and walked into my future.

It was busy. A snooker table surrounded by about two dozen males in various stages of undress – civilian clothes and police uniform. Everywhere, piles of clothing. A hum of excitement. I gave my name and handed my letter of appointment to the civilian inside. He ran his thumb down the list. 'Strange,' he said and looked at me. 'You're not here.'

That was a good start. 'But I've given you my letter telling me to report today.'

'Just a sec., Sergeant Staunton?'

A uniform sergeant excused himself from a conversation with a well-dressed elderly gentleman and turned towards me. 'Just a minute. Did you say, Blake?'

'Yes, Sergeant,' I said, 'Brian Blake.'

'It's all right, John,' he said to the civilian. 'He's an addition. I'll deal with him.' He turned to me. 'Right, Blake, find somewhere to dump your stuff then come back and see me.'

'It's because of your degree,' I was informed on my return. 'Once the Chief had carried out your interview he wanted you on the first available course. A vacancy occurred so you were tagged on the end of this one. This,' he indicated the pile of uniform on the bench behind him, on top of which was a pair of handcuffs and a truncheon, 'is yours.' He handed me a foolscap envelope. 'Looks a lot and it's all going with you. Go and get dressed then come back and bring this envelope. By the way, your service number is 547. You'll find confirmation in the envelope'

That startled me, '547, Sergeant? That was my father's service number,' I replied.

His smile was sympathetic. 'Yes, I know. You've got his cuffs and staff as well. You'll find 547 stamped on both.'

'You know the history, Sergeant?'

'Yes, I do. Come back when you're dressed.'

That gave me a jolt. Perhaps I would have more assistance on the course than I thought.

Before I could turn away the elderly gentleman chipped in. 'I couldn't help overhearing, Mr Blake, but when did you leave university?'

'Ten days ago, sir. I had my interview with the chief constable last Monday.' It might have been a clue but I was measured for my uniform immediately afterwards.

He smiled. 'Strike whilst the iron's hot?'

'My sentiments entirely, sir.'

'Well, good luck,' he offered his hand. 'Perhaps we will meet again.'

'I look forward to it, sir.'

Another half dozen or so joined us. It took another twenty-five minutes before everyone was in uniform. One or two had never seen collar-detached shirts before and tried to strangle themselves by putting the collar studs through sideways instead of from back to front. Quite funny but not a pretty sight. Everyone now dressed. All forms, charitable and otherwise completed. Although one or two did complain about having to join the pension scheme and the Police Federation.

The elderly gentleman, Clarence Charlton, chairman of the local magistrate's bench, had sworn everyone in. We were fully fledged, ignorant and totally clueless police officers; at least I was. The next three months would be telling.

Two

To call the police coach archaic was polite, but it did its job even though it picked up every rut travelling through Leeds City Centre. There were thirty-four on board, including the driver, Sergeant Staunton and John Oxford from Personnel. The remainder - recruits. I got chatting to Andrew Powell, a twenty-five year old, married with two children, former warehouseman from Ossett. Our conversation drowned by half a dozen noisy young lads in the three rows behind us, led by one in particular who held strong opinions about many things, including women.

'But that's the whole point, Dumbo,' he said to one of his friends. 'You learn the definitions, then you can work out your strategy in advance. If there are any problems you know exactly what to say. Your word against theirs. Game over.'

This was ridiculous. I turned in my seat. 'I couldn't help overhearing,' I said, 'Are you sure you're in the right job?'

Writ large the look on his face broadcast, *what's it to do with you?* 'What?'

'From what we and the rest of the coach have heard it sounds as though you're planning to use your position as a constable to manipulate females into sex, whether they like it or not.'

'I wouldn't put it like that,' he protested.

'You already have,' said Andrew.

The smirk was lascivious. 'Well, you've got to use all the advantages you can.'

'There's more to life than sex. And I suspect far more to becoming a police officer. You've got to be an adult.' That didn't go down well. 'Plus, you'll open more doors by knocking than trying to kick them down.'

The conversation was halted by Sergeant Staunton. 'What's the problem?'

'Nothing Sergeant,' I replied. 'I was just about to offer advice to our young colleague here on more appropriate methods of dealing with the fairer sex.'

'That won't be necessary, Blake. Turner, come with me.'

To be fair the sergeant kept it quiet. I turned to the five remaining members of the group. 'You're obviously friends. But what's your background?'

They looked at each other. 'I wouldn't put it as strong as friends,' offered one. 'We were all police cadets. It's just him. We're not all like that.'

'I'm pleased to hear it. But, police cadets?'

'School-leavers sixteen to eighteen,' said one. 'We wore police uniform but had no police powers. Worked in police stations and headquarters departments doing admin stuff and answering the 'phone. Studied very basic criminal law plus bolstering our education at technical colleges.'

Another cadet chipped in. 'We also visited various industries to get an idea of what non-police work is like. Coalmine, steelworks, Manchester airport etc.'

'So, you got a grounding in what the police was all about.'

'Yes.'

'Did it help?'

'It gave us an idea of working conditions and what the job is about. To that extent it did.

'And you're all nineteen?' They were.

I don't know what Sergeant Staunton had said but Turner came back a few seconds later, gave me a filthy look, parked himself and ignored everyone.

The remainder of the journey was peaceful. The weather sunny. Some distance from Harrogate we turned left from the A61 Leeds – Harrogate Road into Yew Tree Lane and Burn Bridge. Narrow, tree-lined and uphill. A few minutes later the view to the left opened. A huge mansion with considerable outbuildings and grounds appeared. 'Our destination, Lads,' came a voice from the front. 'Colditz!'

Even Sergeant Staunton was laughing. 'It's not as bad as all that.'

'No Sarge, it's probably worse.'

It looked fabulous and each yard took me nearer the dream I'd had since before my father was murdered. The dream that put paid to any future that Pamela, my co-alumna at East Midlands and I might have foreseen. Her father was a cardio-thoracic surgeon and being a Bobby wasn't good enough for her husband. That, was non-negotiable. So was my joining the police.

The coach turned right as we approached the main building exposing what, if the head hadn't been moving, could have been a cut-out. Five feet eleven. Immaculate uniform. Chevrons on the sleeves. Creases in his trousers like knives. Boots like mirrors. A half-smile breaking the scowl. Before the wheels had stopped, he began in a voice that could rupture eardrums.

'COME ON. MOVE. YOU'RE NOT HERE TO ADMIRE THE VIEW. GET A MOVE ON. LEFT-RIGHT-LEFT-RIGHT. GET YOUR GEAR. FALL IN.'

'Oh, my God,' came the voice from the front. 'We've got a Drill Pig. Ah well, always remember lads, bullshit baffles brains.'

Three

It didn't take long to collect our kit and be *marched* to the rear and into the entrance hall to be greeted by an Inspector and three further sergeants. It was our Drill Instructor again. 'All right put your kit down.' No sooner had that happened than we were called to attention. 'Ready, sir.' Immediately stood at ease and stood easy. I suppose there was a point to this but it did seem unnecessary.

'Good morning gentlemen and welcome to No.3 District Police Training Centre, Pannal Ash. I'm Inspector Pierce your course Inspector. This is course 234. Remember it. There are three classes, in your case 2,3 and 4. They will be your friends and colleagues for the duration of the course.

A little bit about the house. It was built in the last quarter of the 18th century as a private house. During World War 2 this was a convalescent home for RAF Officers, many of whom suffered from extensive burns and, whether you believe or not, the house is believed to be haunted. It may be pure imagination but figures have been seen on the staircase in the East Wing. That's on your left as we stand. And, for those taking their turn on the duty section, which you all will at least once, during the night voices are regularly heard and the sound of what appear to be sliding slippers around the area where you now stand.'

Apart from a few shuffles there was absolute silence.

'Seriously, sir?' The anonymous question interrupting everyone's thoughts.

'Yes. I've never seen anything but I have heard the voices. It's like a distant murmuring. And I have heard what sounded like people sliding their feet. But with almost two hundred years of history, who knows?

If you do hear anything you're not the first, and I dare say you won't be the last.

Now, a couple more things and we'll get you started. Your class instructors.' He indicated each one as they raised their hands. 'Sergeant Bell – class 2. Sergeant Masterson – class 3. Sergeant Vincent – class 4. They will fill you in with anything else in due course. Your classrooms are all down this corridor to my left,' he indicated with his left hand. 'Outside each one is a notice board, find your way round each one. The one with the list containing your name is your classroom. Outside the dining room there is a large general notice board, keep up to date with that one as well. There is a small office down here on the left manned by a civilian between the hours of 8am and 6pm. Anything you want or need such as report forms, should you have to fill one in, from steam irons, darts, to keys to the snooker room etc. Between the hours of 6pm and 8am it is manned by students in two hours shifts. Familiarise yourselves. Sergeant Faulkner.'

'Sir. Right, collect your kit and we will allocate you somewhere to sleep.'

Like thirty-one overburdened pack mules we climbed to the top of the house and turned right into the dormitory, some occupied beds either side. A scattering of individual rooms on the right. At the far end, the five of us who were left passed down a short staircase into an ablution block. To the right, a steep narrow staircase which we were told in no uncertain terms was out of bounds to students. On the left of the stairs, behind the ablution block, a small dormitory – eight beds with five awaiting occupants.

'Blake, in the far left corner next to Bradbury.'

'Powell, the other side of Bradbury.'

'Foster next to Powell.'

'Burrell next to Foster.'

'Mosley, the empty spot. Everybody, get as much of your kit put away as you can and make the rest tidy. You're all course 234.'

I introduced myself and shook hands with the aforementioned Bradbury. He looked fit. 'John,' he said. 'Five years in the army. You?'

'Brian. Three years at university,' I said. I must have looked guilty because he laughed.

'Clever lad,' he said. 'I wish I could. What did you do?'

'Exercise physiology and anatomy.'

'Brilliant. That's what they call sports science, isn't it?'

'It is. But with your experience you could do well at uni. Don't think you need to be a genius because you don't.'.

'All right,' Sergeant Faulkner broke through the chatter. 'You can make friends later. Housekeeping. This is your dorm. Your responsibility. *You* keep it clean at all times. No litter. No pissing on the floor. If you do, you clean it up or you will all pay the price. So, take responsibility. Saying someone else did it is not an excuse. It reflects on you all. There is an ironing board and cleaning utensils in the cupboard behind me. Waste bin by the door. Irons you can sign out from the office. You sign anything out it's your responsibility to return it, against signature.' We then received thirty minutes tuition into how to fold bedclothes into a neat taut rectangle, sheets on the inside - boxing the bed - which had to be carried out every morning. Why? Because we had to. Just part of the process of turning us into a working unit. Not quite sure about that but it had to be done.

Four

Three classes of eighteen lined up in rows of nine. A right-marker, ex-army, in position. What the purpose of a right-marker was not obvious to me at the moment. I was in class two and our right-marker was John Bradbury. An inspection by the Commandant, Chief Superintendent Andrews, with comments to Sergeant Faulkner in particular concerning length of individual's hair. A situation he assured the Commandant that would be rectified after dinner. I'd had mine cut two days ago, so I should be all right.

Commandant out of the way Sergeant Faulkner took centre stage. 'In eight weeks you will be the senior course,' he paused to let the information sink in. 'On the Thursday of that week Her Majesty's Chief Inspector of Constabulary will carry out his annual inspection of this establishment. In all my time we have never received a black mark and, we-will-not-receive-one-this-year. I require volunteers for my drill squad. Although you may have two left feet I guarantee that by the due date you will be able to hold your head up with pride.' He paused and scanned us. 'I would also stress that all volunteers will be smiled upon. There is a table by the door, those interested should enter their names on the paper provided.

Thirty minutes later we lost our first recruit. Gerald Dobson, from Rotherham Borough Police. After thirty minutes of marching practice he explained to Sergeant Faulkner that he wanted to be a policeman and not a soldier. Surely, he didn't need to learn to march.

'Dobson,' the sergeant said in a soft voice. 'There is only one syllabus and learning to march is a prerequisite. If you are adamant then your only course of action is to resign, forthwith.'

'I'll resign, Sergeant.'

'Very well. Stand by the door.' We watched as Dobson left us. 'The rest of you, 'Atten-shun ... Stand at ease ... Stand easy. I'll be back shortly. Bradbury, you're in charge.'

'Thanks, Sarge,' John said under his breath as Sergeant Faulkner took Dobson away. Class two was one member light.

The food was good. Well-cooked and plenty of it. I would have to be careful. Leaving the dining room I saw a sergeant pinning a notice to the board. They had a rugby team. I caught up with the name on the notice, Sergeant Breen. 'Excuse me, Sergeant,' he stopped, turned and smiled.

'Yes?'

'Pc Blake, Sergeant, class two. Do I have to get permission to use the sports field to train in my own time?'

'What sport do you play?'

'Rugby, Sergeant. I'm also a martial arts instructor.'

That fired his imagination, especially when I told him that I had captained the East Midlands varsity team in my last year. And had turned out for Leicester twice as an emergency substitute outside-half. He took me to the office where he introduced me to Ken, the duty clerk, and supplied me with a general report form – a Minute Sheet, explained how to complete it and authorised my request. It would be submitted to the Commandant for his information.

'What time did you intend running in the mornings, Blake?'

'I thought about six, Sergeant.'

'That's fine but limit it to thirty minutes, otherwise you'll be short. And, if you've no objection I'll come with you.'

How could I object?

We almost lost our second recruit. A local barber attended every month to provide what was decreed a suitable police haircut. Everyone had neat hair but ... Mine was short but not short enough. And, *we* had to pay two shillings each for the privilege of being scalped. However,

Bob Grover objected. His was cut by a prize-winning hairdresser at a cost of £5.

What?

He had an image to protect. With what he described as a shaven head he would be mocked.

'Why did you joint the police, Grover?'

'To make a difference, Sergeant.'

'Do you think that wearing a police uniform makes you stand out? Makes you different?'

'Of course.'

'Your hair will grow back. But what makes you stand out more, you in your uniform complete with helmet or the fact that your hair is short and not cut by a prize-winning barber?'

He had his hair cut.

Each *volunteer* was only in the chair for about sixty seconds, at least that's what it felt like. Afterwards, the classroom, followed by a guided tour of the complex. Gymnasium, theatre gallery, outside sports rooms, heated swimming pool, The Bull - student and staff bar. A licensed hostelry which doubled as a training area – for licensing laws not drinking. Finally, our very own mock-up of a court room, where most of us would make first class chumps of ourselves. It's different being the focal point in a prosecution – or so we were told.

The first lessons concerned the structure of the police force, rank structure etc.

Evening meal was just as good as lunch. We wouldn't lose weight.

Free time? Taking a lead from John Bradbury and Andrew Priestley, both ex-army, we learned to bull our boots – get that brilliant shine on the toe-caps. Someone fetched an iron from the office and several pairs of trousers were pressed. Not everybody was as keen. No studying to do so it was repair to The Bull to make some new friends. There were 150 students and most of them appeared to have the same idea. Sergeant Faulkner made an appearance at eight sharp. The conversation died as he smiled and made for the bar. Beer was a great lubricant at university, why wouldn't it be here? I stood up. 'Here Sergeant,' I said. 'Let me. What are you drinking?' There were a few scowls and shocked expressions. Why? He was only doing his job. 'Then you can come and tell us about this inspection.'

It worked. Within fifteen minutes there were about two dozen standing round our table. Not only did we have a lot more information regarding the inspection but many stories of his time in the services in barrack room language. He didn't buy a pint all evening.

Five

Woke at 5.45am. Outside the sun was shining. Quick swill. Clean teeth.

'Where are you going?' John said as he sat up.

'For a run, coming?'

He looked round at the heads on pillows. 'Ok, let's get the beds done first.' Once you'd got the hang it was simple, just easier with two.

John gawped at me. 'Black belt?'

'Yup, Shukokai second dan, hence the tags. You're into karate?'

'I've done a bit in the past, but not since the kids were born. Any more surprises?'

I returned his grin. 'I don't know. Time will tell.'

There were a couple of puzzled looks as we ran through the big dorm.

Sergeant Breen in his kit waiting by the door. 'You look impressive. Bare feet?' I nodded. We jogged out to the sports field. 'It's about 1100 yards around the perimeter. Can I suggest we do just one lap today? Then I'd like to see some of this karate of yours.' There was no rush although we made the last uphill stretch a sprint. John won; I was last. It took four and a half minutes.

'Right, Sergeant what would you like to see?'

'A cross-section plus a couple of katas.' I talked them through a series of blocks and punches and then the kicks from the simple mai geri – front kick, to a mawashi geri or roundhouse kick. Ran a few combinations together and a couple of simple katas - a choreographed series of exercises from very simple to the opposite. Good practice.

It was different on our return. We'd had an audience. There were a couple of derogatory comments but mainly interest:

Can you teach us?

Is it expensive?

Do we have to wear one of those suits?

'If there's enough interest I'll have a word with the PTI, Sergeant Breen, and ask him. If someone gets a sheet of paper write your name and number and give it to me. And these *suits* are called *Karategi,* or *Gi* for short. Cost £4 if you're going to stick with it,' I said fingering mine. 'They're imported from Japan. Non-returnable. You can get cheaper ones but the quality may not be as good. The belt will be white. Anything else you have to earn. Remember, if I do get permission to run a class it's on top of everything else.' I said and smiled. 'You train in bare feet. Counting and commands will be given in Japanese. Lastly, I teach karate, a mixed style of Shotokan which is Japanese and Shukokai which is based on the original from Okinawa. I do not teach death blows, punches, kicks or anything else in isolation. Last point, courtesy, respect and discipline at all times. And, no obscenities.'

John and I made our way through the crowd only to be confronted by three of course 232, the senior course. They'd been in the bar the previous night. They were all big lads, the biggest in the centre.

'Think you're clever, don't yer?' the biggest one sneered.

That took me by surprise. 'What?' The conversation behind faded.

'You heard,' he said. 'We saw you in the bar licking Faulkner's arse. Teacher's pet,' his tone didn't improve.

'I bought him a pint. What's your problem?'

'Arse licker. All this crap about karate,' he said. 'Waving your arms about like a bleedin' fairy.'

'Personal choice. Where's this going, I need to get showered and changed.'

They were still blocking the aisle. He wouldn't let go. 'See this face,' he said and pointed.

'Of course,' I'd had enough. 'It looks as though somebody's used it as a doorstop in a revolving door. Hasn't improved matters, has it?'

'Cheeky fucker,' he replied. He didn't like the laughter and was getting angry. 'Let's see if you can take a punch.'

'If you think ...'

'Grab him!' His two goons stepped forwards and grabbed me by the arms. 'Make sure the little rat can't get away.'

I'd no intention of getting away or being a punchbag. 'Hold me tight now,' I said and wriggled a bit so they tightened their grip even more. Their friend took a pace towards me, his right fist raised. In one continuous movement I whipped both feet up to chest height, twisted to my left and planted a yoko-geri, a side kick, in the middle of my would be assailant's chest propelling him backwards. Pulled my feet in and completed the backwards roll, dragging my support onto the floor and leaving me on my feet to a chorus of laughter and a few 'bloody hells'. My assailant lying across the bed staring at the ceiling. As I stepped forwards, I heard two voices behind me.

First, John. 'Stay put. Move and I'll drop you.'

Secondly someone I didn't know. 'Same applies to you Widdowson. Three against one? How low can you get?'

Then I heard the dreaded words, 'Yes, Sergeant.' I hadn't a clue which one.

I bent over my supine attacker. 'I'm going for a shower,' I said. 'If you want to continue this conversation, although I don't recommend it, let me know where and when.' He didn't reply.

I hadn't gone three paces. John's voice. 'Look out, Brian,'

He didn't look pleased and was lunging towards me. A full-blooded chudan-zuki - stomach punch. I blocked his right arm and held his wrist, rotated beneath and swept his feet away putting him in an arm-lock as he fell, blood running from his nose. 'Enough, before you get hurt,' I said. 'And you'd better hope that nothing happens to my kit or I'll come looking for you.'

With the exception of a measured tread it had gone very quiet. I glanced to my right. The footsteps stopped. There was only one man that I could think of who had boots like that. 'Sergeant?'

'Blake. Everything in order?'

'I think so, Sergeant.'

'I understand you were going for a shower. Be about your business or you'll be late for breakfast.' I acknowledged and left followed by John.

'Now, Marsden, on your feet.' Holding his abdomen and wiping his nose Marsden waited. 'Before you say anything, Marsden, I witnessed this entire sorry episode. Get yourself cleaned up. Go and see Matron and after breakfast wait outside the Commandant's office with Widdowson and Smith.'

'Who the Hell taught you that?' laughed John.

I grinned in return. 'No-one. I've wanted to try it for ages. Once they had a firm hold I knew it would work, providing they didn't let go.'

'Great stuff, time for a hot shower.'

'You're an optimist.'

'The only reason that I'm not sending you all back to your forces is that so far you have a clean sheet. And, your final exam is less than three weeks away. However, should there be any further breaches of discipline or trust, I will not hesitate. You're lucky that Pc Blake does not want to press matters. Dismissed.'

The door closed behind them. Chief Superintendent Andrews looked at Sergeant Faulkner and slid a beige manilla folder – Pc 547 Blake – across his desk.

The sergeant read the file and looked up. 'DS Blake? Fourteen years ago, sir. I remember that. It was a telex for information, regarding his death ... Well, from the little I've seen so far, sir, he's a fine mature young man. It will be interesting to see how he progresses.'

Six

Wednesday of the first week. Straight after the evening meal John invited me to accompany him on a flying visit home. Consuming the offered cuppa and a piece of cake we made good our escape when the family photos made an appearance.

Katharine, John's pretty younger sister, was looking for a boyfriend, or worse.

John gave me a conducted tour of Harrogate town centre, pointing out The Exchange, the one town centre pub that was out of bounds to police recruits. Every town has its salubrious areas and others not so. The Exchange being the haunt of the 'not so'. Being caught in there attracted a one-way ticket home. Plus there was an element of vocal anti-police who frequented it. Still there were plenty of watering holes. After a few drinks we decided to walk back to Pannal.

So far so good. Half way along The Drive, passing the instructors' houses, Sergeant Breen was walking his dog. 'You've cut it fine, Lads,' he said, chuckled and checked his watch. 'They locked the back door five minutes ago. Sergeant Faulkner is duty officer or had you forgotten?'

With a quick expletive and thanks over our shoulders we legged it. By rights we should have rung the bell and pleaded guilty. There were other ways. We saw Phil Burrell from our Dorm, working the 10pm to midnight shift, standing in the Foyer tapping his watch and gesticulating that we should use one of the emergency access points. A quick thumbs up we sprinted towards the far end of the block. It was fairly simple. An extension to the kitchen had a flat roof with a window cum fire escape next to my bed. The dorm lights were off. John gave me a leg up. I pulled him up. A quick tap and we're in. 'Bloody

Hell, Faulkner's almost here.' Our beds were still boxed. A quick shake of the blankets and sheets. Shoes off and into bed fully clothed. Not a moment too soon.

Sergeant Faulkner's measured tread stopped when he reached my bed. There was silence. Then. 'Bradbury. Blake.' Silence. 'I know you two are awake.'

'Yes Sergeant,' we said together.

'Three things. One, that window squeaks, get it oiled. Two, if it happens again I won't wait for you to get in. Three, when you catch a weasel asleep you can piss in its ear.'

There was a general splutter from around the dorm followed by a growl. 'Quiet'. Sergeant Faulkner left and descended the back staircase wearing a broad grin.

Seven

Lessons began on time and if you weren't there for any reason you made it up. The only exception being swimming or lifesaving. It was a hundred yards to the pool. We had to obtain the Royal Life Saving Society Bronze Medallion qualification within two years of joining. Better now than later.

We didn't have access to the full syllabus but from overhearing what more senior students had said it was going to be relentless. Enough to make your brain ache. We were getting used to seeing those on Duty Section patrolling like automatons outside the school in the evenings carrying the little booklet of definitions donated by the Police Mutual Assurance Society, in recitation practise. No doubt our turn would come.

On top were the practical exercises. Simple scenarios to give context to the legislation and to learn procedure. That was a form of natural break along with drill, swimming, gym and football or rugger. On the horizon possible karate lessons. I had a list of sixty-three names to discuss with Sergeant Breen which he took to the Commandant.

Pannal Ash had 152 students, all male. Female recruits attended Bruche in Lancashire. The vast majority of officers under the age of thirty, most of whom were single and all away from any constraints of home. The domestic and catering staff were all female, the majority under twenty-five and single. It produced some interesting scenarios.

Apart from being an atheist, or Humanist, I'd been no angel at university. Pamela was a very pretty ash blonde with a great figure. She had seen me training at uni and had a laugh with her friends as to what I would look like without *my pyjamas*. We'd been friends for about a month, she was in my room whilst I went for a shave. When I came out her clothes were neatly folded on a chair. She was in my bed wearing a smile, bedclothes round her waist. 'You're going to need this,' she threw me a condom. I was eighteen and a virgin. Our relationship developed to such an extent my work began to slide and I missed a couple of lectures. My work was late.

Joe had taken over his father's butcher's shop. Now there were five plus a pie making business. Everything I needed he funded without question. I felt huge guilt and changed my priorities. That caused problems.

Joining this pack was not on my agenda.

There was a situation developing involving Matthew Turner, the former police cadet with his views on women. I'd heard from others that he was *going to get his own back* over my comments on the coach, even though his voice could be heard by everyone on board. One of his *friends*, Fred Rolands, was in my class. After a coffee break he appeared at my elbow. 'Don't go running in bare feet tomorrow, Brian.'

'Bare feet? What's he going to do, Fred? Scatter drawing pins?'

Fred smiled and raised his eyebrows.

The little bastard. 'Great. Thanks for the warning.'

'Any time, Brian,' he smiled. It was nice to know who your friends were.

At lunchtime a notice on the board outside the dining room from Sergeant Breen:

All those interested in playing rugby
meet on the sport's field at 6pm. Wear your kit.

More of the admin type stuff after lunch followed by a first aid class: How to deal with bleeding and pressure points. That would be useful.

Class over, back to the dorm and bull the boots. First lesson – never miss an opportunity to get the chores out of the way.

It was the first time I'd been on the playing fields with time to spare. Across the valley, the magnificent half-timbered Jacobean mansion with manicured grounds looked very expensive.

Sergeant Breen's voice snapped me back to the present. 'All right everybody, gather round.' There were about thirty on the field including Turner, one or two others from course 233 looked familiar. That could wait.

'Right, gentlemen, we play union, not league, but we don't hold grudges providing you stick to the rules.' There was some general laughter. 'All right, first a warm-up, one lap round the playing fields. Off you go.'

For me it wasn't a race. Others held a different view. The first two back were both cross-country runners. The winner, a member of the Yorkshire senior team. The second, one that I knew from my schooldays, albeit a different school, a former Yorkshire schoolboy champion, Max Fielding. There was no substitute for fitness. Everyone back, Sergeant Breen said. 'Forwards on my left. Backs on my right. Half-backs in the middle.' There were two left. 'And you two?' he queried.

'Never played before sergeant, but we'd like to.'

He nodded and smiled. 'Ok. First, two captains. We lost our captain last week when Colin Digby graduated. So, we'll have a couple of half-backs, Mark Vickers, the former deputy captain and, new-boy Brian Blake, who captained East Midlands University and played a couple of matches with the Leicester first team.' We had one of the non-players each and ten minutes to sort them out.

'The ground is like iron so the game is touch-and-pass. Usual rules but no tackling. If you are carrying the ball and touched by a member of the opposite team you must stop within three paces and pass the ball, preferably to one of your own side. No fouling. Be warned.'

There's always one. I put Mathew Turner at right centre. We'd been playing about ten minutes. I collected the ball from the scrum, put it in the air just behind their backs and followed through. Mark Vickers, their outside half, back-peddled to take the ball and was crash-tackled by Turner who passed me at full tilt. Mark Vickers' left shoulder was dislocated. Turner's apologies were effusive, for all the good that did. Vickers was shipped off to hospital by the Matron. Sergeant Breen told Turner he was off the squad for being an idiot. I became Captain. Once Mark Vickers had left, training was resumed without any further stupidity. He returned to us two hours later, heavily strapped. However, being right-handed he could still wield a pint glass. He was excused everything physical.

Eight

Turner was *advised* regarding his behaviour by the Commandant. Word got back to me that in Turner's eyes the incident had been my fault. What his logic was I hadn't a clue.

Our first visit to the *heated* indoor swimming pool. Indoor, yes. But *heated?* That must mean that the ice had melted. Non-swimmers learned and swimmers learned life-saving. I was in the latter group. A further rugby practise on the Thursday. A pre-season friendly been arranged with a team from The Heifer in Burn Bridge next week. Played at the Heifer's ground. On the Friday the Commandant sanctioned my karate classes. I could hold two weekly sessions in the sports hall or outside, weather permitting. Plus, he wanted to see all the paperwork regarding finance. Fair enough. I put my notices on the various boards. The initial session would be Monday, 6pm.

Transport home on Friday was courtesy of Mum and Joe's van, the adverts on the sides eliciting the expected comments about *mate's rates* for pies and sausages.

I had anticipated being grilled like a sausage that evening. Wrong, I didn't get through the door.

The welcoming committee struck:

'Where do you sleep?'

'In a bed.'

'Ha, ha. Any good-looking men?'

'Yes, me.'

'Oh, you are funny.'

'Kitchen, I'm dying of thirst.'

Dinner out of the way, I sat with my sisters and brother facing me as if I'd been arraigned. 'Is that all? You've done nothing. Haven't you even discussed murder?'

'Believe it or not, Frankie,' Frances was the eldest of the three. Woe betide anyone who used her Sunday name, even on a Sunday. 'In a building housing over one hundred and fifty police officers there aren't all that many murders. And it is quite advanced. I've been there five days.'

I was becoming Frankie's new bone. 'I know that, but even so all you've done is learn to walk in step. Make your bed. Who to salute. A bit of first aid and go swimming. It's a doddle.'

'That just about sums it up,' I replied and winked at Clive. I got a grin in return.

'I saw that,' said Frankie.

'We were meant to,' said Jen, short for Jennifer, the youngest, sitting next to her.

The sound of the phone being replaced signalled Joe's return. He tossed me my jacket. 'Come on, let's go for a walk.'

'You're going to the pub, aren't you? Can we come? We'll just drink lemonade.'

'If you were coming with us, Anne,' laughed Joe, 'that would be true, but you're not.'

He gave Mum a quick kiss. I followed him out to a chorus of spoil sports and rotters'.

We walked in silence to the end of the street and turned right, away from our objective, The Spotted Cow. 'I take it what you said was true.'

'More or less. We do have a drill pig ... '

Joe burst out laughing. ' .. you actually landed a yokogeri then pulled yourself over the top?'

'Yup, his mates made sure I couldn't get away. I thought, why not?'

'Perfect,' he was still laughing when we reached The Cow.

Nine

It had been a fun weekend but I suspected that in future it would necessitate some studying. I returned to Pannal on my bike, two holdalls strapped behind me. One with my kit the other with nine *G's*, Joe's entire stock, an invoice, a duplicate for Sergeant Breen and receipt book.

Monday evening arrived. Surprise, John was a brown belt – Shotokan. There were fifty-three in the sports hall, including Sergeant Breen wearing his black belt – his was for Judo. Did I mind? Not really. He was there to learn. There were three other instructors – tyros.

Ten minutes of exercise including my favourite for beginners – duck walking, it broke down inhibitions. With a little help from John that first session was basic front kick – *maigeri,* punch and block. Finishing with a basic kata. Imagine one square yard of floor and simply practise within that arena. I sold all nine *G's* and took orders for thirty-seven. I rang Joe. He delivered them on Thursday during the class and took the money for the lot.

Into the second week the level of work increased. Traffic law, criminal law and administrative law – firearms, licensing and procedural. On top of which were the practicals – fairly simple and where we made our mistakes.

Ten

We had had our first two practical exercises: Reporting a driver for a defective light. And, a pedal cyclist for having no lights at night; although the exercise was in broad daylight. Pocket books were made up immediately following the offences and, we had to learn our evidence by heart. If we had to seek permission from the Magistrates to refer, the defence solicitor could ask to see it. Something to be avoided if at all possible.

Now we were to give evidence for the first time in Pannal's own courtroom mock-up.

'You are centre stage,' Said Sergeant Bell. 'You may be the only witness or one of many. But when you are in the witness box you are a police officer. All eyes will be upon you and you have to present your evidence succinctly and accurately. Inspector Pierce will act as the Magistrate.'

'Right, Blake,' said a smiling Sergeant Bell. 'Your turn.'

I cleared my throat as I stood. Third from last. I turned as I entered the witness box and faced Sergeant Bell. 'I'd like to affirm, please, Sergeant.'

There was an almost startled silence.

'Yes, you can. Is there any particular reason?'

'Yes, Sergeant, I'm an atheist.'

'An atheist?' Gordon Kennedy was the first to react. 'How can you trust someone who won't swear on the Bible?'

'Enough,' rapped Sergeant Bell before I could respond. 'Blake.' He pointed to my chair.

All settled. Sergeant Bell wasn't smiling. His tone terse. 'Advice. And there will be no discussion. I hope I make myself clear. There are two subjects that you shy away from. They are religion and politics. The two most divisive subjects known to man. If you don't believe me look at the situation in Ireland and Parliament. Religion and politics divide families and nations. You, as police officers, have to be even-handed. You have to be able to react rationally and not allow anything to inflame anyone's passions, especially yours. So be warned. Consider this. Quakers refuse to swear an oath because of Mathew 5:34 where it tells you not to swear. This has applied since 1695. It is now accepted by the courts across the board. Affirming is acceptable. Also consider that there are many people in Britain and Northern Ireland who are not of the Christian persuasion ... Blake?'

I took the card and read. 'I, Brian Blake, do solemnly, sincerely and truly declare and affirm that the evidence I shall give shall be the truth the whole truth and nothing but the truth.'

That was out of the way. I thought it was good. So why were Inspector Pierce and Sergeant Bell smiling like Cheshire cats?

'Train spotter, Blake?' said Inspector Pierce.

That was strange. I frowned. 'No sir.'

'Because every time you took a breath you went up a gear. When you finished your evidence you sounded like the Flying Scotsman on a speed run.'

That brought the house down. 'Slow your delivery. The magistrates or the judge and jury have to be able to understand what you are saying. Not to try and keep pace, All right?'

'Yes sir,' I grimaced and left the box.

An hour later I was in the Commandant's office. Sergeant Bell was standing to one side.

'You can stand easy, Blake ... Sergeant Bell tells me you're an atheist.'

'Yes sir. There's a problem?'

'Not with us here there isn't. However, many of the old school, by that I mean senior officers, are deeply religious. A high percentage members of the Roman Catholic faith. I've even known junior police officers take religious instruction when they found out that their divisional commander was a Roman Catholic as a means of cementing their career path.

This is not a warning, just advice. Tread carefully.'

Eleven

9.00pm. Thursday of the second week. It was busy. It had been a dry, fine and warm sunny day. It was still dry and fine. Karate was finished. John was paying a flying visit home. I was staying away from Katharine. She didn't need any encouragement. John and I had arranged to meet at the Sealed Knot pub at 21.30.

It looked as though half the students from Pannal were out on the town, standing out if only for our *chosen hair style.* Which seemed to encourage a certain amount of verbal interaction from some groups. Nothing physical. I'd had a couple of halves and rejected invitations from some of my classmates to splash the town. The girls were out in force wandering about in groups. Safer that way although their skirts were shorter than our pelmets at home. Many of them didn't look old enough to drink despite their rolling gaits.

John had told me how beautiful the Valley Gardens were. There they were. I had twenty minutes to kill before we were due to meet. It was full daylight so I decided to take a wander. Inside the park the path split into three so I took the right-hand branch. To my surprise it was almost as busy as the town centre, in the main young couples. I smiled to myself wondering why, or was I being cynical.

The gardens were beautiful, but what would you expect from a town with the wealth of Harrogate.

The path led uphill through a long colonnade lined at regular intervals by ornate seats. Each one occupied. I'd never been called a pervert or a Peeping Tom before. I made my escape adjacent to a large pavilion taking the cross-path to the left.

'Excuse me, old chap.' Snapped me back to the present. I turned to face a man aged I would say fifty. Rugged good looks. Around five eleven, hair brushed straight back and sporting a clipped moustache. Very smartly dressed in a grey three-piece suit, regimental tie and well-polished black shoes.

'Yes?'

'Are you looking for clients?' he said, as if it was the most natural thing in the world.

Was he offering himself? 'Are you a police officer?'

He was affronted. 'Most certainly not. The very idea.'

'Well I am,' I replied. 'Might I suggest you depart before I arrest you for importuning.'

He didn't even say good bye.

I was chuckling to myself when seconds later I heard the shouting and the scream cut off in mid cry. At a guess about fifty yards in front. I was there in seconds. To the right of the path was a stream, shrubs and trees on the far side.

No sign of any assailants.

A young couple. Both appeared to be out cold and both in the stream. She had a split lip but her boyfriend had taken a pasting. I don't know about the rest of his body but he had a cut to his left eyebrow and bleeding from his mouth.

I stepped into the stream; the ground was soft but I didn't sink. I managed to get my arms under the girl's legs and back and lifted her out of the water as four men dashed up. The front runner was angry and drunk. 'Your name Blake,' he demanded.

'Yes, why?'

'Oh, you've 'stayed around have you?' he ignored my question. 'Admiring your handy work.'

'What are you talking about? I've only been here fifteen seconds. Here. Take her and put her somewhere safe. Whilst I get the other one.'

'The coppers are on their way. They'll know what to do with a pillock like you. Beating up a couple of kids.'

This was ridiculous. 'Are you going to stand there arguing or going to help?'

'I'll help,' said one of the others. 'What do you want?'

'Take her feet then we can put her down.' Safely on the path I checked for the carotid pulse. Fast and weak.

'Keep an eye on her. Put your sweater over her keep her warm. Is there an ambulance coming?'

'Don't know,' said the argumentative one.

Stupid pillock. 'Will you go and find out then. Make yourself useful. I'm not going anywhere.'

With a bad grace he set off. 'Run,' I shouted after him. 'This is serious.' He lumbered off.

The girl covered up it was time to rescue her friend.

'Right. Let's get this other one out. I'll take the head.'

Between the three us we manhandled him as gently as possible to the path.

Fingers to the throat. There was no carotid pulse. I looked at those beginning to gather round. 'Does anyone know artificial respiration?'

Silence.

I had a clean handkerchief in my pocket. I opened it and spread it over the victim's mouth. Gave him a thump on his lower sternum. Check carotid – Nothing. One hand on top of the other fingers interlinked in the centre of the chest. Ten compressions.'

'What are you doing?'

'His heart's stopped. I'm trying to keep him alive.'

'Bloody hell. We was told you were the one that beat him up.'

'Do you think I'd still be here if I was responsible for this?' I turned back to my task. Extend the neck hold the chin, which felt loose. Two exhalations and back to the chest.

'Who said that?' I said as I continued the compressions.

'Don't remember his name. Widdy something. There were three of them came into the Sealed Knot and rang the police.'

'Widdowson?'

'Aye, that's the name he gave the cops.'

Then the voice I needed. 'Brian, what's happened?'

I looked up. 'You're a sight for sore eyes, John. Cardiac arrest. Can you do CPR.'

'Just about.' He said and knelt beside me. 'The handkerchief?'

'His face is a mess,' I said and managed a grin. He nodded and grimaced. 'You do the breathing. I'll do the compressions. But be careful his jaw grates. It might be broken. ' I looked up at the crowd. 'Somebody get down to the gate and find out where the police and ambulance are.'

Several sets of footsteps clattered down the path.

John had done the breathing. I had my hands on the lad's chest when there were running footsteps. I looked up as a sergeant and two Pcs arrived. 'Sergeant would you check the girls carotid?'

'Sure,' he said, knelt and put his fingers against her windpipe. 'It's there ... Are you doctors?'

'No Sergeant,' I said. 'We're at Pannal.'

There was some confusion. 'Initial course?'

I nodded and began to count to ten again.

John looked up. 'Hello Sergeant Jones,' he said and grinned at him.

'Young Bradbury. So you got in?'

John nodded and began the exhalations.

A couple of ambulancemen arrived and began work on the girl. 'How long's she been unconscious?' asked one.

'Five to ten minutes,' I said.

'Can I have my sweater back, please?' came a voice from the crowd.

Sergeant Jones turned to his other officers. 'Get details of who was first here then get this crowd out of the way.'

One of the ambulancemen tapped me on the shoulder. 'Stop a minute,' I complied. 'How long have you been doing CPR?'

'Six or seven minutes. He was in the stream..'

His colleague felt for the carotid. 'Nothing.'

'Ok, you can leave it with us. But well done. We'll do the best we can. Do either of you know who they are?'

Neither of us did.

'There was some shouting and I heard the girl scream. When I got here he was in the stream. She was half-in half-out.'

The ambulanceman removed my bloodstained handkerchief. 'Is this yours?' he said, handing it over.

I pocketed it. 'Thanks.'

Sergeant Jones looked at the boy's face and grimaced. 'Good God. He's taken a pasting,' he turned to the ambulancemen. 'Right you get off. We'll be in touch ... Now, you're at Pannal, do either of you know a Brian Blake?'

John and I looked at each other and laughed.

'Something funny?'

'You're talking to him, Sergeant.'

'You're Blake?'

'I am, and it's the second time my name has been mentioned in the last few minutes. The first time by the guy who leant his sweater. He also mentioned the name Widdowson. Well, he said Widdy. He was in the Sealed Knot when the call was made. Whoever it was said I was responsible for the assault.'

'That's ridiculous,' said John. 'Brian's a martial arts instructor. He wouldn't need to do this. Besides if Widdowson is involved then so are Smith and Marsden.'

'The guy with the sweater said there were three. And if they were near enough to identify me why didn't they intervene And, if I was responsible why did I stick around?'

'Why indeed. He didn't mention anyone else when he made the call,' the sergeant frowned. 'Is there some history between you?'

I nodded. 'Very much so,' I said.

'That's for later. How come you were here?'

I pointed up the hill. 'I was killing time. John and I were going to meet in the Sealed Knot. I was about fifty yards away when I heard some shouting and a girl scream. When I arrived ...

'Can you prove you were where you said you were?'

'I think so. I'd just been propositioned. By a man.'

'Can you describe him?'

'Fiftyish. Hair slicked back. Clipped moustache...'

The sergeant interjected. 'Smart three-piece suit and regimental tie?'

'Yes.'

John laughed. 'That's Chase-me-Charlie.'

'It is indeed,' the sergeant laughed. 'Would Charlie have heard the scream?'

'I don't know, Sergeant. It was only a few seconds after I told him I was a police officer. He turned tail and ran.'

'That would put the fear of God into him,' he said and laughed. 'Come with me.'

After turfing a young couple out of the phone box Sergeant Jones spoke with Inspector Robertson. 'Sir, this is a bad one, quite possible fatal. The man who made the call fingering Blake? It's not cut and dried. Chase-me-Charlie is a possible witness. Will you call the Duty Officer at Pannal. Three students: Widdowson, Smith and Marsden. They need isolating. Not to confer. Not to change their clothes, wash or visit the toilet. We'll need forensic to do their best. Also, if any of them have bruised knuckles.'

'Leave it with me. I'll call the DI.'

'Before you go, sir. Will you let Pannal know that Pc's Blake and Bradbury are witnesses. We can get them back later.'

'Were you C.I.D, sergeant.' I said as we walked back to the sergeant's car.

'I was. One murder too many. It gets to you given time.'

The girl, seventeen year old Gail Daniels, was now conscious but couldn't be interviewed until tomorrow.

The distraught parents of seventeen year old Gavin Carter had just identified his body.

The interview room door opened. We stood as a plain clothes officer entered. 'D.I. Vellander.' He said. 'Which one of you is Blake?'

'I am, sir.'

He looked at John. 'Wait outside.'

'Sir,' he replied and left.

He sat and pointed to the chair opposite. 'I'll caution you. You are not obliged to say anything unless you wish to do so but what you say may be put into writing and given in evidence. Why were you in the Valley Gardens?' he said as I sat.

'John's local. He'd told me how nice it was. He went to visit his wife and family.'

'You didn't go with him?'

'No, sir. His sister is single and over-eager. She doesn't need any encouragement.'

He laughed. 'I get the picture. And?'

'We'd arranged to meet at the Sealed Knot at 9.30 and I had some time to kill. It was a nice evening so I decided to walk through. Got called pervert and peeping tom a few times walking through that colonnade, though.'

He nodded and smiled. 'You would. Then what?'

'I sped up, cut down on the epithets. Then took that cross-path and met this Chase-me-Charlie character.'

'Yers,' he said and paused. 'You're in your second week at Pannal. How do you know about importuning?'

This time I smiled. 'An assistant professor at uni was ... of a different persuasion. Went into Leicester one evening and tapped up a member of the Vice Squad. His appearance in Magistrates Court made the local rag. Bearing in mind what I wanted to do I went into the library, did some reading.'

'You got your degree?'

'Yes, sir. Exercise physiology with an additional module of anatomy.'

'That's good. Now, tell me about the issue between you and this group: Widdowson, Smith and Marsden ...'

I explained as succinctly as I could.

'And it's Marsden who is handy with his fists?'

'Yes, sir. The other two tag along, especially Smith. Marsden and Widdowson are from the same force. I think it's Hull. Smith, I'm not sure but their helmets are different.'

He nodded. There was a pause for several seconds. 'Let me see your hands.'

I held them out. He took hold and examined both backs and palms. He let go. 'Now clench your fists,' he looked at my fists and turned my hands over. 'Ok relax. I'm happy you haven't hit anyone hard enough to cause those injuries ... But I'll tell you now that the boy, Gavin Carter, is dead. Both he and his girlfriend Gail Daniels were seventeen. This is now a murder enquiry.'

I felt terrible. 'But ... If I'd got him out of the water first, sir, would it have made any difference?'

'Don't worry. The PM will tell. That's at 10.00 tomorrow. In my opinion no. Was there any water running over his face?'

'No sir. His face was wet. I would think because of the splash when he landed. It was only an inch or two deep.'

'It is very shallow in places. It normally is in summer. For the sake of clarity why did you move the girl first?'

'She was laid on her back on the far bank with her legs across his. If I'd tried to move him first.'

'That could have caused her to slide or roll into the stream,' he interjected. 'Fair enough. Then what happened when you picked her up?'

'The first group ran up. They knew my name and accused me of the assault. There was one gobby one there. I told him to go and make sure there was an ambulance en route. One of the others, the one who loaned his sweater to keep her warm helped me to get her out. She had a pulse so I went back for the boy,' I paused. The thoughts didn't get any better. 'They're the same age as my sisters.'

'How many?'

'Sisters? Identical triplets. Step-sisters.'

'Step-sisters?' he iterated and looked at my statement. '547 Blake ... Your father was a DS?'

'Yes, sir.'

'I knew him,' there was an awkward pause as it he had touched some raw nerve. 'I'm sorry ... Now then you were saying. You went back for the boy and that's when you got your feet wet.'

'Yes, sir. The same man helped. We laid him on the path. The boy had no carotid pulse. I'd just begun CPR when John Bradbury arrived. About a minute later Sergeant Jones arrived.'

'Before we take you back to Pannal I shall require your clothes. Jacket. Pants. Shoes and Socks. For forensic who will be here very soon and will swab your hands.'

'But the blood is obvious,' I held my arms up. There were small streaks of blood on the sleeves.

'Not that sort of stain.'

I thought for a moment. 'Spatter?'

'Exactly. The sort of injuries the lad had will have donated something in return. We need to check,' he grinned. 'Cross your fingers. Any questions?'

'Sir, this tie that Charlie wears. Is he ex-military?'

'You mean the Rt Hon Montague Charles Christopher Wilberforce Collins? If you were to meet him in a social situation you would find him highly intelligent, affable and a good conversationalist. He's good company. His forebears have served in the army since before the Crimea. Charlie on the other hand, is colourblind.'

'They wouldn't have him?'

'Not a chance. Anything else?'

'Is he a homosexual?'

'Yes, he is. However, being a homosexual is not illegal. Indulging in homosexual acts is. Importuning. Cross-handing in the gents or any act in public. In private? Still an offence but there's more goes on than most would believe. What he said to you was only a question. However, your reply was enough to frighten him. It's a learning curve as you're finding out. Is there anything else?'

'No, sir.'

'Ok. Wait outside and send Bradbury in.'

Twelve

Chief Superintendent Andrews was concerned. The telephone call from Inspector Robertson to the effect that two students were currently at Harrogate police station as witnesses in an assault case. And, a request that three more be placed in isolation and kept incommunicado was unprecedented. No further explanation had been forthcoming. Now a crew bus had arrived bearing Inspector Robertson, Sergeant Smith and three constables.

Door closed Inspector Roberson turned to Sergeant Smith. 'Let me know as soon as Dr Hawkins arrives.'

'Yes, sir.'

He faced the commandant. 'Good evening, sir. Could I have a word in private?'

'Of course Mr Robertson. Mr Reynolds, Sergeant Faulkner.'

Sergeant Faulkner closed the commandant's office door.

'Now Mr Robertson,' said the chief superintendent. 'What's all this about?'

'About an hour ago a three nines call was received from one of your students. He gave the name, Widdowson. The call was made from the Sealed Knot public house to the effect that he had witnessed an assault on a young couple in the Valley Gardens. He named Brian Blake as being responsible.'

'Blake?' interjected the commandant. 'Most unlikely.'

'Yes, sir. When Sergeant Jones reached the scene which was in the stream about a hundred yards from the gates. Blake was present, in company with a Pc Bradbury, they were performing CPR on a young man, Gavin Carter. The girl, Gail Daniels, was lying at the side. The first thing Blake asked Sergeant Jones to do was to check the girl's carotid pulse. Not in my honest opinion the actions of a guilty man.

It appears that Blake had removed both the girl and boy from the stream. Both were unconscious and both with facial injuries. The boy's very severe. The girl has regained consciousness and we interview her tomorrow. The boy? Death was certified thirty minutes ago.'

'That explains a lot. This is a murder enquiry.'

Yes, sir. The PM will be held at 10.00 tomorrow. Blake claimed that he was at least fifty yards from the scene of the assault when he heard shouting and a girl scream. This has now been confirmed by an independent witness. Further evidence has been forthcoming from those who had been in the pub that Widdowson was accompanied by two others. All big lads with police type haircuts. He never mentioned he had company. When the name Widdowson was mentioned Pc Bradbury said that if he was there then so were Marsden and Smith.'

'That is a reasonable assumption,' said Chief Inspector Reynolds.

'And Dr Hawkins? Forensic?'

'Yes, sir. Biologist, to swab their hands before they had a chance to wash.'

'What about Blake?'

'Because he was accused he is currently being interviewed by DI Vellander, as a potential suspect. He also will have his hands swabbed and his clothing sent to forensic as will the others.'

There was a brisk rap on the door. 'Answer that, Sergeant,' said the Commandant

'Doctor Hawkins,' announced a fresh voice. He stepped inside. 'Chief Superintendent. Gentlemen. I have been briefed. I understand there are three people here and one at the police station. Have those you want examining had the opportunity to wash at all?'

'No Doctor,' said Chief Inspector Reynolds

'Very well. I will do the hands first and then oversee bagging the clothes. Unless you have an alternative suggestion.

'Whatever you require, Doctor,' said the Commandant. 'What course of action do you propose Mr Robertson?'

'We will start with Marsden. I will arrest each one in turn. When Doctor Hawkins has completed the taking of the swabs, then one at a time, I suggest that Chief Inspector Reynolds as Deputy Commandant and Sergeant Faulkner accompany us to the dormitories, along with one of my officers, releasing your member of staff. Once the clothing has been bagged they will be taken to the waiting van. They will be kept in custody overnight and interviewed once we have the initial pathologist's report and preliminary results from Doctor Hawkins.'

Sergeant Faulkner opened Class two's door. 'On your feet, Marsden.'

He was frightened. For the first time in his life this was one problem that his fists couldn't fix. A chief inspector. two inspectors, Faulkner, a tall copper that he didn't know. And a civvy.

Inspector Robertson stepped to the front. 'William Marsden, I am Inspector Robertson. I have to caution you that you are not obliged to say anything unless you wish to do so but what you say may be put into writing and given in evidence. I am arresting you on suspicion of causing grievous bodily harm to Gavin Carter and Gail Daniels. Have you anything to say?'

He made no reply.

'Doctor.'

Jack Hawkins stepped to the fore. Placed his case on a neighbouring desk. 'I'm Doctor Hawkins, a forensic biologist, I'm just going to swab your hands. It won't hurt. Hold your hands out please.'

Widdowson like Marsden remained mute.

Smith almost broke down. He looked at Inspector Pierce. 'Sir, Marsden threatened to kill me if I spoke out of turn.'

'It's out of our hands, Smith. All you can do is tell the truth when you are interviewed.'

Led by Sergeant Faulkner and followed by Marsden they climbed the stairs. Students clustering round the dormitory doors. 'Back to your dorms and your beds. Keep out of the way. This is nothing to do with you.'

Sergeant Masterson, who had been minding Marsden, ensuring that the stairs were kept clear.

There was total silence as the party entered the dormitory and made for Marsden's bed. Garment by garment, under the instructions of Doctor Hawkins Marsden removed his clothing dropping each into a separate paper evidence bag, until all he was wearing were his underpants. He dressed again and was escorted downstairs and out into the van. The Harrogate Pc and Sergeant Smith standing guard..

The same procedure followed for Widdowson and Smith.

Sergeant Bell, on the instructions of the commandant, collected a change of clothing for Blake.

'Sergeant, what the hell's happening.'

'You'll find out in the fullness of time. Now, I suggest you do some studying.'

'Are Blake and Bradbury all right?'

'They're witnesses. They'll be back later.'

'I hope they hurry up I'm bursting for a pee.'

'You're not the only one Brian ... Hang on, that sounds like Sergeant Bell's voice.'

The door opened. Sergeant Bell stepped back allowing a man in civilian dress to enter. Sergeant Bell followed. John and I stood.

'You've had an interesting evening, Blake,' Sergeant Bell said and smiled.

'That's one way of putting it, Sergeant.'

'This is Doctor Hawkins,' he said indicating the civvy. 'He's going to swab your hands.'

'Then can I go for a pee. I'm bursting?"

They both laughed. 'I'll be as quick as I can, sit down and hold your hands out.'

It took thirty seconds. Three minutes later we were back.

'Feeling better?'

'Yes, thanks Sergeant.'

'I've brought you these,' he said handing me a carrier bag.'

Doctor Hawkins stepped in with a paper sack in hand. 'Shall we begin with your jacket?'

It was methodical. I suppose it had to be. That way there would be fewer opportunities for cock-ups.

Ten minutes later I was fully clothed. Wallet, warrant card and cash in my pocket.

'Right, shall we get back?'

'How do you know about CPR?' Sergeant Bell asked as we left the police station.

On our return we were shown into the Commandant's office.

'Blake, I hope you understand why you had to undergo this procedure?'

'Yes, sir. DI Vellander explained why. I knew I hadn't done anything I shouldn't. It was an experience. One I'm sure will stand me in good stead.'

'I think you're right. Sergeant Jones thought you were doctors?'

'He did, sir,' said John. 'He also asked if either of knew a Brian Blake.'

'Did he now?' he and Sergeant Bell smiled. 'That's all for now. Your colleagues will want their curiosities slaking.'

'How much can we tell them, sir?' I said.

'I will address the students and staff in the morning but you can tell them your story.'

Thirteen

We were almost dragged into the lower dorm and peppered with questions until someone shouted. 'For God's sake shut up and let him tell the tale or we'll be here all bloody night.'

That worked. I told my story and John added his. Almost satisfying their curiosities. The Commandant would bring them up to speed in the morning.

'How are these kids that were assaulted?' that was an anonymous voice.

'The girl regained consciousness and she'll be interviewed tomorrow morning. But all three were arrested for causing GBH, so?'

'What about the lad?'

'He never came round. His PM is 10.00am tomorrow.'

There was a chorus of, 'Oh for fucks sake.'

'He died?'

'I hope so,' said one voice from the back of the dorm. 'It's going to bloody hurt if he didn't.'

'Ken, you're a Smart arse. You know what I meant.'

'Do Marsden and the others know?'

'Haven't a clue,' I said. 'I was interviewed by DI Vellander as a suspect.'

'But why?'

'Don't you listen,' said another voice from the back. 'He said that Widdowson told them he witnessed Blake committing the assault. Got to look for evidence, one way or the other.'

I nodded.

He was persistent. 'But it is murder?'

'The GBH certainly,' I said. 'He took a real pasting. But the PM will dictate how. It could have been the assault or a number of other things.' Now they were all listening.

'Such as?'

'Could have been an aneurism that ruptured.'

'What's that?'

'A weakness, swelling, in an artery wall and it's ruptured. Could be anywhere. In the brain. The heart. Anywhere. It could be something else. The PM will tell.'

'I heard you did sports science at university,' said Ken. 'How do you know all this?'

'I tagged on a module of anatomy. One of the bodies that we had to learn from had a ruptured aneurism in the descending aorta. In a major artery death from a ruptured aneurism is pretty quick. The tutor took it from there.'

'You witnessed a dissection? Ken again.

'Several. And participated.'

'Lucky bugger.'

Upstairs it was worse. I put my hands up.

'Whoa. Let us tell you what happened from our side. Then you can ask your questions, when we're finished. All right?'

'We'll be lucky,' said John.

John and I noticed as we passed that Widdowson's, Marsden's and Smith's beds had been stripped and their lockers emptied. They would not be coming back.

We told the tale without any interruptions. Then the questions came thick and fast along the lines of those from the lower dorm. Part way through Sergeant Faulkner appeared in the doorway happy to wait. For now.

The wait had gone on long enough. 'All right, gentlemen,' he said as he strolled through the dorm. 'Lights out was thirty minutes ago. You have a full day tomorrow and I'm sure that Blake and Bradbury would like to get some sleep. If they can. The Commandant will address you all after breakfast and bring you up to date with events.'

He followed us into the ablution block. 'Thanks Sergeant,' I said. 'It was beginning to get a bit trying.'

He nodded. 'Your comments about CPR have raised an interest. And well done to you both for what you did. Try not to dwell on the boy. You did what you could. Finally, five minutes ago a phone call was received from Doctor Hawkins. Strictly between you and me. And I mean strictly. All clothing and all hand swabs bar Marsden's are clear. Five minutes.' He turned and descended the forbidden staircase.

Even though I knew I was in the clear it was a relief to have it confirmed.

Fourteen

I had a new friend at breakfast. Ken Holmes. 'Do you mind?' He pointed at the chair opposite.

'Help yourself.'

He asked so many questions about university his breakfast would be going cold.

The Duty Officer was Sergeant Palmer. 'The Commandant wants you all in the Sports Hall in five minutes.'

'Damn, this breakfast is cold.'

'I'll see you later, Ken,' I said and smiled as he tucked into the congealing mass on his plate.

The only person not present was Ken, the man who manned the office.

All police personnel – students and instructors alike.. All domestic, catering and admin staff by the doors. The Commandant and Deputy entered. We were called to attention. As he reached the podium he nodded to Sergeant Faulkner.

'Stand at ease. Stand easy.'

'I will keep this as short as possible,' he said. 'Everyone is aware of yesterday's event which led to the arrest of three of our students for causing grievous bodily harm to two teenagers in the Valley Gardens. Those students will not be returning. I will not dignify them by the title of police officers. A three nines call to the police reported the assault and pointed an accusatory finger at Pc Blake. An independent witness confirms he was at least fifty yards away at the time of the assault.

The victims, both seventeen years of age. Gail Daniels is currently in hospital. She sustained a fractured cheek bone and possibly other injuries. Gavin Carter did not regain consciousness. A post mortem examination will be commenced within the next hour to ascertain the cause of death.'

The sound of sobbing could be heard from one of the civilian staff. Followed by the sound of the door opening and closing.

'In view of the circumstances, Detective Inspector Vellander has intimated that it may be necessary to interview members of Course 232 and the upper dormitory. Should that be necessary then I expect total professionalism from all concerned.

There may be those amongst you who wondered why Pc Blake, was also subjected to forensic examination. The answer is simple. Evidence is used not only to help establish guilt but also to establish innocence. Other than his attendance at the scene in the aftermath of the assault I am sure that everyone will be pleased to know that there is nothing to tie Pc Blake to the scene.

Should there be any further information forthcoming I will ensure that you are kept informed,' he paused and smiled. 'Now I will let you get back to your studies. Sergeant.'

Fifteen

'Yes, sir. I'll keep you posted,' Detective Inspector Vellander put the phone back on the cradle

'That was interesting information from Chief Superintendent Andrews, Gough,' he said. 'Time to make the little bugger sweat.'

Smith stood as DI Vellander and DS Gough entered the interview room.

'Sit down, Smith,' said the DI. He and the DS sat opposite. 'I will remind you Smith that you are still under caution. Do you understand?'

'Yes, sir. I understand.'

'Did you get any sleep last night?'

'A little, sir.'

'Now, the assault that took place in the Valley Gardens ...'

'I was there, sir,' he interrupted.

DI Vellander glared at Smith. 'Do not interrupt me again, Smith. Do you understand?'

'Yes, sir. Sorry.'

The DI nodded. 'The situation is this ... Gail Daniels regained consciousness half an hour later. She is suffering from a fractured left cheek bone. She may lose the sight in her left eye and there may be other issues. Not least, damage to her brain ... On the other hand, Gavin Carter, her boyfriend, is dead.'

The silence was absolute. Smith went white and struggled to maintain his composure.

'One small thing in your favour, Smith, is that the swabs taken from your hands and the examination of your clothes show no evidence of blood. Therefore I accept that you were not involved in the physical assault on the couple.'

'Thank you, sir. That's a load off my mind.'

'Do not be too hasty. This is your last month at Pannal?'

'Yes, sir.'

'Then you will be familiar with section 8 of the Accessories and Abettors Act 1861.'

'A little, sir.'

'I understand that yesterday evening Sergeant Bell told you that your only hope was to tell the truth.'

'Yes, sir.'

'Good. Because if I find out that you have been less than honest or that I can find evidence to link you to the assault then I will charge you as an Accessory. Which you may think is a lesser charge. However, let me assure you that a conviction as an accessory carries the same punishment as a principal. And the charge in this case will be murder. I have no wish to do that. Do not give me cause. Do-you-understand?'

'Yes, sir.'

'Yesterday, you said that Marsden threatened to kill you if you spoke out of turn. Do you still hold to that.'

'Yes, sir.'

'What do you think he meant by that?'

'I believe he would carry it out.'

'He would kill you?'

'He said he would if I opened my mouth, sir.'

'When was this?'

'After he hit that girl last night, sir. I'd had a go at him when we were walking away. He clenched his fist and said he'd done it before.'

'You're telling me Marsden has killed before, using his fists?'

'That's what he implied, sir. He said one more wouldn't make any difference.'

'Do you know when or where?'

'Hull docks about twelve months ago.'

'Any idea who?'

'No, sir.'

'But why the docks?'

He told us when we first arrived at Pannal that his uncle owns a trawler. He used to crew for him before he joined the police and carries a photo of his uncle and the trawler in his wallet.'

'We will check that out. Now, this bad blood between Marsden and Blake. Talk me through it.'

'It was their first night, sir. The bar is always busy especially first nights. Blake and most of the new guys were there. Sergeant Faulkner came in about eight, he usually did. Blake stood up and offered to buy him a pint and then come and explain about the Chief HMI's annual inspection. Marsden didn't like that. Any fraternisation with the instructors he thought was arse-licking. It got right up his nose. Wouldn't shut up about it.

The next morning there was a bit of a flap when Blake and that mate of his, Bradbury, went for a run round the playing fields with Sergeant Breen, the PTI. Blake was barefoot wearing his karate gear. Marsden was chuntering about Blake was waving his arms around like a fucking fairy.'

Smith paused.

'Carry on.'

'Just sorting the order out in my mind, sir ... Blake and Bradbury came into the dorm to get showered and changed for breakfast. They were mobbed. Most of the dorm wanted to know if he could teach them. He told them to get some paper and give him a list of name and he would speak with Sergeant Breen.

Marsden wasn't happy. Kept going on about Blake and what he was doing wasn't fighting. And he couldn't take a punch. Blake and Bradbury were in the little dorm by the ablution block.'

'Down the steps. I know it.'

'Marsden said, "come on". And we three blocked the way. I thought he was just going to have a bit of verbal. Blake kept his cool but Marsden was getting angry. "See this face," he said and pointed.'

'Blake got smart. He said. "It looks as though it's been used as a doorstop in a revolving door. Hasn't improved matters has it?"

DI Vellander and DS Gough laughed. 'I like that,' said DS Gough. 'Then what?'

'Everybody laughed. Everybody except Marsden, Widdowson and me. Marsden has no sense of self-depreciating humour. Can't stand anyone taking the piss. I knew he would react. He called Blake a cheeky fucker and said "Grab him". Like a fool I grabbed Blake's left arm and Widdowson his right. Marsden pulled his right fist back and as he stepped forwards Blake whipped his feet up to chest height, planted a kick on Marsden's chest and did a backward roll. Marsden ended up on his back across his bed and Widdowson and me on the floor. Blake was on his feet. There was uproar. They were all laughing and applauding.'

'I take it Marsden wasn't too happy.'

'No, sir, he was not. But what we hadn't seen was Sergeant Faulkner standing in the doorway, watching. Blake said something to Marsden about if he wanted to continue let him know where but didn't advise it. And headed for his dorm. Marsden was furious and charged after him. Bradbury shouted a warning. Blake turned punched Marsden in the stomach, grabbed his arm twisted underneath and swept Marsden's feet away. I've never seen anything like it. Sergeant Faulkner intervened and we got a reprimand from the Commandant.

As far as tonight's concerned, no matter which way this goes it's the end of my police career. If I'd known what was going to happen I would have stayed at Pannal.'

'So what did happen?' said the DI.

'We'd had a few drinks in town and decided on a whim to visit the gardens. When we arrived we saw Blake was about forty yards in front walking up the right-hand path. If he'd been on his own Marsden would probably have followed Blake. But we took the path on the left. It was just a nice stroll. Then we heard the laughter. Seconds later I saw a young couple walking towards us holding hands and laughing. Why I don't know but Marsden became incensed. When we all met, Marsden said. "What the fuck are you laughing at?" The lad asked him to moderate his language. Marsden grabbed his sweater and said. "I asked you a fucking question."

'The lad said. "Take your hands off ...it's nothing to do with you, But if we were having a laugh at you it would be about your hair. I hope you didn't pay to have it cut like that." That did it. Marsden still had a hold of him with his left hand. Before we could do anything he punched the lad hard in the face with his right. The girl pitched in telling Marsden to let go and leave them alone. Voices got raised. Marsden told her to fuck off before she got hurt. The lad tried to prise Marsden's hand from his sweater. Marsden lost it. He hit the lad three more times in the face. Let go and the lad fell in the stream. The girl screamed and Marsden punched her as well.'

'Then you legged it.'

'To my shame, sir, I did. We walked out of the gardens faster than we walked in. I asked Marsden what the hell he was playing at and said we should have stayed with them. One of us should have telephoned for an ambulance. That's when he stuck his fist under my nose and threatened me. "We'll go to the Sealed Knot; you can call from there. Tell 'em you've seen Blake beat these kids up." I said, "Oh no. This mess is yours sort it yourself.' The Widdowson pitched in. "I'll do it, Smithy's shitting himself."

'When Widdowson made the call he didn't mention that he had been accompanied. Why?'

'They agreed between them that it would be Widdowson.'

'Even though there were about two dozen regulars drinking?'

'Yes, sir. They overheard what Widdowson had said and a group of them set off to have a look for themselves.'

'They didn't ask why you didn't intervene, or if you were going back to the scene?'

'There were a few who chuntered a bit but nobody made a fuss. At least not that I heard.'

The DI thought for a moment and nodded. 'How did you get back to Pannal?'

Taxi from the railway station, sir.'

'What do you think, Sergeant?'

'For the most part, sir, I think he's telling the truth. What about these allegations he made about Marsden?'

'I agree with you. The allegations? Can't not check them out. He's had the hard word. He knows that if he's caught lying we won't be easy on him. There's still the accessory after the fact if needs be. I know a DI in Hull I'll check Marsden's property see if that photo is there.

Sixteen

Stuart Prentiss caught sight of himself in the mirror. Sagging chin and bald. Only five years to retirement. If I live that long. The phone began to ring. 'Here we go again. I wonder what the Super wants this time. Deep breath. 'Prentiss.'

'Stuart. Keith Vellander how are you keeping?'

'Bloody hell. Where did they dig you up from. It must be what? Ten years? I heard you'd landed some cushy job in Harrogate.'

He snorted a laugh. 'Harrogate? Cushy?' he retorted. 'We've a USAF base less than ten miles up the road on top of everything else. And it's fifteen. At the Federation Conference in Bournemouth.'

'So it was. What can I do for you?'

'Got a possible interest in a trawler – Betsy Lee and its owner.'

'Get to the back of the queue.'

'Anything in particular?'

'Sidelines. Import and export. But what's your interest?'

'We've got his nephew and two others locked up. Goes by the name of William Marsden.'

'Marsden? Will you describe him?'

'Six two. Twenty five. Heavy. Maybe seventeen stone. Quick tempered. Fast with his fists. No sense of humour.'

'Description fits but he's not called Marsden. The owner of the Betsy Lea is Allan Bruce. He has a brother, Clive. Another malcontent. Has two daughters and a son. The boy's name is Peter, Peter Bruce. There's a photo in Police Reports dated, just a minute ... 17th November 1965. A good likeness. What's he in for?'

'We arrested them for GBH. Beat a couple of teenagers up. I'm just waiting for the PM report when it should be murder. I was hoping I'd have a prelim earlier. But wasn't to be.'

'Harrogate is a bit out of his league what's he doing over there?'

'You're going to like this. He's a student at Pannal.'

There was an explosive. 'You must be bloody joking. Check the photo, Keith, if it is him he's an enforcer for some fairly big names over here although he's kept a low profile over the past two years or so.. Him in uniform doesn't bear thinking about. Give me the details of the three. Call me back in fifteen. I've got some enquiries to make.'

'Stuart, it is Bruce. A few years older and heavier but it is him. Right, our enquiry relates to something he allegedly said to Smith after he'd beaten the kids up. He said he would kill Smith if he stepped out of line. Intimated that he's killed before and nothing to lose. Beaten them to death twelve months ago on the docks. He's crewed for his uncle and I wondered.'

'So do I. Have you interviewed Bruce yet?'

'No. You want to come over? It will be tomorrow, probably pm.'

'With pleasure. We have no record of Smith. Widdowson has no previous that we know of but he is flagged in our intelligence index. A few years ago he ran with a group of idiots; into all sorts of problems. But nothing that would stand up in court. In the meantime I'll have Bruce's prints checked out. Those he provided when he joined against those we have at Wakefield taken in '65.'

'Great. Smith is from Lincoln, so I'm not surprised. Widdowson? Don't know. I'll let my Super know but I won't inform the Commandant yet.'

Superintendent Larkin, Harrogate Divisional Officer sat back in his chair. 'No Keith,' he said, 'I'll Call Mr Andrews, he's a former senior detective. He will have to know and there's 150 students and staff who deserve to be made aware. I'll ask him to stick with what we know until we get some more information from DI Prentiss.'

'Fair enough, sir. And Smith?'

'Queen's evidence? Possible. But I will leave that to you for later.'

Seventeen

Widdowson stood as DI Vellander and DS Gough entered the interview room and sat. Widdowson in the chair opposite.

'I am Detective Inspector Vellander. On my right is Detective Sergeant Gough. Before we begin proper, Widdowson, I'll caution you. You that you are not obliged to say anything unless you wish to do so but what you say may be put into writing and given in evidence. Do you understand?'

'I understand.'

'Good.' This was some progress. At Pannal he remained mute. 'Just to salve my curiosity, Widdowson, how long have you and Marsden been acquainted. Your first day in the job? Six months? Since childhood?'

'About five years, sir.'

'Would you describe your relationship as being close?'

'Yes, we were good friends. I applied to join the police when he did.'

'Ok. Then you are aware that his real name is not William Marsden but Peter Bruce.'

The bombshell exploded in Widdowson's mind. 'What? No, sir. I was not aware. I've always known him as Bill Marsden. I had no idea.'

'Why do you think that someone might change their name and then apply to join the police?'

Widdowson was still trying to process the information regarding Marsden, or whatever his name was.

'Don't worry about it,' said the DI. 'We can come to that later. I will tell you what we know. Evidence that is backed up by statements from independent witnesses. In the long run it will save a lot of time. In your call to the police you made the claim that you had witnessed constable Brian Blake assault two young people in the Valley Gardens – Do you still hold that to be true?'

There was a lengthy silence. 'Well?'

'No, sir.'

'Good. We're making progress. We have statements that put Blake at least fifty yards from the scene of the assault at the appropriate time. Furthermore, statements that confirm Blake ran to the scene of the assault when shouting and a scream was heard. But you were present during the assault, weren't you?'

Widdowson nodded.

'Was that a yes?'

'Yes, sir.'

'Good. So why, when you made that three nines call from the Sealed Knot public house did you say what you did and, why did you fail to mention the fact that you were in the company of Smith and Marsden?'

'I can't think of a good answer, sir.'

A half smile wandered onto the DI's face. 'I understand that originally Marsden told Smith to make the call. He refused. You said that you would do it because, and I quote. "Smithy is shitting himself".

There was no answer.

'Smith also told us that he had a go at Marsden when you abandoned the young couple in the stream. He thought you should have stayed to assist and telephone for an ambulance. Marsden stuck a clenched fist under Smith's nose and threatened to kill him if he "spoke out of turn". Something he had done before.'

The was no answer.

'Care to make any comment as to why you took the actions that you did?'

Again no answer.

'You will be pleased to know that the tests carried out by Doctor Hawkins reveal no blood on your hands or clothes and, I can see there is no bruising to your hands. So in that regard you have nothing to worry about. The only person with blood on their hands and clothing with bruising to their knuckles was Marsden. Why did he attack the young couple?'

'He thought they were laughing at him.'

'Why would he think that?'

'You know what happened in the dormitory, sir?'

'When Blake humiliated him?'

'Yes, sir. He couldn't stand being laughed at. He hated Blake.'

'What has that to do with the couple he assaulted?'

'He demanded to know why they were laughing. He grabbed hold of the lad who said that they weren't but then mocked our haircuts. Then he hit the lad three times. When the girl screamed he hit her as well.'

'And as trainee police officers instead of intervening and stopping Marsden, you did nothing. Just walked away and tried to lay the blame on one of your colleagues.'

'Sorry.'

'Sorry. What use is that? You haven't asked me how the young couple are. Don't you want to know?'

'He didn't hit them all that hard, sir. I thought they'd be all right.'

DI Vellander bristled. 'You thought? Did you stop to check? You've done the first aid. The fact that you were arrested for causing grievous bodily harm has told you nothing?'

There was no answer.

'Well I will tell you. The girl was unconscious for over thirty minutes. She has a fractured left cheek bone and the doctors are concerned there may be as yet undetected problems. The boy is dead. The post mortem examination revealed that he had a broken jaw and fractured skull. That is murder. When the police arrived Pc Blake and Pc Bradbury, not knowing this, were trying to resuscitate him.'

'I'm sorry, sir. I didn't know.'

'No. You were only interested in getting away. I will tell you this Widdowson, what you did in telephoning the police and pointing the finger at Pc Blake makes you an Accessory to murder. And, I'm sure you remember from class, a person convicted of being an Accessory could well receive the same punishment as the principal. In addition, that phone call diverting responsibility is perverting the course of justice. You, young man are going to prison for a long time. Your only hope is to admit your guilt and hope that a show of contrition will attract a more lenient sentence ... Think about that.'

Eighteen

Our evening meal was finished, but before the table was cleared the girls demanded to know what I had been up to over the past week ...

'Well, hello sailor,' said Frankie with a limp wristed salute. 'An old man tried to pick you up?'

'Very funny. I didn't say that. He asked me if I was looking for clients.'

'That's just splitting hairs, Brian,' said Anne.

'Are you going to let him finish this tale?' said Joe. 'I'd like to get to bed before midnight.'

Anne grinned at her sisters. 'All right, dad. Carry on, Æsop.'

'Oh very droll ...'

I finished telling what happened to total silence.

'They tried to blame you?' said Mum. 'That's awful'.

'I wasn't impressed. The sergeant called the police station who passed a message on to Pannal and the three were put in separate classrooms. They were arrested for causing grievous bodily harm and a biologist from the forensic science lab took skin swabs and seized their clothing to check for blood. Then they did the same to me.'

'But why, if you were innocent?'

'Because I'd been implicated. Forensic examination is not just to help prove guilt but to eliminate as well. If this house was broken and the police fingerprint officers came, they would want everybody's fingerprints to eliminate those who had a right to be here. Any others might be the burglar.'

'So, what's the score?'

'With a bit of luck I'll find out on Monday.'

'Just a minute,' said Jen. 'Why weren't they arrested for murder?'

'Because until the pathologist has completed a post mortem examination they won't know the cause of death.'

'But what about the facial injuries?'

'They still need to confirm the cause of death. You couldn't take a case to court because you thought it was, or, it looked like. You need certainty ... Nothing more? Right, I want to get some studying done then Dad's taking me for a pint.'

Joe laughed. 'Oh, is he?'

Nineteen

There was a different air in the Interview Room that Saturday at 2pm. A stale smell of unwashed bodies and fear.

Marsden knew he was the last of the three to be interviewed and not knowing what the others had said worried him. Widdowson he was sure of – he knew too much. Smith? Too much of a goody, goody. Hadn't the stomach.

He sat facing DI Vellander and another, older police officer. An officer with a Hull accent. Why?

File closed DI Vellander looked across the table at Marsden, or was it Bruce? It was time. 'Marsden, I am Detective Inspector Vellander and on my right is Detective Inspector Prentiss from Hull.'

A DI from Hull? 'Sir,' he acknowledged.

The DI cautioned him. 'Do you understand?'

'Yes, sir, I do.'

'You and Widdowson are from the same force. How long have you known each other. Was it the day you joined? Six months? Since childhood?'

'Don't rightly know, sir. It's a long time. Maybe fifteen or twenty years.'

'So you would describe yourselves as being good friends?'

'Yes. I told him I was going to apply and he decided to join as well.'

'Yesterday I spoke at length with Chief Superintendent Andrews. He told me that until you had that fracas with Pc Blake on their second day your discipline had been excellent. What happened?'

This he hadn't expected. 'I didn't like the way he was sucking up to Sergeant Faulkner, sir. I don't like that sort of thing.'

'You think of all sergeants and above as the enemy?'

'I wouldn't put it like that.'

'I understand he bought the sergeant a pint and asked him to tell them about the Annual Inspection. Plus, according to Sergeant Faulkner, that night he drank five pints of beer and didn't buy any himself. No student bought more than one. Did you take a dislike to them all or was it just Pc Blake?'

'It was next morning, sir. Somebody saw him and Bradbury running round the sports field with Sergeant Breen. That got up my nose a bit. That he gave a demo of this karate. Looked like a bleedin' fairy waving his arms about. Most of the others gawping out of the window saying how great he looked. Enough to make you sick.'

'It was Sergeant Breen who asked if Blake minded him accompanying them. And, it was also Sergeant Breen who asked Blake to demonstrate karate. But you decided to intervene.'

'All this nonsense about karate. Waving his arms about like a bleedin' fairy. That's not fighting. Just posing. When he and Bradbury came back to the dorm they all clustered round like kids. Will you teach us?' he sneered. 'Do we need one of them suits? Sickening.'

'So you blocked the aisle so Blake and Bradbury couldn't get showered.'

'I wanted to make a point, sir.'

'And you said?;

'I pointed to my face. What I was going to say was. See this face, I can take a punch can you?'

'But Blake interrupted.'

'Yes, sir. I said. "See this face", and he interrupted me. He said it looks like somebody's used it as a doorstop in a revolving door. Hasn't improved things has it.'

'Everyone laughed but you didn't like that, did you?'

'No I didn't. 'Would you, sir?'

Ignoring the comment Vellander continued. 'You called Blake a "cheeky fucker" and told Widdowson and Smith to grab him. Which they did. An arm apiece.'

'I just wanted to see if Blake could take a punch. Any man would.'

'You think that the ability to take a punch is a measure of manhood?'

'Yes, why not?'

'Blake is five nine and about thirteen stone . You're six two and what? Seventeen stone. And you expected him to stand there whilst you hit him? It didn't work out did it.'

'It was a circus trick, sir. Doesn't prove a thing.'

DI Vellander's eyebrows raised a notch as he smiled. 'A circus trick?' he iterated. 'He landed a karate kick on your chest propelling you backwards across your bed. Completed a backwards roll dragging Widdowson and Smith onto the floor leaving himself standing. Then he advised you not to pursue the matter.' Marsden balled his fists. 'What annoyed you most? The fact that you hadn't been able to teach him a lesson? The humiliation? Or the laughter and the applause?'

If looks could have killed.

'But you weren't happy. You couldn't accept that could you? You didn't realise that Sergeant Faulkner was standing in the doorway, watching, when you charged after Blake. Bradbury shouted a warning. Blake spun round, punched you in the gut, blocked your intended punch and,' the DI slowed his delivery, 'put you in an armlock on the floor with a bloody nose. The hard-man of the course taken out by a shrimp like Blake. In your parlance - a bleedin' fairy. How humiliating was that?'

Marsden was beginning to hyperventilate.

'So Peter,' he didn't react to the change of address. 'Two days ago when you, Widdowson and Smith saw Blake heading for the Valley Gardens you followed. But Blake walked through the Colonnade. That was too busy so you walked up the other side. You heard laughter and saw a young couple walking towards you and it started to get to you. Were they laughing at you? Had word spread of your humiliation? The nearer you got the more they seemed to be laughing. You couldn't have that. These were kids. It wasn't allowed. Laughing at you. So you demanded to know what they were laughing at. But you already had made you mind up – it was you. You were the object of their laughter. You grabbed hold of the boy and hit him. Then he mocked you saying that if they had been laughing at you it would be because of your haircuts. All three of you. And he hoped you hadn't paid for it. You snapped. You hit the lad three more time on his face and head. When his girlfriend screamed, you hit her as well. Legged it and tried to get Smith to make a three nines call to the police pointing the finger at Blake. He refused. Widdowson, your long-time friend, said he's do it because Smithy was shitting himself. When Smith said you should stay and see it they were all right and call for an ambulance you stuck your fist under his nose and told him you'd kill him if he spoke out of turn. You'd done it before. One more wouldn't make any difference. That's the truth of it, isn't it, Peter?'

He had been determined not to lose his temper. A resolution disappearing in the distance. 'Yes, all right,' he snapped. 'I hit them. So what. They won't do it again.'

'You're almost correct, Peter. *You* won't. The girl is in hospital with a fractured cheek bone and other injuries. The boy is dead. You killed him.'

Peter stared at the DI in disbelief. 'What? That's rubbish.'

'Oh no. You caved the lad's skull in. He is dead. You will be charged with the murder, and because of the phone call, with conspiracy to pervert the course of justice.'

All the bluster gone, he sat there chin on chest, eyes closed.

DI Prentiss said. 'Peter, when did you change your name to William Marsden?'

He opened his eyes and looked at the DI from Hull realising now why he was there. 'About eighteen months ago, sir. It was done properly by deed poll. Uncle Alan said it might be a good idea after what happened to Alex Gillespie.'

'Gillespie?' iterated DI Prentiss. Gillespie had been a thorn in the side of the police forces on Humberside since he was fifteen years of age. A Prolific burglar who thought nothing of using violence. His body, with half his skull missing snagged on the line of a day fisherman three miles of Mablethorpe. Gillespie's death was no loss to society. 'Tell me about how he died.'

'He was one of Mum's boyfriends. Used to knock her about. When I was little I couldn't do anything about it. Then he disappeared. Good riddance. He turned up eighteen months ago after twelve years and started throwing his weight about again. This time I gave him a bit of a pasting and he ran of towards the docks. Looked over his shoulder to see how close I was and tripped over his boots. Took a header off the quay onto the Betsy Lee, Uncle Allans trawler, split his head open on the winch. Dead as a dodo.

'How close were you?'

'About forty yards. Gillespie was always good at running.'

'What happened to the body?'

'Uncle Allan dumped him in the sea and left it to the currents. Why, am I in trouble for that as well?'

'Ongoing enquiry, Peter,' said DI Prentiss. Although he probably deserved a medal.

He shrugged.

'And you used this death to put the frighteners on people?'

'Sure, why not,' he smiled. 'It was an accident but it served its purpose.'

'Now, you had a conviction for theft. How is it you were accepted for the police?'

He smiled. 'Uncle Allan sorted it. Friends in high places, he said. Somebody owed him a big favour.'

Twenty

Sunday afternoon. After 'representations' from the girls and Clive it had been decided that they would follow me to Pannal – the girls wanted to see the place. Followed by a visit to Harrogate, they had never been before. I wanted to visit the hospital to see how Gail Daniels was progressing. And they *all* wanted to see the Valley Gardens. Bloodthirsty or what?

3pm. 'It looks very posh,' said Mum.

'It was built as a private house in the late 1700's, Mum,' I said. 'And it was a convalescent home for RAF officers during the war. It's gone downhill since then.' The intended joke fell flat.

Anne had her camera in hand. 'Can I take some photos?'

I took them round the front and pointed out the interesting bits whilst Anne snapped away. Then it was inside. 'Right, wait here in the foyer while I go and change,' I said.

'Visitors Blake,' Sergeant Faulkner appeared from the library passageway as I reached the staircase.

'Yes, sergeant.' I told him who was who, although the chances of his remembering which of the girls was which were remote.

'You get changed. I'll give them the sixpenny tour.'

The dorms were empty so it only took five minutes. 'What a nice man,' was the comment as we left Pannal.

'You wouldn't think so if you heard him on the drill square. There have been complaints about his voice from people across the valley.'

'Where next, Brian?'

'The hospital. I want to check up on the girl who was assaulted.'

The hospital carpark was very busy but at last, a space. 'Don't run away. I'll only be five or ten minutes.'

According to the clerk Gail Daniels was in Women's Medical.

I had a brief word with Sister Taylor, the ward sister, showed my warrant card and told her why I was there.

'Third bed on the right,' she said. 'Her parents were asking about you. Just wait a minute I'll have a word.' The third bed on the right was screened.

Seconds later the screens parted. A stocky man about my height aged about forty with dark greying hair dressed in a smart light-grey suit, who I took to be Mr Daniels headed my way. 'Doctor Daniels,' he said. 'You're the officer who helped my daughter.'

'I am, Doctor,' I said. 'I was first on the scene after I heard your daughter scream.'

He seized my hand. I thought he was trying to dislocate my shoulder. 'Thank you so much, we can't thank you enough.'

'Other than checking her carotid pulse there was nothing that I could do.'

'But you were there which is what counts.'

'When my colleague arrived we used CPR on Gavin. But to no avail.'

'So I heard. They've been inseparable since they attended infants school. Childhood sweethearts. There were rumours of an engagement. Now? What happened was ...' I thought he was going to break down. ' ... Here, will you take this?' He put his hand into his inside jacket pocket. It was a cheque for £25 - almost two weeks salary.. 'It's not a lot. But we'd be delighted if you would accept it.'

'That's very generous Doctor. But I can't accept it. I do appreciate the gesture but I'm not allowed to.. Might I suggest, if you do want to make a donation, write to the chief constable, Mr Barton, making the cheque payable to the Police Widows and Orphans Fund, with a covering letter.'

'Well if you're sure. I just thought ...'

'Thank you and I do understand ... How is Gail?'

'Very tired and in pain. She doesn't know about Gavin yet. She will be devastated. Which is why I came out here instead of inviting you to see her. I hope you don't mind. Do they know the cause of death?'

'I don't mind at all. And, no, I don't know the cause. All I was told was that he was probably dead before I arrived.'

'Really?'

'Yes. I'm sorry but this is a flying visit. I just wanted to know how Gail was. I knew she had a fractured cheek bone, was there anything else?'

'Thankfully, no. There was some concern that the damage had been more extensive but it appears not. Whoever it was must have been very powerfully built to punch so hard.'

'He is. Six feet two, seventeen stones and angry. More than that I can't say but there will be a statement or a press release tomorrow. And now I must fly.'

'He wanted to give you a cheque for twenty five quid, and you turned it down?'

'I did. We can't accept gratuities.'

'Does that mean we don't have to buy you birthday presents?' said Jen with a laugh.'

'No Jennifer,' said Mum. 'It does not. But what's the reason, Brian?'

'If he had to be arrested at some time in the future he could turn round and say this officer takes bribes I've had to pay the police in the past. In fact ...'

'I suppose so.'

We parked in the car park of the King George III.

'Are we residents?'

'Of course not,' said Frankie. 'But whilst you were getting changed Dad asked Sergeant Faulkner where we would be able to get a meal. He very kindly called here. And here we are.'

Everyone agreed that the Valley Gardens were superb. Moderated by Clive's, 'They're ok.' A walk through the Colonnade, across to the stream and down to where the assault took place. Blood lust sated we meandered back to the King George III for afternoon tea.

Monday morning. We were lined up in the Sports Hall. Civilians down the side as before, waiting for the Commandant and Chief Inspector Reynolds. The door opened. Sergeant Faulkner called us to attention.

The Commandant mounted the dais. 'Good morning gentlemen, and ladies. I won't take long. I want to give you the latest information on the events of last Thursday.

William Marsden has been charged with causing grievous bodily harm to Gail Daniels. The murder of Gavin Carter and conspiracy to pervert the course of justice. This relates to the attempt to blame Pc Blake for the assault.

Widdowson with being an accessory after the fact in regard to the murder of Gavin Carter and conspiracy to pervert the course of justice.

Any decision in relation to Smith is, for the time being, in abeyance. I am sure that your class instructors will answer any questions that you may have. Thank you.'

Twenty-One

Sunday seventh of July. Two weeks after the murder. Not that I needed an excuse but I'd left home early to get some more studying in at Pannal. My Super Hawk ate the miles. After the rain it was fine with a strong wind and scudding clouds. A steady fifty. Admiring the countryside. Harewood Bank. Cross the Wharfe. Passed the turnoff to Dunkeswick. Now the gentle climb towards Harrogate.

About three-quarters of a mile shy of the junction with the A658, Bradford road, I became aware of a high-pitched motor cycle engine closing from the rear. Seconds later a maroon Honda Benly, my bike's smaller cousin, zipped past. The rider too slim to be anything but female. Dark red close-fitting leathers. Low over the tank. She lifted her left hand in acknowledgement. That raised a smile. I tweaked a little more from mine closing the gap. Two hundred yards ahead the road swung to the left between embankments and high hedges. There was no cross-view. She eased to 40mph. I followed.

Barely visible coming round the bend at about 15mph was a farm tractor towing a trailer laden with several tons of potatoes

The world slowed to time-lapse as a red MGA appeared, overtaking the tractor, travelling at I guess 60 mph blocking the road. A closing speed of fifty yards per second. The driver laughing over his shoulder. The front nearside passenger kneeling and half turned to his right giving two fingers to whatever was behind. Both oblivious to what was happening in front.

The tractor driver, in all probability, couldn't hear a thing because of the noise and didn't appear to have seen the bike.

A hand-cranked motion picture. Frame-by-frame. Except. I wasn't a member of an audience. I was an actor. My view crystal-clear. The result inexorable. How bad was it about to become?

Frame-by-frame. Yard-by-yard the participants closed. The motor cyclist swung her bike to the right and ripped the throttle open in an attempt to get out of the way of the MG and the tractor's sedate progression of 24 feet per second. A collision with the hedgerow preferable to the alternative.

A double-manned police car appeared behind the MG. I swung across to the offside, dropped the anchor and the bike. I have never felt so helpless.

Too late.

The MG driver looked to his front. For the first time aware of what was happening. In horror wrenched the wheel to the right as it struck the rear wheel of the bike and reared up the bank rolling over before sliding down and across the road. Both occupants trapped.

I watched, sickened. The bike spun 180 degrees and disappeared beneath the tractor. The driver stood on the brakes and buried both bike and rider.

The motion picture stopped.

Total silence.

All Hell broke loose.

The police car slithered to a halt.

I didn't care what was going on behind me. All I cared about was the girl on the bike. Was she dead or by some freak of timing alive? I took one look at what lay before me. The tractor was parked with its wheels on the bike wheels. The rider still astride her bike – right leg trapped. She was not moving. Lying diagonally under the axle and sump, her head behind the tractor's front offside wheel.

A rattled tractor driver leapt out of the cab. 'I didn't stand a chance. Is he all right? I'll reverse.'

'Don't move. She's at your feet.'

'Bloody hell,' he said as he looked down. 'I'll try to get these cars shifted.

It was impossible. The space beneath the axle was full of the bike and rider. The handlebars in front of the axle.

From the nearside it was possible. The commando crawl beneath the sump claustrophobic.

She was motionless. Lying on her right side. Her full-face helmet inches from the tyre. 'Hello, can you hear me,' I said with my hand on her shoulder.

No response.

I pulled my left gauntlet off with my teeth. Worked my finger under her helmet and found her throat. I breathed a sigh of relief. Carotid pulse. Rapid but there. I almost said, 'Thank God'.

The bike engine had stalled. I ripped the ignition key from the switch. There was no point in taking chances.

Twenty-Two

The light dimmed as a policeman knelt in front of me. 'I'm Pc Jefferson.'

'Pc Blake, Brian Blake, initial course at Pannal. She's out cold but there's a carotid pulse.'

'Cheers. Welcome to the club, Brian. You look after her. Try and protect her neck.. We'll have to get her head stabilised before we move her. We'll see to this lot ... Oh, bloody hell. Where does this clown think he's going.' I slid my right arm beneath her neck for support and felt for the pulse again then took hold of her left hand with mine.

A blue Mercedes saloon had pulled out of the line of cars and was driving towards us. The driver stopped and opened the window. 'Let me through, officer. I have an urgent appointment.'

'The road is closed, sir. There has been a serious accident or hadn't you noticed?'

'I don't like your attitude. I can get through. Now, move out of the way.'

'I don't like yours either, sir. The only place you're going is back.'

The driver looked in his mirror and smirked. 'My space has been closed. I'll make it worth your while.'

'Then you will have to go to the rear, won't you?'

He wasn't happy. 'I shall report you to the chief constable.'

'Good, then he will know that I'm doing my job. Now are you going to reverse or do I have to arrest you? Your choice.'

With a bad grace he complied.

'Stupid bastard,' Pc Jefferson muttered and made a note of the driver's registered number.

'Let that be a lesson, Brian. Keep your eyes open for those who think they're entitled.'

I heard Pc Jefferson bellow. 'There's a girl trapped under the tractor. Let the Mercedes get past then get some of these cars on the verge. The rest of you back up. Where's the tractor driver. ... You are? Right, get back on the tractor and be ready. Do not start your engine.'

I looked at my charge. 'Well, I can't keep thinking about you as the rider, I've got to give you a name.' I paused then smiled. 'You look floppy like my ragdoll years ago. So, I'll call you Loobylou. Is that all right? ... Good ... Now, I know you're beautiful because you're slim, wear close-fitting leathers. Don't tell anybody I said this but they do turn me on. Plus, you ride a Benly, and very well. But if you wanted me to put my arm round you and hold your hand you didn't have to go head-to-head with that MG.'

The shout of FIRE broke through my conversation with Loobylou. I glanced over my shoulder. The MG was less than ten yards away and fast becoming a bonfire. I could feel the heat and hoped that the fire brigade was on its way. I wasn't bothered about the tank exploding, that only happened in American films. There was too much petrol and not enough vapour for that, but if the fuel in the tank caught fire? Both Loobylou and I were exposed. That was out of my hands. I managed to get my feet under the axle to protect Loobylou's legs then concentrated on my captive audience. 'Right, where were we? What can I tell you about *me*?'

It seemed an eternity. I'd reached the point in my story where I'd gone to university. The flames were now so high I thought the tank must have split. It was very warm. A gust caught the flames pushing them towards the tractor. The heat was intense. In seconds my feet felt as though they were on fire. The wind abated. The heat in my boots didn't. What Loobylou felt I had no idea. Pc Jefferson ran across armed with a small fire extinguisher.

'Are you ok, Brian. Keep still.' He began spraying me and Loobylou and, the front of the tractor.

'My feet and legs are a bit warm.'

'I'm not surprised. Your boots are smouldering. How's your charge?'

'No change.' In the distance I could hear the discordant but welcome racket of several sets of two-tone horns.'

I snuggled down again. 'Listen Loobylou, the cavalry are here. Right, university ...'

First to arrive were two fire engines followed by a couple of ambulances then police cars. How many I couldn't see. I was conscious of people running around. Two ambulancemen knelt at the side of the tractor. 'My name's Larry.' He indicated his colleague. 'This is Jack. What happened?'

I explained as succinctly as I could. 'She's got a carotid pulse.' I said.

'Have you moved her at all?' said Larry.

'I might have moved her head a bit when I put my arm under her neck, but not much.'

'Good. We're going to put a neck brace on her, then see about getting her out.'

It looked like some contraption from a medieval torture chamber.

'Right, Brian,' said Jack. 'Keep your right arm where it is. We've got to remove her helmet can you unbuckle it.'

She was beautiful. Very pale but beautiful. Jack put her helmet behind him and took hold of her head in both hands. 'Brian,' said Larry. 'If you don't feel you can do this that's all right but you're in the best position. Or, I'll change places with you.'

''No I'm fine.'

'Good. Carefully slide your arm from beneath her neck.'

Completed. 'Good,. Here,' Larry passed the neck brace across. 'This opens at the back. Place it on her upper chest and slide it so that her chin rests on the padded edge.'

It was awkward.

Larry fastened the buckle at the back.

'Brilliant, Brian. We've got her now. Wriggle out backwards. And thanks.'

It was uncomfortable standing. I hobbled out of the way. The MG was just about out and for the first time I noticed the pervading aroma of what I hoped was not human remains. Sickening. But if the occupants hadn't managed to get clear, probably was. The last cars behind the trailer were being turned round. A couple of police inspectors were talking with their counterparts in the fire service whilst several firemen set too and dismantled the bike with hydraulic shears. Once the job was complete Larry came and held Loobylou's left leg. The main section of the bike removed he crawled underneath with a stretcher. In a couple of minutes she was ambulance bound. I was impressed by their professionalism. As they drove away I wondered who she was.

'All right, Blake.' The voice of Inspector Pierce behind me.

'Oh, hello sir. Apart from my feet I'm okay. Force control let Pannal know?'

'Indeed. Yes, I saw. Your feet took a bit of a roasting. I'll run you to hospital once I've made arrangements to have your bike transferred to Pannal.

The nurses thought that a policeman dressed in leathers was kinky. It was a pity that I didn't get chance to demonstrate. Still, never mind. The verdict? First degree burns. However, because they were on the soles of my feet, I was ordered to Sick Bay for two nights. Then they would see. As for Loobylou, there was a good chance she would be transferred to the Leeds General Infirmary.

Twenty-Three

I'd only seen Matron in passing a couple of times at Pannal. Late thirties, attractive and slim. She read the letter from the Hospital and laughed. 'So, you like playing with fire do you, Pc Blake?'

'Not with my feet Matron I don't.'

She smiled and pulled the screens round the bed.

I had a few visitors one of whom came bearing a welcome pint. I had to use the crutches to get to the loo.

I don't know what the time was but I woke up to the accompaniment of some very pleasant but unprofessional stroking. A hand over my mouth, 'Shh. How long since?' she whispered.

'Matron?'

'Shh. How long?'

Was this one of matron's sidelines with whom she chose if the opportunity presented itself? I pushed the covers down. She knelt on the bed and straddled me. 'Four or five months.' I stroked a naked breast then slid my hand across her belly into her bush and reciprocated. 'How long?'

'Too long,' she gasped. 'This treatment is not available on prescription or on demand.'

'I understand and gentlemen do not tell.'

'Thank you. Now, lie still. It's time to play with fire.' There was no pretence of romance, just uncomplicated consensual fucking. What the commandant would have thought, never mind done, doesn't bear thinking about.

Matron was nothing if not energetic and it was fortunate that the mattresses in sick bay were interior sprung, unlike those in the dormitories. She stayed for round two. 'Tomorrow morning you will remember a very pleasant dream.'

'Tomorrow night?'

'That depends how many patients I have. I don't want an audience.' Funnily enough, neither did I.

Twenty-Four

I'd slept like a log. It was if it had never happened. Matron never batted an eyelid. Probably a good thing. An excellent breakfast was delivered and devoured.

The Commandant and Sergeant Bell arrived and after a quick word with matron.

'In the wars, Blake.'

'Just a little, sir. I'll be back on my feet in a couple of days.'

They both laughed. 'Yes, very funny. I've read Mr Pierce's report. A Pc Jefferson will be here later but, what happened?'

I explained as succinctly as possible until the ambulance departed carrying Loobylou – I didn't use that name.

'You weren't pushing her at all?'

I hadn't mentioned about the rider being female. 'You know the rider was female, sir?'

'Yes, her name is Lucy Vernon. Her father is William Vernon. The winner of the Senior Manx TT some years ago.'

'That explains a lot.'

'How so?'

'She was an accomplished rider with reactions like a cat. But to answer your question, sir. No, I wasn't pushing. She would be travelling at about 65 when she passed me. And slowed to 40 as she approached the bend. In retrospect the tractor would be doing 15 when the MG appeared. That's a closing speed between the MG and the bike of near enough 50 yards per second. Another millisecond and she would have cleared the MG. If not the offside verge.'

'Closing speed. How do you work that out?'

'Yes, Sergeant. Road speed in yards per second is almost half of miles per hour. I'd guessed 60 for the MG. Pc Jefferson confirmed it. Therefore thirty for convenience. Plus twenty for her.'

'I see. That's handy to know.'

'Had I been pushing her she would have been much further forwards, right on the bend and nowhere to go. The closing speed in those circumstances would have been 60 or thereabouts. It's unlikely that either of us would have survived.'

There was total silence.

'So, when did you realise?'

'It's all fractions of a second, sir. She saw the MG and began to take evasive action before I became fully aware. But when she did it gave me a safety margin of about 35 yards. Time enough to get out of the way as the two collided and she disappeared under the tractor.'

'Wasn't there a danger that the bike she was riding would catch fire?'

'A chance. But the engine had stalled and once I confirmed she had a carotid pulse I removed the ignition key. That reduced the risk.'

'But it was still there.'

'I suppose so. But it was only once I got beneath the tractor I could confirm that she was alive.'

'Very well. Well done, Blake. Sergeant Bell will let you have sight of his notes so that you can make your own as long as you are incapacitated. Inspector Pierce will sit in whilst you make your statement. And before we go, have you called your parents yet?'

'No sir.'

'Would you like Sergeant Bell or myself to call or, do you prefer to do it yourself.' I had intended to leave it for now but that option had just been removed.

'I'll do it myself sir. I need a new pair of boots.' I called Joe.

It was five past ten, I was copying Sergeant Bell's notes on Theft when Pc Jefferson arrived with Inspector Pierce and pulled up a couple of chairs.

'Before we begin,' I said. 'Can you tell me why you were chasing that MG.'

'Simple. Not for the first time Christopher Griffiths and his younger brother Mark drove off without paying for petrol. We dropped on them at Spacey Houses ten minutes later and gave them a tug. As we got out of the patrol car they made a break for it. The MG was in crap order, flat out at 60. It was madness when he pulled out to overtake that line of cars. We backed off. Well, you know the rest.

It was a solemn moment. 'How much did they owe?'

An unsmiling Pc Jefferson looked at me. 'A lousy £2. They died and nearly killed that girl for a lousy two quid,' I didn't know what to say. 'But how about you, Brian? It was a bad one. Has it put you off the job?'

I managed a weak smile. 'If I had to deal with those on a daily basis it might. Yesterday I was more interested in finding out if the motor cyclist was alive. The force of the impact and the way she went under the tractor I fully expected her to be dead.'

'She was very lucky. I called Leeds General this morning. She's unconscious but stable with no apparent fractures. You did well. Most would panic.'

I breathed a small sigh of relief. 'Thanks. I have to admit it was a claustrophobic squeeze crawling under the sump. When the MG fired I was apprehensive, but all I did was to put my arm under her neck for support and check for a pulse.'

I got an answering grin. 'And hold her hand and talked to her.'

I answered in kind. 'I suppose so. There were no complaints. And she was beautiful.'

Inspector Pierce intervened. 'How did you know she was beautiful before her helmet was removed?'

'Sir, the Benly is a young person's bike. High revving and fast. From her leathers she was slim. Her reactions were like lightning. I assumed the rest.' The Inspector smiled.

'Ok,' said Pc Jefferson. 'Talk me through it from when you heard the Benly behind you.' Thirty minutes later I signed my statement. He stopped as he opened the Sick Bay door. 'By the way, Brian. The girl's name was Lucy Vernon and her father's Bill Vernon.'

'The Manx TT winner,' I said. 'The Commandant told me earlier.'

'Fair enough. But he's a tyrant. Very protective of his daughter. Be advised should you come across him.' He nodded and closed the door.

Copying the sergeant's notes meant that I didn't have the benefit of his presentations or class discussions. However, the notes were very interesting and far more comprehensive than was necessary for our course.

At lunchtime I had a full meal and no doubt it would be the same for the evening meal. I was getting no exercise. The Michelin Man had better watch out.

Mickey Gardiner called in with John Bradbury. John, living in Harrogate, had missed the accident but Mickey hadn't.

He sounded very unsure. 'We were the first car in the queue. The MG was on fire when we got there. I've never seen anything like it. I take it that was your bike at the side of the road.'

'It was. When that happened I was under the tractor.'

'But what happened? How did you know what to do?'

'I just reacted, Mickey. I saw the whole thing in slow motion. It wasn't her fault. I crawled under the sump supported her neck and checked for a carotid pulse. Just like we were shown last month,' I paused and smiled. 'Then I spent the rest of the time until the ambulance crew arrived holding her hand and talking to her.'

'Talk? What about? Wasn't she unconscious?'

'She still is. Anything that came to mind. It was something I felt was positive. Whether she could hear me or not.'

An hour later Joe and Mum arrived with a new pair of boots and set of leathers. Matron arranged for tea and biscuits. Once Mum had heard the story and was satisfied that my feet weren't on tonight's menu she was happier. Joe in his normal sanguine mood. They left about an hour later after a chat with the Commandant.

Twenty-Five

Chief Inspector Reynolds came to see me half an hour later. Lucy Vernon was still unconscious. A request had been received from Professor Lightman, Head of Neurology at Leeds General. I was the last to talk with Lucy, would I be prepared to attend at the hospital? They thought that my voice might resonate with her. I agreed to do what I could.

An hour later I was wheeled into a sideward in the neurological wing. Loobylou, eyes still closed, a lot of bruising now visible on her right arm and left shoulder, looking as beautiful as I remembered but no leathers, just a bra and nightdress. A drip in her right arm and what I was informed was a nasogastric feeding tube up her nose and down the oesophagus to her stomach. There were also the leads of an ECG coming from the right sleeve of her nightdress. The operator two yards away from the bed.

At the Professor's request I talked him through what I had seen and the action taken. Although I felt slightly embarrassed when I explained what I called her and why.

'Don't worry about it, Brian,' he said. 'The fact is you made contact at a very friendly level. That could be important.' What he said next was staggering. 'What I would like you to do is to lay on her bed with your arm behind her neck, hold her hand just as you did at the scene of the accident and talk to her.'

'But, it was different at the scene, Professor. She was wearing her leathers not just some flimsy nightdress.'

The Professor's smile was benign. 'You've never been in that situation before?'

'Not with an audience I haven't.'

There were a few smiles from the assembled staff. 'Don't worry. You're dressed and we're here. You'll be safe. And, it might be beneficial for Lucy.'

'I did say I'd do whatever I could, but what should I talk to her about?'

'Whatever ... You both ride motor bikes. Why not take her as your pillion passenger on a ride to some place you know well.. Where she will be safe. Oh, and for continuity call her Loobylou.'

A nurse, ring-free, tall, slim and attractive wheeled me across to the bed. 'Can you stand by yourself?'

'Yes thanks,' using my crutches I levered myself upright turned and sat. The nurse took the crutches. 'Hello Loobylou it's Brian,' I said and I took her left hand in mine. 'You're looking better than you were yesterday. Do you mind if I lay down?'

I slipped my right arm under her neck lowered myself and wriggled until I was comfortable. 'Cosy, isn't it. I hope the nurses are looking after you.' There was no response. 'I know it might take a while but when you get home and are feeling better why don't I take you for a bike ride to Whitby? You can ride pillion. Put your arms round my waist, keep you safe. Why don't we go for a trial ride now. See if you're comfortable.'

'Ok, we'll begin from my home. Feet on pegs. Arms round my waist. Hold tight. Off we go.'

Fifteen minutes later we were back. 'I hope you enjoyed the ride. Where would you like to go tomorrow. Rutland Water in Leicestershire and see the birds. Scarborough or further north to Bamburgh. Or even back to Whitby and spend the day sea-fishing. Let me know. I've got to go now.'

I got back to my feet as a young female doctor arrived. 'If she were your girlfriend you'd give her a kiss when you parted. Just give her a peck.'

'It seems like I'm taking advantage.'

'Isn't that what relationships are about? Taking advantage of the relationship. Knowing how far you can go. It's just a quick peck. Nothing salacious.'

'Okay,' I leaned forwards and kissed her forehead.'

'Whoa. That got a response,' the ECG operator said. 'Increase in heart rate.'

'And her fingers moved.'

'I saw that,' Professor Lightman arrived. 'If you wouldn't mind, Brian, kiss her again. This time on the lips.'

'If you insist.'

I leaned forwards. 'Sorry Loobylou but the Professor says I got to do this,' and planted the gentlest of kisses.

'And again,' said the ECG operator.

'Definite movement of her fingers ... and, she's crying.'

Sure enough, tears formed in the corners of her eyes but not enough to run down her cheeks. I took hold of her hand and squeezed gently. 'It's the first time I've made a girl cry with so little effort,' I smiled at her but there was no response. 'I'll come back and see you tomorrow.' For good measure I kissed her again.

Twenty-Six

Any thoughts of a further clandestine liaison with Matron were dashed. I had company. Greg Mellor from class six broke his arm.

Wednesday, I was able to get around wearing my trainers. Relegated to my dormitory and excused drill, gym, swimming. I could supervise karate but not participate. Instruction was done by John. Bugger, I had to hand Sergeant Bell's notes back.

Wednesday tea time at the hospital there was some change. Her heartrate increased when I took hold of her hand. Our journey that evening was to Rutland Water interspersed with memories of Pamela. Some of them very pleasant. The last thing before I left was to hold her hand and ask, 'Can you open your eyes?'

There was no response. Nor any change on Thursday.

Friday I called in on my way home wearing my new leathers and boots. She was lying there just the same as before. It was heart rending. The first time I saw her was on her bike. Full of life and in control. Now? Who knows what damage had been done. Certainly not the doctors. Apart from the fact that she had no fractures or any wounds all they could do was to provide a secure environment. Ensure adequate hydration. Feed her by tube, and wait.

My identical step-sisters never missed an opportunity. When they got together they could be merciless.

'*You* had a ragdoll called Loobylou?'

'Yes, Jennifer. I did. When I was two.'

'Oo Jennifer. Sunday name. Better be careful.'

'Very funny. But I grew out of mine. Didn't I?'

'Oh, ha, ha.'

Mum bounced in with a paper bag and grinning like the proverbial moggy.. 'This is Loobylou,' she said fishing my old toy from the depths.. A fifteen inch ragdoll. Little red shoes, hooped blue and white legs and, arms with pink hands. A Blue dress with green polka dots. White smiling face with big blue and black eyes, a wide pink smiley mouth and thick bright yellow woollen hair. Just a ragdoll it might have been then but I slept with it every night

'Isn't she sweet,' said Frankie as she pulled a face.

'So cute,' followed up Jen.

Anne bringing up the rear with. 'Shall we put it on your bed so you won't feel lonely?'

Joe kept out of it.

'This is going to be a long weekend,' I said. 'Coming for a pint?'

There wasn't a sound. 'I told you about being treated as a suspect when Gavin Carter was murdered. I've told you about Lucy. So, now you know what it's like being a copper. Now, which one of you is riding pillion?'

'I'm not frightened. I'll come/'

We all smiled. 'No Clive,' I said. My ten year old half-brother was game for anything. 'Not this time. When you're older, perhaps. But it's not about being frightened.'

'And your boots really did catch fire?'

I made eye contact with Joe. 'Yes, Anne,' he said and smiled. 'He had to stay in sickbay for two days and ride in a wheelchair. No karate.'

'No karate? It must have been bad ... Can I come?'

'If you want.'

Forty five minutes later I parked in the side entrance to Leeds General.

Twenty-Seven

There were raised voices as we approached the sideward. Anne looked at me and frowned. 'What's happening?' She mouthed.

I remembered Pc Jefferson's comment about Loobylou's father being an overprotective tyrant. I put my finger to my lips. We waited.

'Doctor,' the decibels were increasing. You could have heard him at the Civic Hall. 'She's been here five days with almost no improvement. I think she would be better off at home where we can look after her. I'll have a room prepared with whatever equipment is required.'

A woman's voice. 'Bill. No. She needs hospital care. Look at her.'

'What do you think I'm doing, Liz? My little girl would be better off surrounded by those who love her instead of this impersonal mausoleum.'

'Mr Vernon, your wife is correct,' it was Professor Lightman. 'It's early days and there is some sign of improvement. In any case which ever agency nurses you hire to look after your daughter it's unlikely they would have the expertise should any emergency occur. To get an ambulance to your house and back here in time could be problematic.'

I tapped Anne's arm and pushed the door open. The tall thick-set bald-headed man who I took to be Bill Vernon had his back to the door. His wife, five four, a honey blonde like her daughter, to the left. The Professor and most of the other staff facing him.

Loobylou lay exactly where she was yesterday.

The Professor looked at me and nodded.

'Professor.'

Bill Vernon spun round. 'Who the hell are you?' he spat the wards out and looked at Anne. 'Is this your tart?'

Anne didn't like that. 'How dare you speak to me like that. I'm his sister.'

'Both of you get out, you're not required.'

I put my hand up as Anne was about to speak.

'The Professor seems to disagree, Mr Vernon. As for who I am, my name is Brian,'

He looked me up and down, 'You young bloods are all the same. See my daughter on the road and you just have to get past. You've got to score points. Go on, admit it. You're the one who pushed my daughter under the tractor.'

He was trying my patience. 'Sorry if it dents your ego but, believe it or not Mr Vernon, I'd never heard of you or your daughter.' He was about to start spitting feathers. 'And, no. I was not responsible. Your daughter had passed me. I was about thirty five yards behind.'

His voice went us several decibels. 'That's right blame her. Anybody but you. The least you could do is admit it.'

I was determined to stay calm. 'Mr Vernon. I was thirty five yards behind your daughter when the MG appeared. She tried to swing to the offside to avoid it and the tractor. Almost made it. Had I been pushing her I would have been close behind. We would both have been passed the point of no return and been killed. I understand you're an engineer, work out the closing speeds for yourself.'

The ECG operator turned in her seat. 'Somethings happening. Her heart rate's increasing.'

A doctor ran across and was pouring over the screen. 'Sinus rhythm.'

The Professor glanced over his shoulder and began swirling his hand. 'Brian, keep talking.'

'Mr Vernon, you must be frightened. But this is a hospital not a mausoleum. Your daughter is not dead. You probably promised Lucy that you would look after her. Always be there for her. You're looking for someone else to blame because you weren't there and I was. Even if you had you couldn't have done any more for her than I did.'

'Of course I could,' he was shouting now. 'I'm her father, who else? I understand you left her under that bloody tractor. I would have gotten her out.'

The Professor began to interject. 'If you had done ...'

'Stop it,' the conversation froze at the husky sound of Lucy's voice. Her eyes wide open. 'Stop shouting, Dad. You're always shouting.'

Bill Vernon charged across the ward and sat on the bed and held his daughter's hand. 'I'm here Lucy. Your father's here.'

'Brian, I want Brian.'

A shocked Bill Vernon was struggling to speak. 'B-B-But I'm your father.'

'Brian,' her eyes closed. 'I'm tired.'

Twenty-Eight

Liz Vernon placed her hand on her husband's shoulder. 'Come on, Bill. There'll be plenty of time later,' her husband rose. Liz Vernon leaned across the kissed her daughter on the cheek. 'Rest, we'll see you later.'

Lucy nodded. 'Mum, tell him to stop trying to marry me off, please.'

'I'll try.'

'No. I mean it. I'll be 21 at New Year. He can't stop me seeing who I want. If he tries he'll never see me again.'

'I'll try.'

That sounded iffy. Lucy's parents were dawdling towards the door. 'If she thinks ...' were the last words I heard Bill Vernon say before the door closed. It didn't sound good.

'Would you wait outside for five minutes, please Brian, whilst we have a word with Lucy.'

Five minutes later she was looking more like a member of the human race. No tubes. No wires.

We sat one either side. I held Lucy's left hand. I nodded at Anne who took her right. Lucy opened her eyes and smiled. A smile that lit up her face. A moment I would always remember. 'I wish I had a comb.'

'If you don't mind, I've got one,' said Anne.

'Oh, yes please ... Sorry, everything hurts.' Lucy said as Anne passed her the comb and she tried to raise her arms.

'Here let me,' Anne jumped out of the chair. Lucy raised her head from the pillow.

'Thank you so much. Human again.' To me it didn't look much different. Perhaps it was just the experience of having her hair combed. Holding hands she smiled at Anne. 'You're Brian's little sister?'

Anne nodded and smiled. 'Yes. It's been a long time but we're step-sisters. I'm one of three,'

'Three?'

'Three,' I iterated. 'Identical.'

'Triplets. Wonderful.'

'My tormentors.'

Lucy smiled again. 'You don't look too bad on it.' She turned to Anne. 'Room for another?'

I was subject to a smiling quizzical look from Anne. 'Of course. The more the merrier.'

'That's all I need.' Time to change the subject. 'Lucy, what do you remember?'

'Everything. I was never unconscious. I don't think so anyway. I could neither move nor speak. But I could breathe.

'Breathing is autonomous. You don't have to think about it.'

'You're a doctor?'

'No, I read exercise physiology with anatomy at East Midlands.'

'Does that mean you could help me to get fit?'

'Once the doctors agree. But it depends, I've got a lot on my plate at the moment.'

'He's training to be a policeman,' said Anne.

'Is he? Just like Jimmy Durante. Stick 'em up you rat, you dirty rat.'

'That's wonderful. Very funny,' Anne joined in the laughter.

I'd never seen anyone trying to laugh and scowl at the same time as Lucy looked from me to Anne and back. 'Why are you laughing at me?'

'We're not laughing at you, Lucy,' I said and squeezed her hand. 'Just what you said. Jimmy Durante was the comedian with the big nose. Jimmy Cagney was the gangster.'

'Ah well,' she smiled, sighed and lay back. 'You knew who I meant. When do you finish your training?'

'In two months.'

'Can I write to you?'

'Of course you can.' I gave my details to the nurse.

'Do you remember anything else,' said Anne.

'Yes, the MG hitting my bike. Being spun round and the tractor running over me. I thought I was going to die,' she paused as tears appeared in her eye-corners. I handed her a clean handkerchief. She dabbed her eyes and smiled. 'When I couldn't move or speak I thought I had. I felt a bump from behind. Brian shaking my shoulder. Asking if I was all right and put his fingers against my throat. Then his arm under my neck and held my hand and began to talk. Called me Loobylou. All the time I was trying to shout and scream but I couldn't,' she said. My memories came flooding back. My eyes welled up. 'I don't know for how long he talked before the ambulance crew took me away. I hung onto his voice.' She paused and smiled at me. 'Your eyes are leaking.'

'I don't care,' I said. 'I expected you to be dead.'

Anne looked at her brother not knowing what to say. 'Would you like to know why he called you Loobylou?'

Lucy nodded. 'That's what my mother called me when I was little.'

I sighed. 'Go on then. Get it over with.'

'Ah well. When Brian was two his mum and dad bought him a ragdoll ...'

'He said I looked like a ragdoll.'

'Wait,' Anne grinned. 'It gets better. Would you like to meet her?'

'Yes please,' Her smile was getting to me.

'Here she is.' Loobylou appeared peeping over the edge of the carrier bag. 'A ragdoll his mother called Lucy. But he couldn't pronounce the 'C'. It came out as Looby, hence Loobylou.'

She beamed at me. 'She's lovely and named after me.'

I raised my eyebrows and smiled. Answered with a grin. 'She's worn out,' I said.

Lucy turned to me. 'You've kept it all this time?'

'Not me,' I protested. 'My mother did. I mentioned it at home and she dug it out of her treasure chest. I had no idea she'd kept it.'

'Can I borrow her?'

'You can have her. I don't have need of it now.' I didn't voice my thoughts but there was someone else I had in mind.

Professor Lightman wandered across. 'I'm sorry, but I'm going to ask you to leave in a few minutes. Lucy's parents will want to return and a confrontation will not be beneficial for Lucy.'

'Doctor, can they come back tomorrow?'

'Yes, I'll make arrangements for tomorrow morning, outside of visiting hours. For a half hour from eleven o'clock.' He smiled at us all.

'Yes. I'll be here.'

'So will I,' said Anne.

'Just a minute,' said Lucy as we stood. 'Haven't you forgotten something?' I looked puzzled. 'Are you just going to walk away?'

I winked at Anne. 'Ah. You remembered.'

'I remember everything.'

I leaned forwards over the bed.

'No. I want Anne to see how we were under the tractor.'

'Ok.' Under the puzzled expression of my seventeen year old sister and the smiles of the medical staff I lay on the bed and slid my right arm under her neck. 'Satisfied?'

'Hold still,' Lucy smiled, lifted her arms and winced.

'Are you ok?'

'Shh,' Lucy clasped her hands behind my neck and pulled. It would have been a sign of cowardice to resist.

I heard Anne's voice. 'So that's what you were doing, is it?'

A round of applause from the medical staff.

At last, our noses almost touching. 'Satisfied?'

Lucy lay there smiling. 'For now,' she breathed.

The professor, wreathed in smiles, stood to one side. 'It is well documented that after a dangerous and intense emotional episode such as you two experienced, you might also share a similar positive emotional relationship. It won't do either of you any harm. Now I have to ask you to leave. Be here tomorrow by eleven.

Lucy's experience had been far more intense than mine but I was not about to disagree.

I couldn't help laughing.

'He did what?' exploded Frankie.

'Climbed on the bed and snogged her.'

Four pairs of eyes swivelled in my direction.

'Guilty as charged,' I said and bowed. 'Now Anne. The truth, please.'

Twenty-Nine

Lucy was subdued. To add to her discomfort from her injuries and the visible bruising, her father had picked another argument with the Professor. What was wrong with the man? He could pick an argument in an empty room. Awkward sod. Now Lucy was devoid of tubes and wires he wanted to take her home, forthwith.

He relented after his wife interjected.

'How did he react to Loobylou,' said Anne.

Lucy brightened. 'He doesn't know. I hid her under my pillows. Mum thought she was lovely.' They shared a conspiratorial giggle. 'He doesn't go in my bedroom so she will be all right there.'

'How long does the professor want you to stay?'

'Open-ended. I think at least a week, maybe ten days.'

'What does your father do for a living?'

'Vernons. We sell motor cycles. Amongst other things.'

'Of course. I should have realised. That's where Joe bought my bike. For my 21st.'

'What's your full name?'

'Brian Blake.'

She thought for a moment. 'No. We haven't sold a Super Hawk to anybody called Blake. When's your birthday?'

'March 21st.'

'March 21st approx. eighteen months ago ... Joe ... Mountain?' She turned and smiled at me. 'Anne said you were step-brother and sister.' She laughed when she saw the look on my face. 'I'm right, aren't I?'

'How on earth did you do that?'

It was good to see her smiling. 'I told you. I remember everything. Unfortunately I'm dad's office manager. I do the numbers. Everything comes through me. It's just a knack.'

'I'm amazed,' said Anne.

'It's outside? I said. 'Care to take a look?'

It was a sedate procession along the corridors

The walk had tired her out. 'Shall I carry you back?'

'No, I feel better for the exercise although everything hurts.'

A few minutes later we borrowed a wheelchair.

'Earlier, you said it was unfortunate that you were your father's office manager, why?'

'Dad's only thought is how can he make money. Everything has a price. In his eyes I'm a commodity.'

'That's appalling,' said Anne. 'Is that what he meant yesterday.'

'Probably. I'm young single and unspoiled. That's how he sees it. It's not quite an auction but I have a value and he wants to capitalize on that. Which is why I'm not allowed to choose my own male friends. He hopes to find someone I'll accept and, providing the joint business venture he hopes he will get out of it meets his expectations.'

'But that's Dickensian.'

'True. However, that's how he sees the world. I don't. He already lost a son.'

'How so?' said Anne.

'Gerald, my older brother. He's very clever but no head for business. He wanted to go into teaching. Dad thought that was a waste of time. It couldn't add anything to his empire. They had a big falling out and dad beat him up. He hasn't been back since. Mum and I still see him but dad doesn't want to know. Gerald's a lecturer in physics at Leeds. I should have met him yesterday. Will you get a message to him for me?'

'I'll do that if you want?' said Anne.

'It's not that I don't trust you, Anne, but on this occasion let Brian do it, please. The fact that there's a man involved ... he will understand. He and Marianne have said that I can stay with them if it gets too bad.'

'I'll give him a call tomorrow.'

'Thanks.'

I checked my watch. 'We're going to have to make tracks, Lucy. Three questions. When do they think you will be able to ride pillion and, where do you want to go. Finally, where do you live.'

'I don't know but I'll ask. And Whitby, never been there. The address is Great Gables, Boston Spa. You know the entrance to Harewood House?

'Yup.'

'Good, opposite is The Avenue, the A659. Follow that all the way across the A1, through Boston Spa. Follow the signs for Tadcaster. It's the last house on the left. Now come and say goodbye.'

'I'll wait outside. You could be some time.'

'What on earth do you mean,' I protested. 'I was dragged into bed.'

'You were not, Brian Blake. I was there. Remember?' Anne scowled at me. 'Don't be too long. I'm hungry.'

We shared our only kiss of the day. 'Have you got a girlfriend?'

'A bit late to ask that, isn't it. No I haven't. Are you volunteering?'

'Yes please. After what happened on Sunday it made me realise just how tenuous our grip on life is,' she bit her lip and sat up close to me. 'Have you ever had sex?'

That was a shock. 'Too soon for that isn't it?'

'I don't know. Is it? I've never even had a proper kiss before. Dad has seen to that. Last Sunday lots of things were flashing through my mind. I would never experience sex. Never have children. Get married. Never be free of my father. Then you arrived. You're not frightened of him are you?

I shook my head. 'No, I'm not.'

'If he finds out about you there will be implied threats and bluster. Then bribery. When we kissed yesterday I wanted more, but ... have you had sex?'

I smiled and nodded. 'Yes.'

There was an answering quizzical smile. 'What's it like?'

'Everything you've ever dreamed of but ten times better. Great fun.'

'Who was it with?'

'Her name was Pamela. We met at university..'

'Were you in love with her?'

'I thought so. But she wanted to control my future to fit in with her vision. Me being a humble constable didn't fit. My joining the police would interfere with the social life of her class as she saw it. That was non-negotiable. For me not joining the police was also non-negotiable. It would never have lasted.'

'Do you think what the professor said about us developing a strong emotional relationship is true?'

'I think we both know the answer to that, don't we?'

She smiled. 'I suppose we do.'

I leaned forward and gave her a quick kiss. 'I'll call Leeds uni tomorrow lunchtime. But when I'll get the chance to see you again I don't know. Your parents will no doubt be here in the evenings. If that's the case I'll call at your house next Saturday.'

Thirty

I managed to get a couple of hours study during the afternoon whilst Anne took the flak from the others. My journey to Pannal incident free.

After our midday meal I called Leeds university physics department and spoke with Lucy's brother and filled him in. He promised to call Leeds General.

I'd just put the phone back on the hook. There was a tap on my shoulder. 'Blake,' Curious. An unusually quiet Sergeant Faulkner. 'Commandant's office.'

Apart from Chief Superintendent Andrews, as usual behind his desk, there were two men in plain clothes sitting between the desk and the window. Looking for all the world like Tweedle Dum and Tweedle Dee. I stood to attention facing the Commandant. 'Sir?'

'Sit down, Blake,' he motioned me to a chair turned towards his two visitors. 'These gentlemen would like to ask you some questions. But before anything else your Chief Constable is aware of what these gentlemen are about to say and has given his permission for them to approach you. You do not have to accept.'

'I understand, sir,' I said as I sat and turned to these mysterious visitors. 'How can I help?'

The one on the left rose, extracted a document from his briefcase and placed it on the commandant's desk. 'Can you confirm that this is your signature?'

The document was a photocopy of the extract of the Official Secrets Act I signed on the day I joined. 'Yes, that appears to be my signature.' He returned the document to his briefcase.

'Are you a Communist?'

What the Hell? I laughed anyway. 'No, I am not a Communist. Neither have I ever read the Daily Worker.'

Neither batted an eyelid. 'Why did you mention the Daily Worker?'

'To save you the trouble. You obviously have some information from my days at university. Yes, I attended two meetings of what transpired to be a branch of the Communist Party. It wasn't for me. I never associated with them after that.'

'Why did you attend the meetings in the first place?'

'I was eighteen. My first experience of life outside of the confines of a family. Other than my parents voting we were not involved in politics. I was curious. That's what being at university is all about. If you're interested, I had sex for the first time at university as well. Why don't you ask me if I'm a rapist?

There was the semblance of a smile. 'Are you a rapist?'

'No, I am not. But who are you? I know that all applicants for the police are checked by Special Branch and no queries were raised. So, can I see your Id?'

> From what little I'd learned at university, Special Branch dealt with internal terrorism and subversion. MI5 was Military Intelligence. The ramifications? What was I about to be exposed to?

'We are members of the security service. The title of MI5 is still used, it's embedded in the public psyche.'

I handed their Id's back. A Lieutenant Phillips *and* a Captain Manville-Jones from the security service? 'Thank you.'

Before Mr Williams leaves,' Captain Manville-Jones said. 'I would just like to say that under any other circumstances we would never dream of approaching someone so young in service. And, as the Commandant said you do not have to participate.'

After ordering refreshments for three the Commandant stood. 'I'll leave you gentlemen to it,' he said nodded to me and left.

'Why the interest in me? Or can't you tell me.'

'We became interested in you, Mr Blake, whilst you were a student at the New College in Huddersfield. It was suggested that you might be of the right material.'

I wondered who that might be.

'Can we call you, Brian?'

'Yes.'

There was a knock on the door as the refreshments arrived.

The lieutenant walked to the desk turned and smiled. 'How do you take it?'

'Black no sugar, please.'

The lieutenant poured the coffee. 'A purist.'

'It spoils the taste of the coffee. Now gentlemen, what's it all about.'

'Before we begin, your contact should you have the need, you already know, Dr Cappelli.'

'My old Latin teacher?' Still waters did run deep.

'Yes,' he saw the look on my face and laughed. 'Don't ask.' He handed me a card. 'His contact details. Remember the telephone number. For use in an emergency. Understood?'

'Yes sir.'

'Now, Brian, tell us what you know about Bill Vernon.'

'Lucy's father?' the lieutenant nodded. 'Very little. I've only seen him at the hospital. I was told, in relation to his daughter, he was an overprotective tyrant. I witnessed as such. He's brusque, very unpleasant with Dickensian views in regard to his daughter.'

'That is true. He can be obnoxious. He is also an undischarged bankrupt with all that implies. Prior to being declared bankrupt every asset he owned was placed in his wife's name. Although he keeps tight oversight he cannot be seen to control anything.

'However, whilst that may be of interest to the geographical law enforcement agencies it is of no direct interest to us. What does interest us is the fact that included in his business empire were the Spartans motor cycle racing team, also in his wife's name. They travel around the United Kingdom and across Europe. Any questions so far?

'No sir. I understand.'

'Good. Now, this relationship that you have with the daughter, Lucy.'

'What about it?' Where was this going?

'In spite of the fact is has only been a few days since you met it is progressing far beyond a simple friendship.'

'I don't know where you got your information from, sir. But it is.'

Neither smiled. 'Are her parents aware of your burgeoning relationship?'

'I have no idea, unless Lucy has mentioned it. I can't see any of the hospital staff doing that.'

'We know Lucy acts as her father's business manager, but as far as we know she has nothing to do with any aspect of the business other than the motor cycle outlets in Britain. Now, we're putting you in an invidious situation. It is, however, a matter of national security. You do not need to know the precise details but top secret information is being smuggled out of the country. Where from does not concern you. The incidents coincide with the departure of the Spartans to the continent. In fact between twenty four and thirty hours prior to the Spartans sailing from Hull. The courier will be a Peter Pederson. He rides a Honda CB77 motor cycle as you do.

'The problem is, we have not been able to establish his contact within the Spartans. Our aim is to track this information into continental Europe. Which is where you come in. Who actually carries the material abroad? What we need is information. Who does he speak to amongst the Spartans. It could be anybody. There is no requirement for you to intervene.'

I took a deep breath and exhaled. 'Nobody mentioned this when I applied to join.' I said. I would have loved to ask my father if he had done anything similar.

They both laughed. 'No Brian. And we didn't anticipate this situation arising. But the fact that you and Lucy Vernon are involved ...'

'Is too good an opportunity to miss?'

'I couldn't have put it better myself. Bill Vernon is volatile. But you appear to be the one, so far, that Lucy has shown interest in. Just play the boy-girl thing. Try and get involved with the family. You have an interest in motor cycles. You were a witness to the accident. Use that to get an invite to meet with the Spartans.'

'Have you any idea when the next event will be, sir?'

'Yes. The Spartans sail from Hull on Friday 9th of August.' That was the week prior to the Annual Inspection.

'And if there is no exchange at Boston Spa?'

'We have the docks and the ferry covered. It is of course possible that it will take place elsewhere, but likely to be done in the hurly burley whilst preparing to leave.'

'So, three weeks to inveigle my way in?'

'You agree to do this?'

'Yes sir. For personal reasons as well as professional.'

'Of course,' the lieutenant smiled. 'And we will be keeping an eye on you from a distance.'

'I understand.' I understood the things they had told me. What had they neglected to tell me?

I couldn't breathe a word of this to anyone.

Thirty-One

The next morning, Wednesday, I received a very short letter from Lucy. Her handwriting was not good. I'm not saying what she had written but she wasn't telling me to go away. She was feeling better and was being treated by physios although everything still hurt. At least she was becoming mobile. She hoped that the professor would allow her home by the weekend.

Several students had seen the two men in suits and asked what it was all about. Informing them that no matter what, I couldn't tell them in the first place didn't help matters.

Members of the teaching fraternity bit their collective tongues.

I rang the hospital on Friday lunchtime to be informed that Lucy had gone home. End of story. I didn't have their phone number.

The fifteen miles from Pannal Ash to the Vernon home took twenty minutes. My heart was thumping as the house, about a hundred yards from the road, came into view. At first glance it was almost identical to ours except ours did not have a large double garage facing the drive with a Bentley Continental in British Racing green parked outside. Yorkshire stone. Double fronted and big. Ours had six bedrooms. This at least the same. The front garden was huge. What the rear garden was like was anyone's guess.

It was with some trepidation I kicked the side stand out, dismounted and removed my helmet. I was unexpected and after what I had witnessed at the hospital I didn't know what kind of reception I would receive. On top of everything else I had my little task to bear in mind. Only one way to find out.

It was the longest ten seconds.

The door opened. She was just as I remembered. 'Mrs Vernon. Sorry I couldn't ring ..'

She had a warm welcoming smile. 'But you don't have our phone number,' she interjected. 'Lucy said you'd come. Come in please, Brian. Straight through to the kitchen.'

'Thank you.'

I hadn't gone two steps when there was a call from the kitchen. 'Brian, is that you?'

'Yes, Lucy,' I said.

Seconds later she appeared in the doorway. Just as beautiful as I remembered. Signs of bruising visible around the top of her sternum. Pyjamas, dressing gown, slippers and wearing the biggest grin. 'Wait there.'

I returned the grin. 'It's lovely to see you.'

She nodded and took the eighteen sedate steps to reach me. 'See,' she beamed a smile.. 'I'm better already.'

That deserved a smile. 'Better is a relative term.'

She could scowl as well. 'Still better.'

'True. And thank you for your letter. I'd be delighted. But not yet.'

'Oh shut up. Hold still.' Her closed eyes and facial expressions told me how much pain she was experiencing. Her hands closed behind my neck. She opened her eyes and grinned. 'Success.'

'I'm impressed.'

'You talk too much,' she said pulling me towards her.

'That's better,' she said, when she came up for air.

'Excuse me,' said a voice from behind.

Lucy looked round my arm. 'You still here, Mum?'

'Cheeky. You know what the doctor said. Shouldn't you be resting?'

She sighed. 'Suppose so. Help me back to the kitchen, will you.'

I raised my eyebrows and smiled. 'Or shall I carry you?'

She looked exasperated. 'I'll walk for the moment. Thanks.'

Lucy lowered herself into her chair. I checked my watch. 'I should be making tracks. I'll be late.'

'So soon,' she looked despondent. 'Can't you stay for something to eat?' she glanced at her mother. 'Mum?'

'You can stay if you want, Brian. Where do you live?'

'Huddersfield.'

'But that's what, forty five miles?'

'Near enough. Could I make a phone call. I'll pay for the call.'

'You'll do no such thing,' Mrs Vernon pointed to the phone.

On the third ring. 'The Mountain residence. How may I direct your call?'

'Brian.'

'Oh it's you.'

'Who else. Apologise to Mum but I've been invited out to tea.'

'Good of you to let us know. Who?'

I turned and winked at Lucy who frowned in return. 'She wants to talk to you.'

'Who is it?'

'You need ask?' I passed the phone to Lucy and mouthed, 'It's Anne.'

'Oh goody,' she put the handset to her ear. 'Hello Anne.'

'Who's ... Lucy?'

'Yes, they let me out.'

'Fantastic. How are you?'

'Better. Although Brian says that's relative.'

'He would.'

'I've a favour to ask. Can I borrow him?'

There was an answering laugh. 'Borrow? You can have him.'

'Yes please ...'

I sat back at the table. 'I'll let them get on with it, Mrs Vernon.'

'Liz, please. Anne? That was the girl with you at the hospital.'

'It was.'

'Lucy has never stopped talking about Anne and her sisters: Frankie, Jennifer and half-brother Clive. Your mother's called Dorothy and your stepfather, Joe.'

'She's got quite a memory.'

'Yes she has. That's quite a family that you have.'

'The girls are all right but when they decide to gang up on me I take shelter.'

'Where?'

'From the outside our house looks remarkably similar to yours. On the left of the hall is our library. No radio, television, records or arguments. It's a haven.'

'It sounds like it,' she said and laughed. 'What does Joe do for a living?

This was a fishing expedition. Was I right for their daughter. 'When Mum met him a year after my father died he had taken over the family butchers. Now he has five butchers shops. Five years ago he bought a pie making factory and after a fire re-built it. I know he's negotiating for the sale of a cooked meats business and also a bakery. He says it makes good business sense.'

'I agree it does. He's a busy man with an eye for business. You're a policeman?'

'In time. I'm five weeks into my basic training but it's going well. I was returning to Pannal Ash at Harrogate when the accident happened.'

'Yes. Thank you for what you did for Lucy.'

'It was my pleasure, Liz.'

'Look, Brian, I'm sorry about my husband's attitude at the hospital. He dotes on Lucy and won't accept that she can do any wrong.'

'On this occasion he was correct. The people responsible were in the MG and died when it overturned and caught fire. I can only hope they died before the fire. I wouldn't wish that on anybody.'

'At the hospital I wasn't really listening. Lucy had said she thought she was dead, until she heard your voice. Do you know what she meant?'

I took her step-by-step what happened. 'She's intimated that some of the things I said I might find embarrassing. But she won't tell me what.'

'I wouldn't worry too much, Brian,' she said and smiled. 'Whatever it was hasn't put her off.'

'So I see.'

'Now I understand. Thank you. She said she hung onto your every word whilst she was trying to shout, but couldn't.'

The sound of the handset being replaced and Lucy's laugh was followed by, 'They've invited us over, tomorrow.'

'When?'

Her eyes were pleading. 'Will you take me?'

'On my bike? Not this time, Lucy. It's too soon.'

'But?'

I crouched, took hold of her hands and looked into her eyes. 'Lucy, it's less than a week since the accident. I'm surprised that the hospital agreed to let you come home so soon ...'

'They didn't agree,' she interjected. 'Dad insisted. Said that he would arrange for a nurse to pay visits daily and for a physio.'

'I understand. But it's a forty five mile trip each way and on the back of a bike? Sorry, it's too far too soon. There'll be plenty of other times.'

Her eyes dropped. 'Can't Mum bring me?'

'That's different. You'll have to ask her.'

'Mum?

'Your father's away until Sunday. We'll go in style. We just need directions.'

Thirty-Two

I left at seven arriving home at eight only to be berated by the girls for not having the forethought to take a camera with me. There are some battles you are just not destined to win.

Liz aimed to arrive at Salendine Nook not later than two tomorrow.

I would love to have been able to have a chat with Joe about what I was up to. Even though his signing of the Official Secrets Act during the war would probably still be in effect it was not an option.

The forecast was for the warm sunny spell to continue. Early breakfast and bike ride the two miles into town. A call at a jewellers in the Imperial Arcade. No, it wasn't for a ring. Not yet.

Following the revelations of the week I needed a run. Living where we did in Salendine Nook it was perfect. A good five mile blast finishing with a final uphill mile. Clear the cobwebs.

They arrived at five to two. Everyone agog as the Bentley coasted to a halt. Being a gentleman I opened the door for Lucy and helped her out. Not wearing her pyjamas, that gave me too many ideas. This time a white long-sleeved blouse with mid-blue slacks and white shoes. Earrings but nothing else.

Even with its cavernous doors she still found it painful to exit. A point noticed by all. The kiss we shared receiving a cheer from the girls who, as usual, were doing their party thing: identical dresses, shoes and hair. Like three peas. What trick would they try and pull today. Clive just stood there looking disinterested. He wasn't, but he tried.

I introduced everyone leaving my three grinning sisters until the last. 'Which of us is Anne?' said Frankie.

'Anne?' Lucy stood in perfect equanimity scanning the line looking for invisible clues. 'Ok. A question that only Anne would remember, I hope. No doubt you all know the story. But, what did Brian say when I asked about my breathing?'

I was impressed that Lucy was able to recall the incident and speak about it so calmly. There were glances along the line. Anne, standing at the opposite end to Frankie, said. 'Breathing is autonomous. You don't have to think about it.'

'Hello Anne,' she smiled. 'We made it.'

There were no over enthusiastic hugs from the girls. Lucy was escorted into the house followed closely by Mum and Liz. Joe, Clive and I examined the Bentley.

'Will you and Dad give a Kendo demonstration for Lucy and her Mum?' Said Frankie when we joined them. The kitchen chairs lined up for the spectators.

We could take a hint and left. 'Can't I join in,' moaned Clive. 'I like Kendo.'

'You like everything,' Jennifer laughed. 'If you want, shorty.'

'I'm nearly as big as you are,' he protested.

'Not yet you're not.'

The natural response being the ritual that begun when Clive was five, they stuck their tongues out.

'This Kendo, isn't it dangerous?' said Liz.

'Not really,' said Jen. 'Unless you don't put the armour on as you should. But you'll find that the armour makes Brian look far more handsome.'

The explosion of laughter said otherwise.

'Here they come. See what I mean, Lucy?'

Lucy clasped her hands to her mouth and laughed. 'Doesn't he just. And doesn't Clive look cute?'

'Don't be fooled by his age, Lucy,' said Jennifer. 'He's tenacious and fast. By the time he's fifteen he'll be better than either Brian or Dad.'

Lucy found this comment strange. 'Do you think so?'

'Just watch.'

We lined up. 'Our warrior-in-chief,' said Joe as Clive took a bow, 'will now demonstrate the targets.'

He stood in front of me. Joe listed the targets as Clive, to the amusement of the others and grinning through his helmet, thwacked me.. 'Head – left, right and centre, above the temple. Side, wrist and throat.'

'That's funny, Dorothy?'

'Not usually, Liz. Normally it's just a tap on the helmet to show the target. Clive has taken advantage and got his own back.'.

'I see. Do you indulge?'

'Er, no. Six warriors in the house is enough. Kendo is the secondary sport. Their primary sport is Karate. Joe runs a class on Saturday mornings. This is playtime. Excuse me a minute whilst I put the water out,' she noticed Liz's puzzled look. 'So they can wash their feet afterwards.'

Tenacity didn't enter into it. Clive could be ferocious. We never let him win for the sake of it. Every point he scored was earned. And, he was getting better. And the better he became ...

'See what I mean, Lucy.'

'Yes but doesn't that sort of aggression lead to violence.'

'You've seen Brian. It leads to confidence. The confidence to walk away from conflict, but the skill to defend yourself should it become necessary.'

'Could I learn when I'm better?'

'You'll have to speak to Dad,' said Anne. 'But I don't see why not ... would you like to try my armour on? See what it feels like.'

'I'd love to.'

'Come on then,' Anne turned to the others. 'We'll be in the library.'

Ten minutes later demonstration concluded and feet washed Liz sniffed the air. 'Something smells good, Dorothy.'

'Tea. Meat and potato pie and peas.'

'Wonderful.'

'A family favourite.' Said Dorothy as she filled the kettle.

'Brian told me that Joe's a butcher.'

'Yes,' he is.

The conversation interrupted by Anne's shout. 'Brian. Mum. Lucy's collapsed.'

Thirty-Three

It had been all hell and no notion. The 999 call. The ambulance followed by a mad dash with blue lights and bells to Portland Street and Huddersfield Royal Infirmary. The new Huddersfield Royal just a mile down the road wasn't scheduled to be open until January next year.

Lucy was being prepped for an op. Almost certainly, according to Senior Surgical Registrar Duncan Donaldson, a ruptured spleen.

'... And you say that the tractor passed over her?'

'Yes, Dr. By rights ...'

'Yes, I understand. Do you know who the Doctor was?'

'Professor Lightman.'

'The best. I'll contact him, but can you tell me why she isn't still in hospital?'

'My husband insisted. He arranged for twenty four hour nursing cover and a physio. Where Lucy is concerned he has a short fuse.'

'His ego trumps medical expertise?'

'Yes.'

'Well Mrs Vernon. A ruptured spleen is very serious. We might be able to save it. If not ...' he left the point hanging. 'As soon as Mr Grayson arrives we can get started.'

'Brian, do you think that Joe and your mother would object to showing Lucy living at your address?'

'I don't see why not, Liz. If it would stop untoward interference.'

'Would that be all right Dr?'

'All right by me. Will you go with the nurse and complete the necessary paperwork.'

'Could we use a different surname. I don't suppose Brian would object if we called her, Lucy Blake.'

'I like the idea. However, you would have to ensure there was consistency.'

Dr Donaldson smiled. 'Good luck. Can I suggest you go home and call back after seven this evening. Now, I must contact Leeds.'

New wrist bands, consent forms and personal details completed we returned to the waiting room.

'What's happening?' said Anne.

'Just waiting for the consultant.'

'It's almost two weeks since the accident why wasn't it spotted before,' said Anne.

'According to the Dr a rupture can happen weeks after the event.'

'Is she going to be all right?'

'All being well, Clive.' I said. and turned to Mum and Joe. 'We've switched her name to Lucy Blake.'

'A bit premature isn't it,' said Mum. Joe Laughed. 'Although we have no objection.'

'Just a little and shown here as her home address.'

'Why have you done that?' Clive persisted.

'It's because my husband is likely to try and find her and he always causes an upset. We're hiding her. She needs rest so she can get better.'

He seemed satisfied and went looking for something to eat. Nothing could blunt Clive's appetite. No-one else was hungry. I put a camp bed up in Clive's bedroom leaving my room free for Liz.

Seven pm. Liz called the hospital. There was a collective sigh. The operation had been a success. A small piece of Lucy's spleen had been removed. Given time all should be well. Liz could visit on Sunday afternoon.

Early Sunday morning I went for a three mile run with Clive. When we returned Liz had phoned the hospital – Lucy had had a comfortable night. I could visit with Liz this afternoon.

A traditional Sunday breakfast: Bacon, eggs, sausage, tomatoes and mushrooms with as much bread as you could put away. Clive, the Gannet, showed the way.

'You might be ten but you ought to weigh ten stones,' said Jennifer. We got the usual response. A cheeky grin and a wrinkled nose.

It was just chit-chat with a leaning towards Lucy until Liz spoke. 'Joe, Brian has been telling me all about your business.'

I was subjected to one of Joe's quizzical smiles. 'Has he now?'

'How you built the business up from one outlet to five and bought a pie-making factory. Plus you are, I understand, in the process of negotiations to buy a cooked meat business and a bakery. That's excellent.'

'Well,' he paused and smiled. 'He's almost right. I bought up Cooked Meats Yorkshire Ltd the first week he was at Pannal Ash. Somerset Bakeries three days ago. The owners were retiring. Both are in excellent shape and ripe for expansion. If you've read Neville Shute's book A Town Like Alice I used the same principals. Draw a wage, treat my staff well, apart from my daughters ...'

'Too right,' came the triple reply.

Which drew the appropriate grin from Joe. '... And ensure that the remainder goes into my contingency fund.'

'I'm sure you treat your daughters very well.'

'Oh no he doesn't.'

'I'm sure he does. Joe, you may think this is impertinent but I'm sure you know what happened to my husband.'

'Yes, it was unfortunate.'

'For those that don't know. Things were a bit rocky for a time and for protection all the business assets were transferred into my name. Bill made some bad decisions and was declared bankrupt. He is working to discharge the debt. Which is why he's bad tempered. However, there is one project that may be of interest to you bearing in mind your own businesses. Would you be open for me to send you a proposal?'

'By all means. Send it to me here, please.'

Thirty-Four

Not a cloud in the sky. The ward windows were open and there was a gentle breeze wafting the curtains. Lucy looked pale. Her eyes closed. Bruising clearly visible down her arms and across the top of her chest. Liz and I sat either side of the bed and held her hands. She opened her eyes and smiled. 'Just having forty winks.'

'How do you feel?' said Liz.

'How about lousy. What happened?'

'Anne said you were trying the armour on when you went dizzy and collapsed,' I said.

'I remember,' she nodded. 'What's all this about.' She lifted her left wrist displaying the name band. 'They keep calling me Miss Blake. I haven't the strength to ask them why.'

Liz and I laughed. 'Ah, you're in Huddersfield Royal Infirmary and likely to be here between seven and ten days. After that you can stay with Brian's parents for as long as is necessary. It's only to prevent your father from finding out where you are and making trouble.'

Lucy closed her eyes and sighed. 'Thanks, that was worrying me.'

'There's no need to worry.'

'I know, Mum but you know what he's like.'

'They have your address as Salendine Nook,' I said. 'You'll use my bedroom.'

'Promising. Anne told me all the bedrooms have double beds.'

'They do.'

'Lucy, you're almost twenty-one. I'm not going to play the heavy-handed parent but please be careful.'

'We will, Mum,' she looked at me. 'Won't we?'

'When you're well enough. And that won't be for a while.'

'An early birthday present,' she winked at me. 'For both of us.'

'Ah, just a minute I almost forgot.' I fished her present from my pocket and handed her the small gift-wrapped box. 'This is for you.'

'What is it?' she said and frowned. 'It's not my birthday until New Year's Eve.'

'Open it love and see.'

She grinned at her mother. 'Right.'

Ribbon and paper removed she open the box. 'Oh, it's beautiful. Look, Mum,' she said and passed Liz the brooch. It was a sheaf of flowers comprised of what looked like diamonds, rubies, sapphires and emeralds. It was only paste but it looked the part.

'Liz stared and turned to me. 'Are these stones real?'

'I wish,' I said. 'It's costume jewellery.' It had cost me nine shillings and sixpence.

'It does, thank you so much. For that you get a kiss.'

I sat on the bed. Lucy reached up and winced. 'Ouch. Better not.' A brief peck was the order of the day.

Mum, mine that is, and Anne deputised that evening. I returned to Pannal.

Liz? She went home taking Lucy's brooch with her for safekeeping. Visiting was put on a rota by the girls. Lucy wouldn't go short of company.

The air at Boston Spa was fraught with tension.

Bill Vernon was not happy. 'What do you mean she's in hospital? She was fine.'

'She collapsed. Needed an operation on her spleen because of the accident.'

'Then why didn't they find it before? I'll sue them. She was fine.'

Hackles raised an angry Liz Vernon rounded on her husband. 'What do you mean? She wasn't fine. Professor Lightman wanted her to stay in hospital for at least another week. This is your fault. If you'd left well enough alone she would still have been safe in hospital. But oh no. You always know best. Well you don't. Stop interfering in things you know nothing about.'

'Well, which hospital is she in?'

'I'm not telling you. She needs hospital care and rest. Not to have you charging round creating havoc.'

'She's my daughter. There's nothing they can do that I can't arrange.'

'That's stupid talk. It's all arranged. She's safe and that's all you need to know.'

'We'll see about that.'

'If you try and interfere I'll let the court know about your little enterprise with Geordie.'

'You wouldn't dare.'

'Try me. Now, leave-her-alone.'

Thirty-Five

It was back to normal at Pannal, almost. Because of our now common surname I could get information when I called the ward but that was all. A little more when I called home. It appeared, however, that Frankie was reticent to visit on her own – the usual practice was to attend in pairs.

There was no indication that Lucy's father had contacted them.

Everything Pannal oriented continued as normal. We played a local rugby club and scraped a win.

It was good news when I arrived at the hospital on Friday evening. Another two weeks to go before I had to be at the Spartan's base. Lucy would be allowed 'home' the following Monday. Plus Liz's business proposal had arrived. It concerned development of the Spartan's training track on the edge of Tadcaster, including what was described as a business centre complete with restaurant. Joe thought it interesting. The first thing would be a visit, arranged by Joe for tomorrow. We would all go with him. Everyone warned not to be free with information with regards to Lucy.

Perhaps it was an omen. The sun broke through when we arrived at 1pm, greeted by the large burgundy, royal blue and white sign:

HOME OF THE

SPARTANS

MOTOR CYCLE RACING TEAM

It was days away. I was only supposed to be looking for someone called Peter Pederson who rode a Honda CB77. The nerves were starting to have an effect. Perhaps it was the interest of MI5. Just who amongst those connected with the Spartans would become suspects?

I strained to absorb every detail. Fifty yards away, behind what appeared to be some kind of Grandstand, the doppler effect of high revving bike engines. Visible down the lefthand side a smaller open stand. To the right, adjacent to the track, a line of garages, doors open. To the left of the garages, a double line of sheds. Behind the sheds what appeared to be a control tower, similar in size and shape to those you see on airfields.

A door in the Grandstand opened. Liz came to meet us. Could she be one? Come on Blake, stop playing mind games. Get a grip. 'Glad you found us all right, Joe,' she smiled. 'When we get through to the track would you come with me. Some of the boys will show the rest of you the facilities. And we have a treat in store.'

From the top floor of the Grandstand the perspective changed. 'Bill, this is my wife Dorothy. I'm finding it harder to be everywhere at once these days and Dorothy manages the business on a day-to-day basis.' Introductions complete Joe looked round. Everywhere looked tired. A spruce up was definitely on the cards.

Liz was about to speak when Bill jumped in. 'Joe, what I propose.'

'Whoa. Bill, you're an undischarged bankrupt. I heard it was 50K. You can't get involved in anything without a court order. Do you have one?'

Bill Vernon drew himself up to his full height. 'Nonsense.'

'Thanks, Joe,' interceded Liz. 'Bill, I've been telling you for months. But would you listen?'

'No Bill, Liz is right. You need that court order. I'll deal with Liz but you can't be a party. See your solicitor and make the application. Sorry to be so dogmatic but I'm not putting any part of my business at risk for the sake of expediency.'

Thirty-Six

The girls, Clive and I were standing behind the barriers as one bike after another flashed passed.

'Hello Brian, I thought it was you.'

I spun round. He hadn't changed one bit. Resplendent in Spartan racing leathers. Five six. Broad shouldered. Black wavy hair. Still the same smile. I'd known Neil Greeley since we were eleven years old. His father was a mechanic. Neil used to help out. He was a bright lad and we were all surprised when he dropped out of college on his sixteenth birthday to work for his father. In retrospect we shouldn't have been. He had his own motorbike when he was nine. Could strip and re-assemble it by the time he was eleven. Taking up racing seemed like a natural step. To his right another Spartan in his racing leathers.

We shook hands. 'Neil, great to see you. It must be what? Seven years.'

'Near enough.' Then he caught sight of Anne. 'Well,' he said looking at the three girls and sang:

'Tell me pretty maidens are there any more at home like you.'

I'd forgotten Neil had a good tenor voice. Seven years down the line it hadn't deteriorated. He always played the male lead in the school music society.

Anne responded in kind. '*There are a few, kind sir*,' she indicated Jen and Frankie. She looked him up and down, 'Aren't we enough for you?'

She got a grin and a quizzical look. 'You were a Florodora girl?' said Neil.

'Good grief, no. A fetcher and carrier. I have a voice like a corncrake.'

'Not from where I'm standing you haven't. You have a nice voice.'

Anne blushed and switched emphasis. 'Were you in Florodora?'

'I was one of the six. But which one are you? You three were about eleven the last time I saw you. You've grown.'

'We all have. I'm Anne. This is Frankie and Jen.'

'Hello,' he nodded and smiled. 'And you young man must be Clive? You've grown as well.'

He got an answering cheeky grin. 'Hi.'

'Hello everybody. I'm Neil, Neil Greeley. Brian and I were in the same class at the New College. It's a small world. I'm the Spartan's engineering captain and work more with Liz. I get it in the neck if the bikes aren't up to scratch. On my right is Vance Pickering. He's the race captain and gets it in the neck if somebody falls off. Works more with Bill.'

'Hello everybody,' Vance said and smiled.

Everyone responded.

'Right, let's go to the grandstand so you can see the layout.'

The track was low down not much higher than the nearby River Wharfe.

All the riders back in the pits it was quiet.

'You can see the layout. The track is 2.1 miles. Not huge but it's testing. Those are the Pits opposite. They're going to be extended. There's a fair selection of obstacles and a tricky hairpin in the distance to the right. You can see tyres and hay bales where they are needed. There's a couple of gravel run-offs for those who can't handle gravity. And, of course the mini-grandstands. Only scaffolding at the moment but over time who knows. There are the garages and sheds to the right and the tower at the back is for commentaries and announcements when we get going. We have the superstructure but no guts as yet'

'What's that for, Neil,' I pointed at a smaller track in the centre. 'It seems a bit small.'

'Ah. You've heard of Go-carts?'

'I have,' said Clive. So had I but the girls hadn't.

It's a racetrack for Go-carts,' he said and smiled. 'Would you like a go?'

There were no dissenters.

'Ok everyone,' said Vance. 'A quick recap. No ramming or barging someone out of the way. There will be plenty of opportunities to overtake. You've all got proper footwear – nothing open-toed. Don't brake too hard. Keep both hands on the wheel. And, remember there is no reverse gear. If you get stuck do NOT get out of the Kart wait for us ... Helmets on and take your seats.'

There were four karts. Jennifer first. Frankie second. Anne third. Clive last.

Neil and I were standing together. 'Who's going to win, Brian?'

I kept my eyes glued on the grid. 'Clive. No question. Watch.'

The flag dropped. Clive, foot hard down zipped past Anne weaving between Frankie and Jenifer. He was away.

'I thought he hadn't driven a kart before.'

'He hasn't. He's very competitive and these are his big sisters. They need to learn not to be polite.'

'Very true. Whilst we're on our own, Brian. Your name cropped up in relation to Lucy. I take it you heard?

I wondered if this might crop up sometime. 'I witnessed the accident.'

He sounded shocked. 'You're joking?'

'Nope,' I told him as much of the story as I thought he ought to know.

'And you don't know where she is?'

'No. Sorry, can't help. But perhaps you can tell me what the trouble is with Liz and Bill?'

'Simple. All the businesses, even the Italian ones, are in Liz's name. She's the brains. Bill? Great rider. Brilliant at bringing riders on, but he hasn't a business bone in his body. Got himself into all sorts of problems. Everything he touches turns to shit. Doesn't get it.'

'Ok, From what I've seen and heard that makes sense. He's volatile.'

Neil laughed. 'I would have put it stronger than that. But the girls,' he said changing the subject. 'Are they involved in the business?'

'Not Frankie, great with languages. Wants to go to Uni and read English or modern languages. She doesn't know yet. Jennifer is at college studying marketing. Anne is working with Joe and studying business management.'

Neil smiled. His eyes drifting to the Go-cart track as they lapped. 'Anne's nice. And, in spite of what she thinks she has a good voice.'

'And you like her?' I teased.

'What's not to like?' His brow furrowed. 'Trouble is, how do you tell the difference?'

They were my sisters and it was a long time since I'd seen Neil. 'Practise, concentrate on her voice. You've got nobody in tow?'

'Not for a while. Has she?

'Just the one. Kenneth.'

'For how long?'

'Six months. But as far as I can tell it's not serious. I wouldn't rule anything out. So?'

'You think?' He sounded hopeful.

'Just don't take anything for granted. You might be talking to the wrong one. They like to play games.'

Neil looked at the three girls vying for second place. Clive was half a lap ahead. How on earth did you tell them apart? 'Oh great.'

Clive buried the front of his kart in a hay bale in the final two hundred yards, but he was so far ahead, even though it was only a three lap race the result was a foregone conclusion.

'Before I forget, Neil, I spotted something in the Yorkshire Post that you're travelling to the continent shortly.'

'Yup. A week on Friday. We're catching the midnight ferry from Hull to Rotterdam. We come back on the Monday. Should be a good session.'

'Sounds great. Seeing everybody's tied up why don't you introduce me around. We can leave Clive to gloat in peace.'

Joe and I were in the next race with a half dozen Spartans. We fought it out for last place. It was great fun.

The day was over.

The door was hardly shut when the questions started.

'How did it go? I'll let your Mum tell you.'

'First. Did you enjoy the go-karting?'

There was a multitude of: 'Silly question.'

'Ok. Nothing is settled. Mrs Vernon wants your dad to come back in a month with suggestions and costings for *all* the catering at the track. Far more than we have seen today. That is as much as you're going to get at the moment.'

That was it.

Visit to Lucy in the evening. Anne played gooseberry.

Lucy put her foot in it. 'The Spartans are travelling to Rotterdam a week next Friday. Why don't you get Brian to fetch you over? You can wave Neil off.'

'If you want, Anne.' I said. Thank you Lucy. Still it wouldn't hurt.

Sunday: Run. Dinner. Hospital visit to Lucy. Early tea. Return to Pannal.

Monday. I received a warning to attend Coroner's Court on Thursday re the road accident and deaths of Christopher and Mark Griffiths. Totally different from magistrate's courts. The Inquest was to determine the cause of death and not to apportion blame.

Chief Inspector Reynolds once again provided transport.

The Coroner, a gaunt looking local solicitor called Winterton entered. The jury of ten men were sworn. Inspector Nelson, the divisional prosecutor managed the hearing.

Lucy was a bit miffed because I couldn't sit next to her.

When I was called I asked to affirm which had the Coroner looking at me over his glasses. He made no comment. When I had given my evidence Inspector Nelson sought permission for me to be released, which was granted.

Lucy looked even more miffed.

When Chief Inspector Reynolds got me back to Pannal the month two exam had already begun. I was taken to the library for the privilege. The Library was closed. Sergeant Faulkner had the stopwatch.

It wasn't a good experience. I wasn't sure about several of my answers. Too late to worry now.

The inquest verdict was misadventure.

Thirty-Seven

Thursday evening just one more week to the Inspection.

Frank Whittaker stuck his head round the dorm door. 'Come on you two there won't be any tables left.'

'As long as there's some beer.'

The bar was full. We got the last table just inside the door and squeezed seven chairs round it. I found myself next to John Masters from Sheffield City, 'How did it go, John?' I said. I wasn't going to admit my doubts. There would be time enough tomorrow when the results came out..

'Not bad, Brian,' he said. 'Perhaps someone will catch you.'

'You never know, John,' I replied.

'I should bloody hope so,' commented Frank. 'Who gets 93% in an exam?'

'Those who do the studying,' said John, laughing. 'Anyway, Brian, how did you get on in the library?'

'I'll tell you tomorrow.'

'Sounds griefy,' said Phil.

'He's having you on,' said Frank. 'He'll piss it. Whose round is it?'

'Mine,' I said putting my hand in my pocket. 'Damn, I left my cash on the bed.' There was a chorus of epithets. 'Look, someone get this one, I'll get the next.'

'Go up the back staircase it should be clear by now.'

I glanced out of the window. 'Nope, the lights on in the kitchen and they're still shifting stuff.'

'Well then Speedy you'd better get your skates on,' said Phil Jacques as I stood to leave. 'I don't know you just can't trust some coppers.'

There were several laughs and a couple of, 'Go on get your slates on.'

I looked over my shoulder as I opened the door and grinned. 'Bollocks.'

It took two minutes to reach the dorm and collect the cash. The lights in the corridor below were off. Everything was quiet. I paused at the top of the forbidden staircase and listened. Silence. All the catering staff had left the building. I stepped forward and froze at the sound of a deep sigh vertically below me, followed by quiet male and female voices and female laughter. 'Oh, it's beautiful,' she said. 'Thank you.'

That apart, the voices weren't clear enough for me to hear properly but they were vaguely familiar. I leant against the rail and peered over hoping that the expected creak did not occur.

Immediately below, a bank of personal lockers used by both domestic and catering staff. Leaning against them a female with prominent breasts and wearing a pale dress. Dark brown hair, straight and cut into her neck. Her male companion hands either side of her shoulders supporting his weight. Dark hair, grey at the temples. On his left ring-finger a signet ring. The design? Anybody's guess. Neither was the light good enough to make out his service number. They were either kissing or he was vacuuming her face. She had her hands over his shoulders. I could just make out, draped across his back, a necklace comprised of butterflies. The object of the thanks?

He lowered his left hand. The hem of her dress began to rise. The intensity of the kiss increasing with altitude. He must have had his hand at hip level when she broke the kiss, giggled and grabbed his hand. 'No.' she said and giggled again. 'Not here. Not now. What if a student comes down?' I withdrew my head behind the rail. 'Look, I'll see you in an hour. You know where. I've got something to tell you.'

I drained my glass and looked at the six expectant faces. 'Well,' said Phil. 'Who the hell was it?'

'Don't know,' I said.

There were uniform grumbles from the assembled. 'Fine informant you are. You turn up late with half a tale and leave the interesting bits out.'

'You know what that corridor's like,' I protested. 'There's only that pokey skylight over the door, it's gloomy. I could hardly put the lights on and say, come on smile for the camera. They were up near the door into the corridor. She was wearing a pale coloured dress and had short brown hair. He had dark hair with grey at the temples and a police tunic.'

'You couldn't see his shoulder tabs?'

'Not clearly. But let's face it all stripes look the same.'

There was a stunned silence broken by John Bradbury, 'Stripes?' he gasped.

'It'd have to be, wouldn't it?' said Frank. 'Instructors can move anywhere. If we were hanging about down there for a grope there'd be hell on if we were caught.'

'Oh, I don't know,' said John Masters. 'Remember last month? That sergeant from Lincoln whose contract was up? Nigel Perfect, wasn't it? He was single. Knocking off that blonde lass from the kitchen, Carole. They were having a fumble in the same spot. We just dashed down the stairs, said, "Evening Sarge," and out of the door. Nothing happened. If whoever it was who had his hand up her skirt even recognised you, he's not going to say anything. Too much to lose.'

I had to admit he was correct. 'Didn't Carole leave about a week after he left?'

'Yes, I think she did. Rumour was she followed him to Lincoln.'

'She was fit, I'd have given her one.'

'She was a very popular girl.'

'But no-one else stood a chance. She had eyes on the prize. Sergeants earn more.'

'Can't argue with that. Anyway, who's duty sergeant tonight?'

'Palmer or Vincent.'

'It could have been anybody.'

'Except Faulkner.'

'By numbers, begin.' There was a spluttering. I looked up, 'The board's free. Time for a 501?'

Thirty-Eight

The Commandant bit his lip. He must have been aching to ask when he sanctioned my early departure. The weather was fine and sunny. Nevertheless traffic heavy. It was half four when I arrived home. Anne was ready and waiting. Liz had collected Lucy at half three and was probably home by now. I wondered how her father would react.. Thirty minutes later I was fed and watered. Tank filled. We were off. With Friday traffic we would be lucky to get to the track by seven. I changed route deciding on Wakefield, Garforth, Towton, Tadcaster. It couldn't be any worse than through Leeds. We arrived at 6.45pm. There was no sign of a second Super Hawk – the Honda CB77.

There must have been thirty cars in the carpark plus several bikes. Parked between the Grandstand and the garages were the coach, with boards back and front announcing The Spartans Motor Cycle Racing Team. Alongside, the van transporting the bikes.

People everywhere. Spartans. Riders, mechanics, even a reporter and cameraman from the local rag milling round as were wives and girlfriends.

I was just about to say there was no sign of Lucy, Liz or Bill when they walked round the end of the grandstand. All peace and calm. Lucy saw me and walked across throwing her arms round my neck and kissing me hard on the lips. A signal to her father? 'Come on,' she said when she came up for air, 'Let's find somewhere quiet.' The applause and whistles from the Spartans and Anne faded as they returned to loading the bus. Smiles from Liz and silence from Bill.

'I'm not losing interest,' I said in an attempt to avoid any kickback. 'We'll have plenty of time when they've gone.'

The reply? A disgruntled, 'Misery.'

The sound of a decelerating bike engine peaked my interest as a silver Honda Super Hawk turned in through the gates. The rider in full-face helmet and black leathers. 'From the bike it's Lester's cousin, Peter,' said Lucy. 'He always comes to see him when they go abroad. They've got relatives in Holland, save on postage.'

I suppose it did, but what was he going to pass and to whom?'

Neil separated himself from the pack. 'Hello pretty maiden. Come just to see me?'

'Yes, she has,' grinned Lucy.

'No, I didn't,' protested Anne but couldn't avoid the blush. 'All right, I did. Lucy, just you wait.' All she got was an answering grin.

'Come on let me introduce you to the others. They were all asking about you the last time you were here.'

Lester's cousin Peter removed his helmet and looked round. Fortyish. Five six. My build. Dark greying hair. Square-jawed. Tanned with a few facial scars. There was something wrong. Lieutenant Phillips told me the biker's name was Peter Pederson. Lucy had just confirmed that. But I knew the face. Where from I couldn't remember. But, the name was neither Peter nor Pederson. Of course I could be mistaken.

'What did you just say? His name isn't Peter?'

> I must have been thinking aloud. 'No, he just looks similar to someone I met at university.

His name was, or the name I had known him by was Rudi. He was the communist. If he recognises me it could get interesting.

For the next thirty minutes or so we meandered round the car park chatting whilst I made sure I kept Rudi in my sights. The first person he handed something to was Bill. Quite a surprise. It was a pair of business sized brown envelopes both of which disappeared into Bill's inside blazer pocket.

It was turned eight o'clock when the van containing the bikes left. They should get to Hull by ten. No doubt Special Branch were waiting. The coach began to load. So far only one package had changed hands. Almost the last to board was Lester, Lester Roberts, one of the mechanics. Rudi walked up to him said something and shook hands. Something fell to the floor. Something that looked like a small rectangular metal container. It must have been palmed and Lester dropped it. Scooped up in seconds and pocketed as if nothing had happened. Last to board was Neil leaving Anne with a kiss on the cheek. Kenneth's days were numbered.

Thirty-Nine

The skies were darkening. The first street lights beginning to glow. The coach left to the waving of friends and family. Within seconds all that were left were Lucy, Liz, Anne and me plus Rudi who sauntered across and stood next to Lucy..

'Forgive me,' he said with a slight but noticeable accent. 'Have you been watching me?'

'Not really,' I replied. 'It's just that you reminded me of someone I knew at university. I can't place you.'

He narrowed his eyes, questioning. 'Which university?'

'East Midlands.'

Rudi pursed his lips and tilted his head to one side. 'Don't think so ... To the best of my knowledge I've never been there.'

He lied.

'He's got a wonderful memory,' said Lucy trying to help. 'He's a policeman.'

I laughed. 'I'm eight weeks into my basic training.' Oh my God Lucy, steady on.

In a single action Rudi stepped behind Lucy wrapping his right arm round her shoulders holding her to his chest. In his left hand he held a pistol to her head. He was completely calm. I was completely cold. I don't think Lucy realised what was happening. Anne and Liz looked petrified. Unarmed combat isn't much use against a loaded firearm and I had no thoughts of testing that hypothesis.

'This pistol holds nine bullets. Dead men tell no tales. Nobody move. Nobody speak unless I ask a question. If anyone does this young lady's next bed will be a mortuary slab.' He looked at us all in turn. 'No-one will get hurt if you do as you are told.'

Why didn't I believe him. So much for MI5's stated aims.

The memories came flooding back. It was the last of the two meetings I attended. Rudi was a political agitator touring universities and speaking to groups of undergrads about the benefits of Communism. He described it as a "fairer system of government – re-distribution of wealth - power in the hands of the people".

I was at the rear of the room. I stood. Pointed at Rudi. 'Why, in 1956,' I said in a voice loud enough to be heard next door. 'If that is the case did the Russians invade Hungary when they wanted freedom from the Russian yoke. Answer that if you can?'

He didn't have a sense of humour. Instead, a face like thunder. There was a brief but violent scuffle as I dealt with the two goons he sent to deal with me. Now. the question in my mind was, have I been set up?

His calmness was terrifying. Lucy was shaking. She and Liz had tears running down their cheeks. Anne now furious and looked as though she might try something. Not a good idea. My mind working overtime trying to work out what his options were. None of them were good for us.

'Now Mr policeman. Special Branch?'

So, it was espionage. I hoped that Captain Manville-Jones and Lieutenant Phillips were close. 'No, I've told you I'm eight weeks into my basic training,'

'No matter,' he paused and turned to face Liz. 'What's in those sheds past the garages?'

'They're just stores.'

He pulled the hammer back. 'You have the keys?'

Liz, even more rattled, lifted her handbag. 'In here.'

'Good. You three,' he pointed the pistol at each of us in turn. 'Turn round and raise your hands. Then walk until I tell you to stop. If anyone does anything stupid you will be the second one to die. Now move.'

I didn't like the look of what was on the far side of the garages one bit. A fuel tank, maximum capacity I would guess a thousand gallons, operated by means of a standard petrol pump. Once the fuel was flowing it was possible to lock the pipe open.

Race tracks use hay bales and old tyres at various points round the tracks. Twenty yards behind the fuel tank was a large stack of old tyres. It wasn't getting any better.

'Stop there. Keep your hands up. Liz, undo the padlock and leave it where I can see it. Open the door and step back.'

Liz, fighting back the tears, fumbled and dropped the keys. 'Be careful,' warned Rudi.

'Sorry, I'm nervous.'

His smile was sardonic. 'Just do it.'

The door open. The padlock hanging from the hasp Liz stepped back.

'Right. You,' he pointed the pistol at me. The penny dropped. The look of astonishment when he recognised me was a picture, I didn't feel like laughing.. 'You? Stand still. How do the English say? The bad penny?'

'If you say so.'

'By the time you get out I will be long gone.'

'If you say so, Rudi.'

He smirked. 'Face me. Back into the shed and keep your hands high where I can see them.' Inside it was gloomy. But for the time being I was more concerned about what was happening outside. There was no way in Rudi's mind we were getting out.

'Now you,' he pointed to Anne. 'Back up. Keep your eyes on me.' She followed suit.

'Now you, Liz. Back into the doorway and wait. Keep your hands up.'

'Now you, Lucy. Go to your mother.' She staggered and fell. Liz walked the three steps, put her arms round Lucy and helped her up. She glared at Rudi. 'Anything else you bastard?'

Rudi smiled. 'Back into the garage and don't do anything stupid or I will shoot Lucy.'

The padlock snapped on our large wooden coffin. I heard Rudi's voice. 'This time English the debate is concluded.'

Forty

I was assailed by a chorus of 'What's going on Brian. Who is this man?'

'Ok, in a minute. Give me a bit of air.'

With Anne and Liz hovering I sat Lucy on a nearby box, crouched and took hold of her hands. 'Do you trust me?'

She managed a thin smile. 'I don't know. I suppose so.'

I smiled. 'Do you love me?'

'Of course I do.'

I let go of her right hand and fished the box from my pocket. Now seemed as good a time as any. There was an overhead gasp as I removed the ring and placed it on the first joint of her left ring finger. 'You told me that after the accident when you thought you were dead, amongst the things that passed through your mind were that you would never experience getting married and having children. This is the precursor. Will you marry me?'

A broad grin replaced the smile. 'The first thing I said I'd miss, Brian, and you know it, was not experiencing sex. And yes, I'll marry you.'

The ring in position. A swift embrace and kiss. I stood. 'Now Rudi, or whatever his name is, I met at uni. He's a Communist. I attended one of his meetings out of curiosity. It ended in a row and a punch up. He had a couple of thugs with him. They lost. He bears grudges.'

'Why did he call you English?'

'He's eastern European and couldn't remember my name. Now, shall we see about getting out of here.' What I didn't say was – the land falls slightly from the fuel tank towards the river. *And before he sets fire to this coffin.*

'Liz, what do you use to mop up oil and petrol spillages?'

She gave me a quizzical look. 'Cement,' she knew what I was thinking. 'You think it's possible?'

'Don't you? Do you have any in here?'

'We're due a delivery but there's a couple of bags in the corner.'

I passed Liz my gauntlets. 'Will you three set about the cement whilst I have a look back here. And Liz, is there any lighting?'

'There's a hurricane lamp and matches on the shelf behind you. Spare paraffin in the corner.'

'Thanks.'

Quite bizarre talking about paraffin for a hurricane lamp and the distinct possibility of several hundred gallons of petrol heading our way. I checked the lamp. The reservoir was full. Liz was giving out instructions.

'Lucy, against the back wall there's a couple of old spades. Anne put your gauntlets on and help me to shift this ....'

Liz was interrupted by a series of bumps against the wall nearest the petrol tank. The first of the tyres had been deposited.

'What was that?' said a fearful Lucy. She had had enough scares for one day.'

'Don't worry Lucy,' said Liz. We exchanged glances. 'Just concentrate on what we're doing. Do not breathe-in the dust, it's dangerous.'

The bumps continued.

> Getting out? Problematical.
> Time?

One spot of luck. I noticed that one board three down from the top right corner there was a large knot. That gave me a weak spot. To have enough room to get out two boards would have to be breached.

I needed tools. It took a while; they were buried beneath a pile of flattened cardboard boxes. It must be where Bill's team stored anything that was no longer serviceable. I was just pleased they hadn't thrown them out. Nevertheless I became the possessor of several blunt and damaged masonry and wood chisels, a sledgehammer with a broken shaft and several saws with teeth as sharp as worn false teeth. Still better than nothing. I stripped to the waist and stood on an upturned packing case.

The bumping had stopped. Not a good sign. Confirmed when the smell of petrol became noticeable. Lucy, her mother and Anne clustered behind me. Nobody spoke but I knew what they were thinking – *How long would it take before the flames reached us?*

Nobody spoke.

It took five shots to shift the knot.

Petrol seeping under the door caught fire, creeping towards us. The smoke from burning cardboard and wood was accumulating and we had no cement left. Liz had her arms round both girls.

'Everybody get down,' I said and coughed. 'The air is fresher near the floor.'

That might have been true but there was nowhere for the smoke to go and I had to stand on the packing case. It was either that, or die.

Fear is a great driver. It was a good job these boards were pine and not a hardwood. Blunt or not in less than thirty seconds I had cut through to the board below.

'Brian?'

I looked down. Lucy was holding a case opener up towards me.

'Brilliant,' I smiled. 'Hang onto it.'

Seconds later I cut through the top of the knot-hole. A couple of belts with the broken sledgehammer loosened the short end of the board.

I held my hand out. 'Lucy,' I pointed at the case opener.

Within seconds I could breathe fresher air. The smoke was pouring out. At least the air was clearing at ground level. If Rudi became aware would he make the link and investigate? Options were few. Surrendering to the flames was not one of them. I managed to get my head out of the gap. There was neither sight nor sound of Rudi.

Another question in my mind. Was there petrol under the floor. I could worry about that later.

This was no time to get tired but I felt myself weakening. Not far to go. One last push. The final stroke and I was through the second

I propped myself against the wall. 'Anne first. Make sure you've got everything. Then Liz and Lucy."

Anne scrambled onto the packing case. The extra weight punching a hole in the base. Could things get any better? I scooped her up and slid her legs through the gap. She threw her helmet as far as she could, twisted, gripped the board and lowered herself. Dropped the eighteen inches to the ground and waited. Liz, carrying my jacket and helmet followed, spreading her weight across the packing case so as to not collapse it. She was heavier but Anne was there to support and help her out of the way. I held my hand out as the flames licked the sides of a can of solvent. 'Lucy, quickly,' I reached down, grabbed her hand and in one movement hoisted her up feeding her feet through the gap and throwing her as far as I could. 'Sorry,' I shouted after her as the packing case collapsed beneath my feet.

There was a WHOOSH behind me. I didn't need to look. It was bloody hot and the flames were licking my leathers. I grabbed at the lower plank and hoisted myself through the gap. Anne and Liz grabbed my left arm dragging me out of way. Burning petrol appeared from beneath the shed. The flames soared skywards and advanced.

Forty-One

'Everybody ok?'

Under the circumstances we were.

Any tears were of relief. But until we knew where Rudi was any thought of escape was premature. I didn't want any of us with a bullet in the back.

Liz had her arms round Lucy.

A now composed Anne lay alongside me. 'What do we do now?' she whispered.

'Rudi still has his pistol. Until we know if he's departed as he intimated we can't expose ourselves. Come on this way. And no talking.' Even out here it was beginning to get hot. I put my jacket on. It was painful. Peered round the side of the hut. Clear. We made our dash to the shed diagonally opposite.

Strange. Rudi appeared pacing to and fro. Why? Was he waiting for someone? If so, who?

'Look, wait here whilst I have a quick look. I won't be long.' Before they could stop me I was laid behind the shed next in line to our coffin. The fire was still yards away. My heart rate was increasing faster. I had toyed with making my way to the petrol pump and switching it off. But again, would Rudi investigate. For the time being we were out of harm's way. The fire couldn't do any further damage, at the moment.

Without warning Captain Manville-Jones accompanied by Lieutenant Phillips walked into view from the direction of the Grandstand. 'Why the fire?' the Captain said.

What the fuck, they're in this together ... I've been set up. The treacherous bastard. To put it politely, this was not good.

'He was a policeman. Recognised me from university,' said Rudi. 'Why didn't you make sure he was clean?'

'He was supposed to recognise you. Once I discovered he was applying for the police and his subsequent meeting with the Vernon girl it couldn't have been better. They are all expendable. All except Blake. I need him alive. What have you done with them?'

Rudi smiled and nodded towards the fire.'

In the light from the flames I could see the look on the Captain's face. He was not happy. 'All of them?'

'Of course. Even that stupid Lucy. Dead men do not talk.'

Whether the others had heard or not there was no reaction.

'What's done is done,' the Captain said and held his hand out.

Rudi reached into the inside pocket of his jacket removed a brown envelope and passed it to the Captain.

'Sir?' Lieutenant Phillips was also unsure.

'You've screwed up too often Mikhail. No-one is indispensable.'

'What you mean?'

'Simply this.' I felt stunned as Captain Manville-Jones put his hand in his raincoat pocket produced a revolver and shot Rudi once in the chest. Peter, Rudi or Mikhail collapsed in a heap. He replaced the revolver in his pocket.

'Sir,' protested Lieutenant Phillips echoing my thoughts. 'Just what is happening?'

The Captain ignored the question and walked to the corpse. Crouching at the head put his hand in the left-hand coat pocket and produced Rudi's pistol, stood and pointed it at the Lieutenant. 'I was trying to save your life Lieutenant, but this spy,' he kicked the corpse. 'was faster than I. I managed to shoot him but, too late.'

The horror stricken Lieutenant appeared frozen as the Captain shot him through the heart. He joined Rudi on the ground. Pistol wiped clean he placed it in Rudi's left hand and stood. 'All nice and tidy. No loose ends.'

No lose ends? There wouldn't be enough fingerprints on the pistol even though he's put it in Rudi's hand. There'll be nothing on the trigger. What the fuck was going on? I glanced across to the other shed. How much they had heard I don't know but the gunfire was unequivocal. Lucy was sobbing. Anne wasn't far behind. Neither was Liz. I put my finger to my lips. If the Captain became aware that any of us were still alive karate wouldn't be much use against a loaded firearm and a man who would not hesitate to use it at distance.

Thoughts were pulsing through my brain. Could I get to the pump and turn it off? Would the Captain react to the cessation of noise? Where the Hell was he?

I stood and peered round the end of the shed. He was standing quite still, back to me. The noise of approaching emergency vehicles getting closer. Lucy and the others watching me and Lucy was pointing at something behind me. I turned. Liz's keys were in the pathway. It only took seconds before I had them and ensuring that our would be executioner was still facing the road I tossed them over.

I made my decision. He thinks we're dead. The others were, in his mind, expendable. However he wants me alive. Insane risk or not it was only twenty yards. Time to give Manville-Jones a shock.

I caught Lucy's attention. Pointed to myself and then Manville-Jones and put my hand to my throat. Without waiting for their answer, which was sure to be don't be so bloody stupid, I set off to travel to longest twenty yards on the planet.

I don't know whether the Captain heard or sensed something but I'd gone about five yards when he turned. 'Brian?' I continued walking. 'Thank God, I heard you were dead.'

I had less than ten yards to go before I could bring this to an end. If he didn't produce his revolver. 'A little premature Captain, although it was touch and go for a while.'

'And the others?'

'All safe and away from here . They might be expendable to you, you bastard, but not to me.'

The penny dropped. Four witnesses too many. To my surprise he spun and made a dive for Rudi's pistol. I was less than five yards away. However, motor cycle leathers and boots are not an aid to mobility. There were eight shots left in the magazine. The emergency vehicles, police car in the lead visible through the fence. I had seconds. Manville-Jones snatched at the pistol and dropped it. Managed to pick it up and rolled over raising the pistol as I threw myself at him. Grabbed his hand pushing it to his left. He fired three shots. The first nicked my leathers. The other two went wide. I applied a choke hold with my left hand as Lucy, Anne and Liz made an appearance. What the Hell were they doing?

I found out when Lucy lifted a three foot length of 3 x 2 and smashed the Captain hard across the right hand side of his face. He opened his mouth in an almost soundless scream. A choke hold does tend to interfere with the ability to make a noise..

Anne slid down beside me and removed the pistol. 'Hello,' she said and grinned. 'Lucy thought you might need some help.'

'You could have been killed.'

'So could you. Then what?'

'Ok, point made. Where did you get the wood from?'

'Liz's keys. And she's got some rope.'

'Check his pockets will you. He's got a revolver somewhere.'

'I'll do that,' said Lucy rummaging through the Captain's pockets. He wasn't in a position to object. 'Pleased to see me?' she sounded happier than she had for some time.

Incredulity didn't enter into it. 'Delighted. But you might have been killed.'

'So might you. We came down the back of the sheds. When we saw him on the ground and facing away we thought it was safe. Besides, it made us feel in control. After being on the defensive? It feels good.'

'Feels good?' I said. Lucy nodded. I shook my head which drew a laugh from both her and Anne. 'It was bloody dangerous. Very brave but bloody dangerous.'

She flashed me her broadest smile and passed me the revolver and the envelope. 'You mean like riding a motor bike?'

The best thing to say was nothing. I shook my head and none too gently tied the Captain's wrists behind his back.

Liz was standing close to Manville-Jones. I held my arms out. 'Come on, we all need a hug,'

Liz burst into tears. 'Sorry,' she said and got herself back under control, 'Like a damp rag.'

'Don't be foolish. It was dangerous. You're entitled to let go. You don't have to try and keep a stiff upper lip.' She sniffed and stood back searching her pockets trying to find a handkerchief.

Lucy threw her arms round my neck. 'Well?'

'Don't do it again. You might not be so lucky next time.'

She flashed me a smile. 'Yes, sir,' she whispered. 'Make love to me. We've earned it.'

Forty-Two

The traffic car came up the back of the garages and slithered to a halt. The firemen dealt with the fire.

As the driver exited the car I handed him my warrant card. 'Pc 547 Blake.'

He looked me up and down. 'Don't know you. Where are you stationed?'

'I've just finished my second month at Pannal. Can you get a message to the Commandant, Chief Superintendent Andrews. He is aware of what I'm doing. So is Mr Barton, the Chief Constable. Oh, and Special Branch.'

The officer looked behind me. The girls in a huddle. The two bodies with blood stains clearly visible and Manville-Jones face down on the floor hands tied behind his back 'Whoa. What the Hell is going on?'

I'll show you.'

;Whisky 133 urgent message.'

'Go ahead.'

'Pips.' He dragged his eyes away from the two corpses and the prostrate MI5 Captain to look at me, 'Those,' he said as a stream of pips began over the radio. 'Block anyone other than the control room staff hearing my message.'

'Go ahead.'

'Duty Officer, please.'

'Inspector Carter, go ahead.'

'Sir, this is a real mess.'

It had been manic. Two ambulances arrived for transport to hospital in York. One for the Captain who left with a police escort. I could have sworn the two officers were carrying revolvers. The second was for us to be checked out because of smoke inhalation. Our escort unarmed.

After initial examination we were placed on oxygen and blood samples were taken so that blood chemistry could be assessed. The left side of my back, left shoulder and left lower leg were treated for mild burns. We were kept in for observations.

It was 11pm. The curtains round my bed parted. A doctor and another man wearing a grey suit with blue shirt and dark blue tie entered. 'Ten minutes, Inspector.' The Doctor left.

The Inspector pulled a chair closer and sat. His voice low he said, 'Inspector Thewlis, Special Branch,' he said, produced his warrant card and smiled. 'Not exactly what you expected on your initial course, Blake.'

'No sir. Not at all.'

'At least you're alive. Now, time is short. This is a matter of national security. You do not divulge any of what we are about to discuss to anyone, even your fiancée. Tell me as succinctly as you can what happened after you arrived at the Spartan's track.'

'... And there were just Bill Vernon and Lester Roberts that he handed objects to?'

'That I saw, sir.'

He nodded.

The curtains parted. The Doctor appeared.. 'Inspector?'

Inspector Thewlis glanced over his shoulder. 'Just coming, doctor,' he said and stood. 'Thanks for that, Blake and well done. Try and get some sleep and with a bit of luck you will be discharged in the morning. We will see you then.'

Blood samples were all within acceptable tolerances. We were released the next morning with advice to contact the hospital should we cough up black sputum or start wheezing.

We were met at the door by two plain clothes officers: DS Mallory and DC Venables.

'Pc Blake,' said DS Mallory. 'You come with me.' He turned and smiled at the others. 'You three ladies go with DC Venables. You'll meet up again at Tadcaster.'

A swift hug with the others and we headed for the cars. 'Blake,' coming towards us was Chief Inspector Reynolds.

'Who's he?'

'Chief Inspector Reynolds. Deputy Commandant, Sergeant.'

'Ok. Mr Reynolds,' he said as the chief inspector arrived. 'I'm afraid that Pc Blake is incommunicado for the time being.'

'I might have guessed,' he said with a half-smile.' Getting information from some is like trying to plat fog. But before you go?

'DS Mallory, sir.'

Thank you. Blake, how are you? We received the message about the fire last evening but the hospital said that you suffering from the effects of smoke inhalation. I took the opportunity to pay a visit to the track about an hour ago. It's a mess.'

'Yes sir. We were kept in overnight for observations and blood tests. The results are all right. And we've been told what symptoms to look for if there is a problems.'

'Very well. We'll see you Sunday evening?

'As far as I'm aware, sir, yes.'

'Excellent. And a word of advice. When they let you go check your fingers and toes. Make sure they're all there.'

That raised a laugh from DS Mallory. 'He'll be fine, sir. And you'll be pleased to know that we stopped applying pressure by pulling finger nails out last week.'

We left Chief Inspector Reynolds heading for his car. 'You're having an interesting course.'

'Too true. This wasn't in the brochure.'

At least he laughed. 'You've got yourself right in the deep end. The conversation that we are about to have never happened. You understand?'

'I'm beginning to.'

'Good. You may find out in due course the ramifications of last night's events. The upshot being that the Assistant Director of the Security Service, a Mr Syme, is here and will speak with you all. Much of what he will tell you is complete tripe. It would be an insult to your intelligence to expect you to believe what he will say bearing in mind what you saw and heard. However, you have to react as if you believed him. All right?'

'I understand.'

'Until we find out exactly how things pan out that's the way it has to be. The fewer people who know the better. No discussions, other than the banal with your compatriots. Do not visit your old school just in case Dr Cappelli is present and although your step-father is still bound by the Official Secrets Act nothing to him either. The more people who know the less control we have over the narrative.'

'Careless talk costs lives?'

'I couldn't have put it better myself.'

Forty-Three

10.00 am: Mum and Joe had been contacted about the smoke inhalation, nothing else.

First things first – the statements. Mine taken by DI Thewlis

An hour later we were all, including Mr Syme and Detective Inspector Thewlis, seated around a table in an interview room.

'My name is Syme. I don't know whether what happened to bring this sorry episode to its conclusion was an example of outrageous courage, self-preservation or a mental aberration. Nevertheless, congratulations for surviving,' he smiled at us all. 'I am an Assistant Director of the Security Service. We have finally got to the bottom of it.'

'There is not and has never been anyone by the name of Duncan Manville-Jones or Leslie Phillips employed by the Security Service. They are respectively Joseph Crozier and Malcolm Clyde. Both professional criminals. What happened was nothing more than a sordid falling out amongst thieves.

'Crozier is wanted on warrant in London and will be transferred at the earliest opportunity.

'Pc Blake, the man you were told was called Peter Pederson and you knew as Rudi is, or was, Mikhail Kuznetsov. A criminal from East Germany in some way, how we are not yet sure, associated with certain elements of the East German state.

'The Id's you were shown are forgeries, very good, nevertheless forgeries.'

Liz was shocked. 'But my husband,' she said. 'Is Bill involved? They always chatted when Peter, or whatever he's called, visited. Sometimes he even took packages to deliver for him.'

'I'm afraid that cannot be ruled out, Mrs Vernon. Enquiries are ongoing. However, as far as we are concerned neither you nor your children are involved. So you can rest assured.'

I might as well play their game. 'Could I ask, sir,' I said. 'What was in the envelope that Kuznetsov passed to Crozier?'

Syme smiled and shook his head. 'It was money. Just money. And, Mrs Vernon would you like us to contact your husband?'

'Are you going to arrest him?'

'Not for the time being, Mrs Vernon. However, he will still have some questions to answer.'

Mind only partially eased Liz said. 'What do you think, Lucy.'

'I suppose he ought to be told. I'm sure I could go back to Brian's. I don't think he would mind,' she said and smiled at me.

'He wouldn't mind at all,' I replied in kind.

Liz turned to Mr Syme. 'Yes, please. As long as it's stressed that there is no urgency.' Liz noticed the puzzled look on the faces of Thewlis and Syme. 'You might think that a bit strange but anything involving Lucy's safety sends him into a frenzy. He would fly back here creating havoc. The last thing that either Lucy or I need.

'As you wish Mrs Vernon,' said Syme still puzzled.

'Just a minute, Lucy,' I said. 'How is it you managed to run the way that you did. I thought you were supposed to take it easy.'

She frowned. 'Oh yes, I was wasn't I. I never thought about it. I just ran. Perhaps I can do all sorts of energetic things now.' She had a wicked grin.

Following advice not to contact the press, or to discuss the matter openly because police enquiries were ongoing, we left. Liz insisting that we freshen up and have a meal at their house.

Thewlis and Syme watched as the Bentley containing Liz and Lucy Vernon turned right out of the car-park followed by Brian Blake and Anne.

'I know that Blake has been told what was necessary, Mr Thewlis, but did the others buy it?'

'They did, sir. And I'm certain he will keep his mouth shut.'

'Let's hope so.'

Forty-Four

After a quick swill and light lunch at the Vernon house I had a lonely ride back home. Anne sharing the rear seat of the Bentley with Lucy, no doubt talking about the probable response to the ring on Lucy's finger.

I was five minutes late having stopped to refuel to be met by Mum bearing a quizzical smile. 'That was a bit precipitous, Brian. She's a lovely girl but you've only known her thirty seconds.'

'I know, but is seemed the right thing to do at the time. Don't I get a hug?'

The library door opened. Joe's head appeared. 'Five minutes?' He closed the door behind me. 'Following the meeting we had with Liz I've been ringing round. This morning I spoke to a contact who lives in York. Last night he was on his way home and drove past the Spartan's track,' he paused when I smiled. 'Police, fire and ambulance?'

Perhaps I shouldn't. 'Police, and others.'

'Others?'

'Others.' I iterated. 'You have signed the Official Secrets Act.'

'You can't say anything, can you?'

'Not a ...'

The door burst open. An angry Frankie stormed in. 'Why didn't you let us know that you were held hostage locked in a shed which Peter or Rudi or somebody set fire to and that's when you proposed to Lucy and what about the shootings?' She stood there hyperventilating.

Thank goodness she hadn't mentioned anything about the gun to Lucy's head. 'So this wouldn't happen.'

A tearstained Lucy and Anne appeared behind her. 'Sorry,' Anne said.

'That's all right,' I said as Anne almost threw herself at her father. Lucy flung her arms round my neck. I put my arms round her. 'Come on let's go in the lounge. I'll fill you in.'

Over the next twenty minutes I talked them through the previous day's events, missing out any possible reference to espionage and the pistol being held to Lucy's head. There were comments about the hole in my jacket. And Lucy, Anne and Liz acting as the cavalry.

'So they weren't spies?'

'No Mum, I know it sounded romantic but they were just common or garden criminals. As we were told, it was a fall out amongst thieves.'

'Violent thugs you mean,' said Jen.

'That just about sums it up.'

There was a mass exodus to the garden. Joe and I hung back.

'Anyway, how are you?'

'Ok, I suppose. It was hairy at the time. But it all turned out well.'

'That's fair enough but these things can have long-lasting effects. And you never know when they will come back and bite you in the arse. If you ever need to talk?'

'I know, thanks.'

'And a word of advice should you be ever in the situation again where you have something like this to reveal. I know you haven't told us everything, but get people together first and you keep control of the information flow. That way you can hopefully prevent the unexpected.'

Martial arts was cancelled. Saturday became an additional day of rest. Except I went into the library to do some studying. Lucy insisted on accompanying me. There were plenty of books to read. If only ...

Clive went off to his friends with strict instructions from Mum to keep schtum. Fat chance.

Forty-Five

It was 4.00pm when the phone rang.

Anne shouted, 'I'll get it ... Hello ... Neil, you sound terrible ... Yes, I'll get her.' There was a clatter as the handset hit the table. 'Mrs Vernon,' she shouted. 'Telephone call for you. It's Neil, I think something's wrong.'

Liz came running from the garden. Snatched up the phone. 'Yes Neil, it's Liz. What's the matter? ... Christ ... how many ... who are they ... which hotel .. the hospital ...Neil, you're in overall charge. Make sure the others know, including Vance.' She put the phone down, took a deep breath and turned towards us. 'As if it couldn't get any worse.'

'Has there been an accident?'

Liz nodded. 'In Rotterdam. About an hour ago. There are five in hospital including your Dad. Neil wasn't sure how many injured in total. I've got to get home and contact the families. I'll get the first flight. Are you coming, Lucy?'

'Yes. I suppose I'd better.'

'Pack me a case whilst I make the calls.'

'Ok.'

'Can we come said Anne? 'Perhaps we can man the phones. Try and answer any queries.'

'I can't ask you to do that.'

'Yes you can. Once word gets out there's bound to be contact. All we need to know is what to say and to whom.'

'I'll come as well.'

'No Brian, your first priority is to finish your training. But thanks for the offer.'

'If you're sure.'

'I am.'

'Please, can I call Gerald?'

'Your brother?' queried Mum. 'Of course you can.'

Liz and Lucy left for home whilst the girls packed their cases in record time and left with Joe. I collected my gear and followed. Mum waited for Clive.

At 5.00pm Neil called. Bill Vernon and Lester Roberts had died of their injuries. Mum called the Vernon's and spoke to Liz. It didn't improve matters for her or Lucy.

I called police headquarters and asked for Inspector Thewlis.

On the fourth ring. 'DC Crosby.'

'Pc Blake. I was with Inspector Thewlis yesterday evening at Tadcaster.'

'What can I do for you?'

'The Spartans are currently in the Netherlands. At around 3.00pm this afternoon there was a road accident in Rotterdam with numerous injuries. Five were admitted to hospital. Bill Vernon and Lester Roberts have since died from their injuries.'

'How do you know?'

'Neil Greeley, their head mechanic and acting Manager, and my sister seem to like each other,' there was a chuckle down the phone. 'He called our home.'

I passed the remainder of the details and explained who was doing what. I would shortly be returning to Pannal. He thanked me. That was that.

Forty minutes later Gerald Vernon and his wife Marianne arrived at Boston Spa to learn of the death of his father. It was a painful time.

I spent the night at the Vernon's. Sunday morning at the track. The afternoon at the Vernon's, studying. There was nothing further I could do. I shared a quiet two minutes with Lucy, said goodbye to the others and left for Pannal.

Forty-Six

Even taking into account being with Lucy, on balance the weekend had been crap. Now it was Monday morning and I had to put events out of my mind and concentrate on why I was at Pannal. There were three more days before the annual inspection. Everything had to run like clockwork.

I was looking forward to demolishing the cooked breakfast in front of me.

'Good weekend, Brian?' snapped me out of my reverie.

I looked up. They would find out soon enough. 'Fine, Tom, been practising?'

'Spot-on,' Tom Gerard gave me the thumbs up and made a bee-line for my table.

Two men in suits, looking like tv detectives, were talking with Sergeant Vincent. He turned and pointed me out which for some reason gave me a feeling of unease. Any family calls would have been made direct; they had the number. After what had happened in the Valley Gardens and over the weekend, perhaps I was a bit hypersensitive. What I was supposed to have done I had no idea but they were now walking in my direction. Numbers in the dining hall were down, the majority of the new course, 236, hadn't arrived yet. There wasn't a sound. No-one eating. No-one talking. Everyone watching. I could feel the tension building.

The one in front, slim, thirty something with receding hair. The other thick-set, fortyish and black hair. 'You're Pc 547 Brian Blake?' the latter said.

'Yes, I am.'

'You're coming with us,' he said.

'Why?'

The thick-set one put his hand on my shoulder. 'Don't argue. Move.'

'I'm not arguing. I'm asking a valid question. Am I under arrest?'

'Move,' my assailant said.

A concerned Tom Gerard stopped at the table. 'What's the matter, Brian?'

'Haven't a clue, Tom.'

Sergeant Vincent arrived at the table. 'You said you wished to speak with Pc Blake. What's the problem?'

'He's helping with our enquiries,' the thick set one replied.

'You've just arrested him.'

'This is real police work. Keep out of our way,' he tightened his grip on my shoulder. 'Come on, move.'

Chief Superintendent Andrews appeared in the doorway and walked towards us. His eyes narrowing. 'Who are you?' He demanded.

'We're taking Pc Blake in for enquiries, sir.'

'I asked you a question. I will not repeat it.'

The was a silence. 'I'm DS Gough, sir. This is ...'

'He can answer for himself,' the Commandant snapped. 'Well,' he demanded.

'DC Cope, sir,' he said. The aggression gone.

'Sergeant Gough,' The anger on the Chief Superintendent's face was obvious. 'It may have escaped your notice but this is No.3 Police District Police Training Centre, a Home Office establishment, of which I am the Commandant. As far as you are concerned this is a foreign country. You do not just march in here and deprive one of my students of their liberty without having the courtesy to notify me or my deputy of your intentions. DC Cope remove your hand from Pc Blake's shoulder.'

The hand left my shoulder faster than it arrived.

He turned his attention to me. 'Blake, were you cautioned or given any explanation as to why you are being treated in this manner?'

'No sir.'

'My office, now,' he snapped. 'You as well Blake,' he nodded to Sergeant Vincent. 'Carry on Sergeant.'

As we left the Dining Room Sergeant Faulkner was walking past. 'Sergeant, come with me.'

Door closed. The two detectives standing in front looked acutely embarrassed. I was standing to the left of the Commandant's desk, Sergeant Faulkner the right.

'Where were you taking him, Sergeant?

'Harrogate police station, sir.'

'Why?'

'Sir,' he replied. 'We have separate statements of complaint from two of your staff that concern this officer.' He nodded in my direction.

What?

'For the moment, Sergeant, I will leave your woeful lapse of procedure. Shall we start with the legal niceties?' He turned to me. 'Blake, allegations have been made and as police officers we must establish the veracity. You understand?'

'Yes sir.'

He nodded to the Sergeant. 'Brian Blake you are not obliged to say anything unless you wish to do so but whatever you say may be given in evidence. Do you understand?'

'Yes, I understand.'

The Sergeant glanced at the Commandant who nodded. 'Pc Blake I have received two separate complaints from members of the kitchen staff at Pannal Ash that you have persistently pestered them for sex. They are Julie Slater and Mary Cartwright. Julie Slater was reported missing last Saturday We need you to answer some questions.'

'What would you like to know?'

The Commandant raised his hand. 'One moment, Sergeant.' He turned to me. 'Blake, wait outside. Sergeant Faulkner.'

I closed the door and stood next to the sergeant. 'Can I ask you a question, Sergeant?'

'Providing it's not about the case in question.'

I bit my lip. 'Yes and no, Sergeant. It's more about investigative procedure.'

'Ask it anyway. We'll see.'

''For argument's sake. Two people have made independent complaints of threats of violence, serious enough for a police officer to take a statement ...'

Sergeant Faulkner interrupted. 'It's a potential minefield. From a practical policing point of view you wouldn't commit yourself to paper straight away. Threats, like pestering are implicit. They are an annoyance. Unlike a punch or a touch, which are explicit. It could be a couple of people in drink. It could be bullying or jealousy. Experience will tell you what to do. Make a note in your pocket book and seek advice. Do not leap into statements and recording crime. That can be a nightmare. See both parties and give advice and make sure you record everything. Domestics. Remain even-handed. Refer them to solicitors or the Magistrates Court to apply for a Binding Over. I've been to domestics and arrested the husband for assaulting his wife only for the wife to defend her husband and attack me. It's bizarre,' he paused and chuckled. 'Remember Blake, it's a learning curve. We're not here to win. Just to make up the numbers. One final point, ask Sergeant Bell about the Justice of the Peace Act 1361.

'1361?'

'Yes, it's one of the oldest active Acts of Parliament.'

Forty-Seven

The Commandant picked the phone up and dialled. 'I'm trying to stop you from getting any more egg on your face, Sergeant,' he held his hand up as the phone was answered. 'Ah, Mrs Nutton, Commandant. Over the past two months have there been any unacceptable behaviour by the students towards any of your girls?'

'No, sir. Nothing that I've entered in the book otherwise I would have told you. Of course there are always those who try it on but I've heard nothing.'

'Will you just repeat that to Detective Sergeant Gough.' He passed him the telephone.

'Mrs Nutton, DS Gough ... Thank you.'

Rain began to beat against the windows as lightning flashed in the distance. Chief Superintendent Andrews looked over his shoulder. 'That will please Sergeant Breen. Put a bit of give in the playing field.' He looked to his front. 'Could I see those statements you mentioned, Sergeant.'

Sergeant Gough hesitated.

'There is a problem, Sergeant?'

'No sir,' he said, opened his briefcase and passed the statements across the desk.

'Thank you.' He put them side-by-side on his desk and frowned. Picked up the phone and dialled. 'Sergeant Masterson, my office please.'

'There's a problem, sir?' said Sergeant Gough.

'You could say that, Sergeant.'

Masterson knocked and entered. 'Sir?'

'What do you make of these?' He indicated the statements.

Masterson peered at the statements. 'What on earth?'

'You had no idea?'

'Not a clue, sir. I've seen no evidence of this at all.'

'That's all, but wait a minute.'

He turned the statements round. 'Sergeant Gough it is now obvious that you did not take these statements.'

'No sir, sorry.'

'Were you aware that with the exception of the signatures and personal details they are verbatim. Almost pro-forma?'

'I knew they were similar.'

'And how you knew that Pc Blake's service number was 547?'

'Yes sir.'

'How is Pc Mathew Turner involved?'

'His parents are friends with the Slaters. He stays with them some weekends.'

'And?'

'He told the original officer when Julie Slater was reported missing that he had evidence that Pc Blake was responsible. The enquiry was passed to me.'

It was a sardonic smile. 'You thought it was an easy collar. No-one thought to check with me or my staff?'

'Sorry sir.'

'Sergeant, we don't run popularity contests here. It's not in our brief, and, I'm not saying this to protect Pc Blake. If he has done wrong he will pay the price. He came here with a BSc in exercise physiology. He's one of the course leaders. He is a martial arts instructor and runs a very popular karate class twice a week. Sergeant Masterson is a member. Are you not?'

'Indeed sir. He's very good as my thighs can attest. I could hardly walk for two days after the first session.'

'Whereas Mathew Turner was a bit of a loud mouth. An ex-cadet who thought the course would be, and I quote, a piece of piss. He is finding it very difficult.'

'Indeed,' said Sergeant Masterson. 'He's become sullen. Nobody wants to be with a moaner.'

'Quite. Now, when was Julie Slater last seen?'

'Thursday, sir.'

'Hmm. This statement purporting to be Slater's is dated two days prior. Mrs Nutton has heard nothing about her staff being unduly harassed. That would lead me to question its veracity. But these,' he wafted his hand over the statements. 'I can tell you that Blake has an unbreakable alibi for Friday night. He was in York hospital being treated for the effects of smoke inhalation following a fire. He wasn't released until 10am Saturday. Thursday I don't know.'

'I can answer that, sir,' said Sergeant Masterson. 'I called in the bar for half an hour on Thursday at 9.30, sir. Blake and his friends were there. There were still there when I left. There were no reported absences when the bed-check was carried out.'

'Thank you, Sergeant. The information about Turner stays in this room. Keep an eye open and see how he reacts when he discovers that Blake is still at liberty.'

'Yes sir,' he said and left.

The Commandant sat back in his chair. 'Before I was appointed as Commandant, Sergeant Gough, I was Detective Superintendent in Nottingham. Not doing too well, are you?'

The chastened detective sergeant looked back at him. 'No sir.'

'How do you propose to redeem yourself?'

'Visit the Slater's and examine his room. Ask if they knew about the statement and check the signature. Ascertain his state of mind and his family circumstances. Why does he prefer the Slater's to home.'

'Good. When you come to interview Anne Cartwright. This is her first job out of school. She's sixteen, a juvenile. Kid gloves and an adult.'

'Thank you, sir. She might be reticent talking about sex in front of her parents would Mrs Nutton do?'

'She will. I won't keep you any longer.'

He picked up the phone, 'Mrs Nutton, Pc Blake is returning for his breakfast. A fresh one, please.' He opened his office door. 'Thank you, Sergeant. Blake there's a fresh breakfast waiting for you.'

Forty-Eight

The conversation stopped as I entered the classroom. 'What was that all about,' said Sergeant Bell.

'Not sure, Sarge. We were in the Commandant's office, he suggested to DS Gough and DC Cope, the pair from Harrogate, that they apply the legal niceties. I was given the short caution and DS Gough told me it was to do with my pestering a couple of the canteen girls for sex. One of them, Julie Slater, was reported missing from home last Saturday. But I can't place her.'

'You know,' said John Bradbury. 'She was in the Sealed Knot last Tuesday with her sister.'

'Ah. Now I remember. Then the Commandant sent me out with Sergeant Faulkner. And that was it really. Sergeant Masterson paid a flying visit. Then the two detectives came out. A minute later he dismissed Sergeant Faulkner and sent me for my breakfast. Now you know as much as I do.'

'I don't believe that,' said Eric Carr. I smiled.

Coffee time. Sheila, the Commandant's secretary tugged my sleeve. 'Pc Blake, Mr Andrews would like a word.'

John Bradbury spotted me leaving the dining room. 'Going on your travels again, Brian?' What the hell was it now? I raised my hand in acknowledgement.

'This fire you were caught in, Blake. I've had the press on the phone. Somehow they have your name and want an interview. They also mentioned shooting. I've spoken with Mr Barton your Chief Constable and they will deal with it and let both me and you know. As it happens I had a call from a Mr Syme yesterday afternoon who gave me some details. He thinks highly of you.'

'He wasn't so effusive when we spoke, sir.'

He smiled. 'He was with me. Fed me part of the picture. You weren't injured?'

'Minor burns to my left shoulder, back and leg, sir, it was hairy.'

'Bearing in mind you were supposed to be working under the supervision of the security services Sergeant Bell will bring you an injury form.'

'Yes sir. To be honest I was more concerned about my fiancée, her mother and my step-sister.'

'Fiancée? Congratulations. I didn't know you were engaged to be married.'

I smiled. 'I wasn't until Friday evening, sir. I know we've only known each other a few weeks but we both think it's right. I had the ring and planned to make it official that weekend. However, once we were trapped getting engaged seemed to be a positive step. Something to look forwards to. And with the death of her father in Rotterdam the next day following a road accident. To put it crudely sir, it was, with exceptions, a bastard of a weekend.'

'I can see your proposal being a distraction. As for her father, that is terrible. Please give her and her family our condolences when you see them.'

'I will, sir. But could I use your phone? I'll pay for the call.'

'You'll do no such thing,' he indicated the phone. 'Please.'

I called Joe and brought him up to date. He promised to call Tadcaster and Boston Spa. At least they would be aware. The girls had their own way of diverting attention.

'Before you go, Blake. There's been a mention of shooting and fire and, I know you were treated for smoke inhalation and minor burns. Now you've mentioned being trapped. Is there anything else I ought to know?'

With the exception of the espionage and Mr Syme's identity I told him.

His expression changed from curiosity to shock as the tale unfurled. 'I had no idea. Do you need some time off to recover? You're entitled to it.'

I didn't even consider requesting a night with matron. 'I'll be fine, sir. I can concentrate on my studies here and throw myself into some hard physical work on the sports field and the gym. But one favour, if I might ask?'

'It goes no further. No doubt the full story will appear following the trial.'

'There's something wrong with that lad's brain, sir,' said Sergeant Gough. 'The signature on the statement is not Julie Slater's. According to her mother it's nothing like. Plus, he has a diary, if you can call it that. It's a diatribe concerning Pc Blake but the language is becoming more violent. And, sir, DC Cope found this under his bed.' He opened his briefcase and placed the knife on the commandant's desk.

'A stiletto?'

'Yes, sir. There's only one use for a stiletto. I think it would be best if Pc Blake were not made aware.'

'I disagree, Sergeant. He ought to know, but leave it with me, I will telephone Superintendent Larkin. But what about the Slaters, had they any idea?'

'Mrs Slater said he had started talking to himself, which she found worrying, but done nothing. She was planning to talk with Turner's mother but hadn't gotten round to it. She'll call this afternoon.'

'Was there any other potential evidence?'

'Plenty, sir, including a box file with three proforma statements waiting for details. We've taken everything from his room and left it in the office. Also had a word with DI Vellander. We'll take Turner in for questioning. See what he has to say about what we found. Let the police surgeon have a look at him. Depending on what we find charge him with perverting the course of justice. We'll return after dinner and interview Anne Cartwright.'

'Very well. Keep me appraised sergeant, but let Turner change out of his uniform before you leave.'

Forty-Nine

It was the first full rehearsal for the Annual Inspection. Gym kit on and *Gi* in hand I ran to the drill square. Course 236 were lined up across the rear. Their first day. Course 235 in front and 234 to the fore. Those doing the gym display off the square next to the gym equipment and, half a dozen in *Gis*. The commandant, deputy and course inspectors at the top.

'Blake,' Sergeant Breen called across. 'Turner's absence doesn't affect you, does it?'

'No sergeant.'

The command. 'PARADE! ... As you were. Wake up ...' Started the ball rolling. All in all it was pretty good. The Drill Squad did their display. We had a couple of hiccups when someone tripped over the tumble mats. Other than that it was fine. It was the first time we had done the karate display outdoors. Everyone knew the routine by heart. There were no cock-ups. Finally, the march-past.

Word was circulating about the fire at The Spartan's track. Some of it grossly exaggerated. I kept out of it.

Next morning as usual, John Bradbury and I went for our six am run round the sports field. Usually half a dozen but today the spirit was weak. Running up the hill towards the house we were about forty yards short of the swimming pool when my right lace came undone. I stood on it. 'Hang on, John.' I shouted.

He was jogging on the spot ten yards away when. 'Bloody hell. Look at this.'

Barely visible, looking at us through the long grass was a fox, blood around its muzzle. Behind it a pile of grass clippings from the latest cut of the field. As I stood the fox turned tail. 'It's obviously been eating something, but what.'

It didn't take long. 'Oh for fucks sake, Brian,' John looked sick. 'Look.'

Apart from Friday night's escapade I'd witnessed and participated in several post mortem examinations at uni. This was different. Walking into a mortuary as a student to observe and later participate in post mortem examinations was one thing. Coming across what lay behind the clippings was another altogether. I don't know about John but it hit me like a kick in the chest. Even moreso than Friday, probably because she was young and naked. Eyes open. About five four. Dark hair cut into her neck. Bruising to her throat. Swollen lips. Signs that something, probably the fox, was making a meal of her right breast and shoulder. 'Look at this.' I pointed at her right eye. 'See those little red specks. They're called petechiae. Signs of possible strangulation.'

'How do you ...? Oh, uni. Do you think it's Julie?'

'Good chance.'

'You know more about this than I do. I'll stay in case the fox comes back. You go tell someone.'

A tracksuit-wearing Inspector Pierce was about to miss his morning jog; astounded wasn't the word. 'Where?'

'Just below the swimming pool, sir. Behind that pile of grass clippings.'

He scrutinised my face. 'Are you all right, Blake?' he said. 'Must have been a shock.'

'I'm fine, sir, really.' After the initial shock and compared to last Friday evening.

'Ok, Go back. You and Bradbury keep everyone below the rank of sergeant off the playing field.' He turned and ran up the stairs. Somebody wasn't going to need their alarm clock.

Sergeants Palmer and Morton were first on the scene. Sergeant Morton took the three steps back to the playing field. 'I thought you did exercise physiology at university, Blake. So, how come you know about petechiae?'

I smiled. 'A module of anatomy, sarge,' I said. 'The one that includes post mortems. The lecturer was only too pleased to pass on little extras.'

'Fair enough ...'

Before he could continue Sergeant Palmer let rip at a group of students from course 235 who appeared from behind the admin block. Perhaps they'd never seen a naked female murder victim before. 'Get back off the field, all of you. Bradbury, take that lot on the right. Get them off.' Sergeant Palmer and John walked twenty yards away to take up their defensive positions.

Sergeant Morton grimaced. 'As I was about to say,' he continued.' That's useful knowledge. Me, I did history. But the pathologist will decide. Come on I'll help you and Bradbury with your pocket books and then your statements before breakfast.'

Whatever was planned for the morning was out of the window. I was back talking with my friends DS Gough and DC Cope. This was different. This was not about sexual pestering. However, I had my alibis. 'Aren't you the lucky one?' DC Cope was almost sneering.

This was ridiculous. 'Really? Apart from my alibi? You've just seen the lividity when she was moved suggesting that she had been kept somewhere lying on her left side. Just where was I supposed to have done that? Under my bed? In my motor cycle pannier? How did I get her from there to where it was found? Next, you'll be accusing me of training the fox to stop making a meal of her as we got near. Then show itself long enough for us to see the blood on its muzzle.

'All right, Ken. That's enough.'

I checked my watch. In two hours I would be transported to Wakefield for a Press Conference courtesy of Chief Inspector Reynolds; Lucy, Anne and Liz would also be there.

Everyone had to write their statements as to what they had been doing over the past two days. Not too bad for the two senior courses but 236 had only been there for two days. Some wanted to know why, when they were innocent, they had to write a statement. Good experience. Doing it in this manner saved a lot of time for the investigators. Nevertheless, with civilian staff they had two hundred statements to add to the file. All had to be read.

Straight after lunch the seven of us from last Thursday had a quick huddle. 'Right, Brian,' said Phil. 'Apart from the fact that he's male what can you remember about this sergeant?'

'Five ten. Dark hair greying at the temples, receding where the parting is. Signet ring third finger left hand ... that's all.'

We agreed to swap notes after evening meal.

Fifty

John Bradbury shouted after me. 'Where are you going dressed up like a dog's dinner?'

'I've got a dinner date, John. I'll see you later.' No doubt tongues would be wagging.

Conversation en route centred around the female body which had just been identified as Julie Slater. I supposed Mathew Turner would be interviewed.

At HQ we were fed and watered in the Officer's Mess, after which we were taken to the Chief Constable's office. What a surprise, Mr Syme was waiting. We were briefed. The press conference would take place in the adjacent conference room.

There were two camera crews present: BBC and Granada, backs to the window. Eight reporters in front facing us across the table. The Chief Constable on the left with his back to his office. The Chief opened the proceedings.

'My name is Raymond Barton and I am the Chief Constable. Numerous requests for clarification of the events that occurred at the Spartan's race track, Tadcaster, on Friday last have been received. As there will be no interference with the legal process Pc Blake, Miss Vernon, Miss Mountain and Mrs Vernon were approached and agreed to this meeting which will cover the time between the departure of the Spartan's team coach for the Netherlands and, the arrival at the track of the first police officer.'

They must have prearranged who was going to ask the questions. There was no fighting to get in first. It was the man on the left.

'It must have been a traumatic experience and we do thank you all for making yourself available ... Pc Blake, there are several rumours in circulation some of which appear outrageous. How did it all begin?'

I took a deep breath. 'Before the coach left the track a motor cyclist arrived. Lucy told me it was Peter, Peter Pederson, Lester Roberts' cousin. Lester is one of the mechanics and Peter always called when the Spartans were travelling to the continent.'

Lucy took over. 'That's right. He often had some envelope for relatives who lived in The Netherlands or Belgium. But he spoke with a lot of people including Dad.' She began to choke at the thought.

'When Peter took his helmet off,' I said. 'I thought I recognised him. Except I didn't know him as Peter. I just couldn't remember. It came to me that it was when I attended East Midlands university. But still couldn't remember his name. When the coach left he came over and asked if I was watching him. I explained. He denied ever having been to East Midlands university. I knew he was lying. The name came to me. I knew him as Rudi. Then someone tried to help. Didn't they?' I squeezed Lucy's hand.

She nodded. 'Hmm. All I said was that Brian had a wonderful memory. He was a policeman.'

'I pointed out I had been on my initial training course for eight weeks. The wheels came off very fast. He stepped behind Lucy put his right arm round her shoulders and the next second he had a pistol in his hand.'

I thought she was going to cry. 'Are you all right?'

She nodded. 'I'm ok. I survived that. I can live with the memory.'

'Take your time.'

'He put the barrel against my head and said, "If anyone moves or speaks without my asking a question the next bed this young lady will have is a mortuary slab.'

You could have cut the silence with a knife.

'That was a terrible moment,' said Anne.

'I really thought he was going to carry out his threat. It was terrible,' said Liz.

'Then Rudi said: "Well Mr policeman. Special Branch?"'

'Those were his exact words?' said my interrogator.

'Yes. Initially I thought it was a strange thing to say. Then it all came back. Why I remembered him. It wasn't strange at all. He had us walk with our hands up past the garages and the fuel tank, to a storage shed. Made Liz open the padlock and the doors and me back in with my hands raised. At that moment he remembered who I was. All he said was, "You". Then locked us in.'

'And then,' said Anne. 'Brian did something totally irrational.'

I chuckled. 'It was not irrational,' I said.

'It was a lovely thing to do,' said Liz.

'He asked me if I trusted him,' said Lucy. 'I said I supposed so. Then if I loved him. I told him I did and he put this on my finger,' she held her left hand up. 'Then asked me to marry him.'

There was laughter amongst the reporters. 'And of course you said, no.'

'I was going to pop the question that weekend anyway,' I said. 'It seemed the right thing to do. To be honest things weren't looking too good. It was something positive. A commitment. Help to lighten the mood.'

'Then Brian had us putting cement down just in case we had petrol coming into the shed,' said Anne. 'Eventually it did and we'd run out of cement.'

'The shed walls were inch thick planks. I was looking for knots. There were plenty of small ones but I found one about three inches across almost near the top at the back. There was a box of old or broken tools: masonry and wood chisels, sledgehammer with a broken shaft and saws. It didn't take long to dislodge the knot. Then I set to with the saws. It was quite warm by this time and burning petrol was trickling towards us. The smoke was bad and getting worse. I cut through two planks. Hoisted Anne through the gap followed by Liz, Lucy then me. It was hairy.'

'Couldn't you have made your escape then?'

'That thought did cross my mind. But we had no idea where Rudi was. Away from the sheds we were exposed. If he checked the burning shed and realised we'd escaped? He still had his pistol.'

'So?'

'I crossed behind the shed next to the one on fire and I could see Rudi walking backwards and forwards. As if he was waiting for someone. I'd thought perhaps it might be a good idea to go round the front of the sheds. See if I could turn the petrol off. But the sudden silence of the pump might have alerted them. The I saw Liz's keys on the path behind me. I picked them up and tossed them across to Lucy.

Seconds later a man in a raincoat walked from the direction of the Grandstand. He stood facing towards me. Rudi had his back to me. That and the sound of the fire cut out some of the conversation. I heard the newcomer say something about the fire as another man, tall, slim, younger walked in and stood beside the older one. But it was obvious the first of the newcomers and Rudi knew each other.

'Then he asked Rudi, "Where are they?" I didn't hear the reply but he flicked his head towards the fire. The older one frowned and said, "What, all of them?"

'An argument developed. The older said, "Can't be helped", and stuck his hand out towards Rudi who handed him a small package which he put in his left-hand coat pocket.

'The youngest of the three was looking unsure and addressed the other as "Sir". I heard the older one say "You've screwed up too often Mikhail. No-one is indispensable".

'That was another name. Rudi threw his arms out wide. What he said I don't know. The response which shocked the younger man was, "Simply this," he pulled a revolver from his right-hand coat pocket and shot Rudi once in the chest. He went down like a sack of spuds. It didn't make me feel too good either.'

I looked across at Lucy and the others. 'Are you ok?'

They all nodded. 'Yes,' said Lucy. 'It's not so bad this time round.'

I took Lucy's hand and gave it a squeeze. 'The next one might be. The younger one protested. "Sir, just what is happening."

'He ignored him, Walked across to Rudi's corpse. Crouched, put his hand in the left-hand pocket and stood. He was holding Rudi's pistol. Said something and shot his colleague once in the chest. He joined Rudi on the floor. The shooter wiped the pistol stooped and put it in Rudi's left-hand – he knew Rudi was left-handed. Then he stood.

'You could just hear the sounds of approaching emergency vehicles, two-tone horns etc. But the shooter was in no rush. He just stood there looking at his victims as if he was waiting.

'It might have been foolish but I reasoned that he shot his colleague with Rudi's gun because the calibre was likely to be different from his own. The striations on the bullet could identify the weapon that fired it. Or so I'd read.'

'It's not an exact science Pc Blake,' said the third journalist. 'However, in essence you're correct. But carry on.'

'He was standing with his back to me. If I could get close enough. He was about twenty yards from where I was. I'd gone about five yards. He must have either heard or sensed something. Turned. Realised who I was, spun round and made a dive for Rudi's pistol. Dropped it. Managed to pick it up and was in the process of lifting it up when I threw myself at him clamping my hand over his. He managed to fire three shots. The first nicking the sleeve of my leathers. The other two went wide. I applied a chokehold with my left hand as the cavalry arrived in the shape of these three.

'Go on Lucy,' laughed Liz. 'This was your idea.'

'Well,' said Lucy with the broadest smile. 'When I saw you take that first step I realised what you might try. Mum had her keys but the door of the nearest shed was unlocked. There was a bundle of pieces of wood tied with cord just inside the. Anne untied it. I took a piece three feet long. We crept behind the back of the sheds just as you tackled him. We could see the two bodies and him on his back facing the other way. I saw the gun in his hand so I ran out and hit him as hard as I could down the side of his head. He didn't like that. But I did and with the chokehold the noise he made was more of a gargle then a scream.' She took a moment to smile at the journalists. 'After all that time being cowed it felt great to do something positive. I didn't know about chokeholds. I won't be in trouble will I, for hitting him?'

The Chief Constable had been sitting there listening. 'I think that counts as an intervention with a view to saving someone's life. So no, you're not in trouble, Lucy.'

'Oh good. I wish I'd hit him harder.'

That made everyone smile. 'Not necessarily a good idea. What would you have done if I hadn't managed to stop him and he had come looking for you?'

'He'd have made for the fire. We could have run down behind the garages and the Grandstand and out of the gate waiting for the police.'

'As simple as that?'

She was going to swallow that grin if she wasn't careful. 'Of course. It would take a woman to think of it. That's all I can think of unless you need clarification.'

'There is one thing, if you could,' said the first interrogator. 'You mentioned earlier that you remembered what it was that made Rudi or Mikhail so memorable. Could you tell us what it is?'

'Of course. I'd never had any particular interest in politics before I went to university. But everything was new, clubs, meetings etc and I attended one particular meeting and found it was the Young Communists. That didn't interest me at all. The following week somebody contacted me and said they had a special speaker coming and I might change my mind.'

'That was Rudi?'

'It was. To be fair he was a good speaker. Communism was the fairest form of democracy. Support of minorities. To me it was a fairy tale. I stood up and challenged him. Free speech. Freedom of the individual. A country's right to self-determination. And if Communism was so freedom loving why had they supressed Hungary and its people by sending in the army in 1956. 2500 Hungarians killed. 200,000 Hungarians fled the country. He wasn't impressed. Two of his minders came to introduce themselves. They lost.'

'Not bad for someone not interested in politics, especially you were what, fourteen years of age when the invasion took place,' came the amused reply. 'But yes. I can see why he remembered you. But you say the minders lost?'

'He's a black belt at karate,' said Anne with a broad grin.

'They all are,' said Lucy.

'All?'

'My two sisters,' said Anne.

'Identical triplets,' said Lucy. She was enjoying this. 'And their father.'

Everyone was sitting up and taking notice. 'And are you going to university like your brother, Anne?'

'Step-brother,' she turned and grinned at me. 'Not that I hold it against him. I'm studying business management at the local college. I work with my father. Jennifer is studying marketing at the same college and Frankie; she has a gift for languages. She does want to go to university.'

'What an interesting family you have.'

'And you, Lucy. What about you?'

'I work with my parents ... Oh.' She said as her face dropped.

I gave her hand a squeeze. 'You ok?'

She nodded. 'I suppose it's just with my mother now.'

That dampened the conversation.

'Sorry. I didn't mean to upset you.'

'That's ok,' she replied. 'I suppose I'll have to get used to it.'

Back to interrogator number one. 'Brian, you said the man you arrested referred to Rudi as Mikhail. Did you by chance hear the name Kuznetsov?'

'No, nothing like that, sorry. But it sounds Russian.' It wasn't a lie because I was told by Mr Syme a long time after the event.

'It's a common Russian name, the equivalent of 'Smith'. A derivative of Kuznets meaning a blacksmith.'

'Are *you* a spy,' said Lucy.

He laughed. 'No, a journalist, but I worked in Moscow and the far east for several years. I came across many interesting people.'

'Was this Kuznetsov a spy?' said Lucy.

'The one I had in mind was a member of the KGB,' he replied. 'But he dropped off the radar a few years ago. Could you describe Rudi, Brian.'

I took a deep breath and exhaled. 'Five six, fortyish, tanned features, dark hair greying at the temples, square jaw.'

My interrogator nodded and looked thoughtful. 'It could be him, thank you.'

I got the idea from his tone he was about to say something else, but didn't.

The cameramen wrapped up. As they were leaving the BBC operative turned to us. 'This will be edited and go out on the six pm news bulletin. Thank you for being so candid.'

Liz had been quiet for most of the session. She stood. 'Before you all go, gentlemen,' the conversation died. 'With the death of my husband last Saturday it's true that our lives are going to change. And once the news spreads all around the motor cycling world there will be a movement to celebrate his life. I haven't mentioned it to Lucy, but I thought a weekend racing festival at Tadcaster next year once I've discussed arrangements with the local police. I take it all of you drive?'

'We do,' said my interrogator, 'But we don't race motor bikes.'

'Mum, are you thinking what I think you are?' She got an answering smile. 'Can I?' There was an answering nod. 'Have you heard of Go-carts?'

'You want us to race Go-carts?' said the BBC cameraman. At least he looked enthusiastic.

'A special invitation race for the news media?' Liz nodded.

'For those who are present or can we substitute?'

'Preferably you,' said Liz. 'If there is the interest an annual Press Trophy.'

'That's very clever,' said out initial interrogator. 'If we don't enter people will want to know why and those who do will milk it.'

'I thought that as well,' said a smiling Liz, looking happier than she had all day.

'It's a great bit of PR. Count me in.'

The general consensus was positive.

Our interrogators, although they didn't do much, had left. The chief constable shook hands and thanked us for attending and was walking us to the stairs. One of the journalists had hung back. 'Brian, could I have a quick word.'

I said I'd catch the others up. 'How can I help?'

'Is your service number perchance 547?'

Strange. 'Yes it is. Could I ask why you want to know?'

'Don't worry. It's the same as your father's isn't it?'

'You knew him?'

'You have the look.'

He smiled and gave me his business card. 'If you want to chat give me a call.'

Fifty-One

Chief Inspector Reynolds had done the Grand Tour of Wakefield and consumed a surfeit of tea. I told him the tale and answered his questions. He would watch the 6pm news. Although he said it sounded more like part of the script of a James Bond movie.

'6.00pm, sir, either BBC or Granada.'

'Thank you Blake. Better go and get changed.'

I closed the commandant's door and walked into half of class two. 'Brian, where the hell have you been?'

'Press conference in Wakefield.'

'Why?'

'Watch the six o'clock news. I'm off to get changed.'

'Aren't you going to tell us?'

'Nope. Watch the news.'

It was the same at meal time. I didn't need a reminder and had intended to give it a miss but I crept into the bar to watch.

The Newsreader Vivienne Crutchley:

'It had been intended at this point to air a recording of a press conference that took place at police headquarters in Wakefield. The details were so graphic it was decided that it would not be suitable for viewing at this time. However, we do have Jason Dexter the cameraman. Jason, what can you tell us?'

The camera panned back revealing a man sitting to the interviewer's left.

'Vivienne, I've been a cameraman for over 20 years. I've been in places where no-one should have to go and listened to harrowing stories that no-one should have to tell. What I experienced today was on a par with the worst. When I left Wakefield I drove to Tadcaster where the divisional police commander made this announcement.'

The scene changed to a shot of a senior police officer standing outside a police station.

'Ladies and gentlemen. I'm Superintendent Deakin. After this announcement there will be no questions. At approximately 8.30pm Friday last ...

I'd seen enough and closed the door behind me. Seconds later John's footsteps caught me up. 'You ok, Brian?'

I took my copy statement from my tunic pocket and handed it over. 'John, you haven't seen this. Read it. Head for the library.'

Page by page punctuated by an occasional, 'Oh for fuck's sake.'. Finally, seated in the library. 'They sound like executions by the military,' he said as he folded the statement and handed it back.

'I'm not sure what it was.'

'But you arrested him?'

'Yup, it was either take that risk or chance being on the receiving end.'

'And all that came out in this press conference?'

'No. It was edited. All possible contentious bits removed.'

'Makes sense. Special Branch were involved?'

'And others.'

'Talking about others, how are Lucy and her mother and Anne?'

'I think in time Lucy and her mother will be ok. However, with the death of Lucy's father on the Saturday it's not going to be a walk in the park. Anne? She's young and resilient. I think she'll be all right. But they didn't witness the two shootings.'

'What are you going to do now?'

'If the phone's free call home and then Lucy. Then risk the crowd and go for a pint.'

'We could always go down to the Heifer.'

'Good idea. And John?'

'I know. I know nothing.'

I took the opportunity to call home and Lucy from the kiosk outside the Heifer. Home was all right but Lucy was struggling and I promised to ride over as soon as I could. Exactly when, I wasn't sure.

It was on page three of most of the daily papers we had access to the next morning, but the articles were light on detail and no-one identified. Although most at Pannal knew I had been involved but not how.

Could it have been the mentioning of the name Kuznetsov during the press conference that had been the determining factor?

There was no point in playing guessing games.

Fifty-Two

Wednesday. The final dress rehearsal for tomorrow's big event. There had been only one topic of conversation. Even that stopped. All minds concentrated.

Course 236 lining the parade ground. Everyone positioned as before. It was almost perfect. It was for me - Sergeant Breen had dropped the Flying Angel on my toes. The box lengthways. Run up to the springboard and aim for a spot about fifteen feet in the air with arms outstretched. My mind flashed back to the conversation I'd had with the commandant half an hour before; Turner had a stiletto? What the fuck? I mistimed my run and almost head-butted the sergeant in the guts. All he said was, 'A little higher tomorrow, Blake, if you please.'

Thursday morning. The big day. John, myself and a few others from course 234 were having a race round the sports field. Mickey Gardiner, one of the rugby team stopped and pointed. 'Look at that,' he said. 'Our lass would love that.' In a bush not ten feet away two magpies were squabbling over what looked like a necklace. A necklace of butterflies.

Sorry,' I said. 'You can't have it.'

'I found it, why not?'

'It was Julie Slater's. I saw her with it a few days before she disappeared.'

'Is that the necklace you told us about?' said John.

I nodded. 'Butterflies. Looks like it.'

'What do we do now?'

'Mickey, pick it up by its chain and drop it in your pocket. Then we find an Inspector.'

'Why Inspector?'

'Because it was given to her by a sergeant.'

Chief Superintendent Andrews sat back in his chair and pondered. 'You say this was commonplace, Blake.'

'I wouldn't go so far as to call it commonplace, sir. It was the second one I've witnessed.'

'Care to name names?'

'The first officer is no longer on the staff and the girl he was kissing followed him.'

The Commandant pursed his lips. 'That would be Sergeant Perfect? Another girl from the kitchen staff. They got married.'

'This time it was more than just kissing, sir.'

'So it seems. But you have no idea who they were this time?'

'No, sir. I was looking down on them. Just a sergeant and a member of staff who was holding that necklace. But her hairstyle appeared similar to the girl that Pc Bradbury and I discovered. I do recall the sergeant had his hands against two of the cabinets. I know the doors on those lockers are touched all the time but is it possible there might be viable fingerprints?'

The Commandant looked at the DI. 'Mr Vellander?'

'Quite possible, sir, if Pc Blake could point them out, I will make the necessary arrangements.'

'And this is where you were standing?' queried the DI peering over the rail.

'Yes sir.'

'I see what you mean. And in bad light ... I'll go down. You direct me to the two lockers.'

Arms at shoulder height and slightly wider DI Vellander called. 'How near am I?'

'Right width, sir but move one locker to your right ... That's spot on.'

'Lockers 14 and 16.'

Several sheets of paper and copious quantities of Sellotape later the doors were protected. Instructions given to the kitchen and domestic supervisors not to interfere. A fingerprint officer arrived within thirty minutes. If word had reached the sergeant responsible he had not come forward to give his side of the story. Could he be the murderer? Yes. But was he? It certainly wasn't Sergeants Faulkner, Breen, Best or Morton, of that I was certain. That left seven possibles.

This afternoon we were going to be busy.

Fifty-Three

From our early lessons on the structure of the police in No. 3 District there were six county and sixteen city and borough forces. Judging by the amount of brass on display, most of the chief constables and their various entourages were present. In addition, various Lord-Lieutenants and Her Majesty's Chief Inspector of Constabulary and entourages. Sergeant Faulkner was in his element. We gleamed, or rather those in uniform did. The rest of us togged up and ready for action.

The drill squad were step perfect. Sergeant Faulkner beamed with satisfaction. Then the gym squad. No-one goofed. Only two displays to go. First, my flying angel. Concentrate. I hit the springboard on the sweet spot and flew. I saw the look on Sergeant Breen's face. If he didn't move and fast I would go over his head. He started to back-peddle down the tumble mat, got his hands on my hips. Turned to his left putting me down on the tarmac, I'd overshot the mat. I don't know who was sweating most, him or me. 'Well done, Blake.' I grimaced and ran back as the handlers turned the box at right angles. Two members of the squad climbed on board, one crouching the other stretching over him. There was a gasp from the visitors as one of the prop forwards, Tom Bradshaw, came to the front – a big lad not noted for speed – ran towards the box, stopped and pushed the others off, bowed to the guests and ran back to laughter and a round of applause. John Masters from Sheffield stepped forwards, took a deep breath and ran. He leapfrogged the box and occupants. Even higher than I went.

Everybody knew the routine, a choreographed sequence of blocks, punches and kicks, nothing fancy just good basic technique. The display closed with a kata. To say they had only been practising for six weeks it was good. Then Joe was introduced to the guests. He was all padded up looking akin to a six feet two-inch Michelin Man. Just me and him. To show what could be achieved with practice. The conclusion being a march past led by Course 234, us at the rear. Course 235.followed. That was it. Joe even received an invite to join the guests for refreshments; He had come in his Gi, and apart from a pair of moccasins, which he wore for driving, he had no other clothes.

Fifty-Four

The final session of the day was for revision. However, I'd swapped a duty period with Johnny Mosley so I was working his 2.00am to 4.00am slot. The most unpopular one of all. Evening was two hours swatting, two more in the bar and bed by eleven. Mosley's was midnight to 2am. If I wasn't there by 1.50am he would come and wake me up. That was the plan.

I was rudely dragged from my slumbers by being shaken. 'Brian,' someone hissed. 'Brian, wake up. It's quarter past two.'

'What?'

John Bradbury shook me again. 'You've overslept.'

'Christ.' I swung out of bed. Mosley's bed was untouched. No time for a swill as I dragged my clothes on. 'Where's Mosley,' I said. 'Why didn't he come and check.'

'God knows. I'll come with you. Just in case.'

I looked presentable even if I didn't feel it. John, a tracksuit over his pyjamas had looked better.

Walter Mundy, the course 235 heavyweight, was still dressed and pissed. 'Little shit said he was going to report me,' he said as we reached his bed. 'Stopped that, didn't I?' He giggled and fell across his bed. Mosley was no push-over, but against Munday?

The paper scattered in the corridor told its tale. John looked behind the counter. 'He's here, Brian, behind the counter.' Mosley was out cold. A gash on his forehead, still bleeding. Peri-orbital bruising. 'John looked at me, finger to Mosley's throat. 'He's got a pulse.'

'You look after him, John. I'll find Matron.'

'I'll call an ambulance,' he said as I ran. Strange, Matron's door was open. Phone off the hook. A light showing beneath her bedroom door. And, two voices. One female and one male. That made me smile – what *was* matron up to? And, in *her* bed. The man spoke again. I stopped dead in my tracks. It was *the* voice. No mistake.

'You'll write to me, Donald?'

'Of course I will, but I've got to get off. I left a note on the commandant's desk explaining about my wife.'

I rapped twice and walked in. Sergeant Palmer was buttoning his flies. Matron grabbed at the covers.

'Get out, Blake!'

I ignored him, picked matron's dressing gown up from a chair adjacent to the door and tossed it to her. 'Pc Mosley's in the office. He's unconscious. A head injury. Pc Bradbury has called an ambulance.'

A naked Matron scrambled out of bed revealing far more than she should. Sergeant Palmer face like thunder.. 'Right, you've passed the message on. Now, get out.'

This was awkward. In front of me was the man I had seen with Julie. Did I comply and let him walk or had I the bottle? I decided on confrontation. 'Donald Palmer, you're not obliged to say anything unless you wish to do so, but anything you say may be put into writing and given in evidence. How long had you been having sex with Julie Slater?'

There was deathly silence. Both the sergeant and matron had gone pale.

'What the hell are you burbling about. I shan't tell you again. Get out.'

'That butterfly necklace. The one that Pc Gardiner found on the playing fields. I was standing at the top of the steps the night you gave it to her. She thought it was beautiful. So how long had you been having sex with Julie?'

'You bastard. Julie was only a kid.'

'You're mad. I wasn't,' he looked across at the matron. 'Valerie, I wasn't.'

'DI Vellander had lockers 14 and 16 fingerprinted. You had your hands there whilst you were kissing Julie. Until you put your left hand up her skirt.'

Now he was looking worried. 'You had your hand under her skirt at hip level. Until then she didn't bat an eyelid. She was getting as carried away as you were. What did she say when she laughed and grabbed your wrist? *"Not here. Not now. What if a student comes down? I'll see you in an hour. You know where. I've got something to tell you."* She was pregnant, wasn't she?'

'How the hell should I know? If she was it's nothing to do with me.'

'Yes, she was,' said matron. 'She came to me a few weeks ago. I thought she was and referred her to her doctor. She was happy, but wouldn't tell me who the father was.' She grabbed her case and ran out of the room.

'Have you learnt nothing, Blake. Even if she were pregnant, you have no evidence. If what you say is true you've not said anything before.'

'Not until tonight. I heard your voice. It was you. Donald Palmer, I am arresting you on suspicion of the murder of Julie Slater.' I took a step towards him.

'You're finished. Take one more step, Blake and I'll batter you senseless. You think you're clever with your karate but I'll show you.'

If I was wrong I probably *was* finished.

The die was cast.

He dropped into a boxing stance and flicked his right hand out. He was a southpaw. I took a step forwards. He did it again. I blocked the punch with my left hand and applied a choke hold with my right, dropping my wrist, pressing my knuckles into his adam's apple forcing him to his knees. It can be incredibly painful. The thought *what the hell have you done* flashed into my tiny mind. 'I never thought I'd ever say this to a police officer. You're spineless. You get the girl pregnant promising her what? If she hadn't objected you'd have given her one against the lockers. How romantic. Then you dump her body for the foxes. I'm going to release the hold, Sergeant. I trust it won't be necessary to re-apply it.'

I walked him down to the office. My right hand under his left upper arm. I got a strange look from John. 'I wondered where you'd got to.'

'I've arrested him.'

His eyes nearly popped out of his head. 'What? You've arrested him?' I'm not sure whether John believed me.

I sat Sergeant Palmer in the corner of the office furthest from the door. 'Yes. It was his voice I heard in the corridor that evening. He told Matron he was leaving because his wife was ill. The only way that I could think of to keep him here was to arrest him.'

John saw the funny side. 'His wife's ill and he stays behind to get his leg over with Matron?'

'So it appears.'

Matron, her back to me, never uttered a single word.

Perhaps she was contemplating the aftermath.

John Bradbury knocked on Inspector Pierce's door. He, Sergeants Bell and Groves arrived at the same time as the ambulance and a uniform inspector, sergeant and two Pc's from Harrogate.

'I hope to God you know what you've done, Blake,' Inspector Pierce looked very worried. 'If you're wrong?'

'Yes sir. I understand.' Everything.

Johnny Mosley was stretchered out accompanied by matron. Followed five minutes later by Walter Munday, still barely awake an officer either side.

John Bradbury watching Sergeant Palmer, Inspectors Pierce, Robertson and Sergeants Bell, Groves and Smith and me had a confab in the foyer out of earshot of the office. Once again I went through the events of that evening.

'We meet again, Blake,' said a smiling Inspector Robertson. Perhaps we ought to have you transferred to Harrogate when you graduate.'

'I've seen worse places, sir.'.

'Quite. Now, Sergeant Palmer. There's no animosity between you?' said Inspector Robertson.

'None sir. I hardly saw him. He's an instructor on Course 236 we're 234.'

'And you say that it was just his voice? You recognised it because there were no other distractions: people or events.'

'Yes sir. Just the voice.'

'And you're absolutely certain it was Sergeant Palmer's voice you heard?'

'Yes sir. There's no doubt in my mind whatsoever. I take full responsibility.'

'Fair enough.'

'It was when I heard him say he was leaving immediately. I had to either walk away or arrest him. It was the only way I could think of.'

'I can't fault you for making a decision, Blake,' said Inspector Robertson, 'Right or wrong his career is finished. If you're correct he goes to prison. If you're wrong, at least about the murder, and he's fathered a child with this girl then...' he left the point hanging. He turned to the sergeant. 'Smith, arresting officer Pc 547 Blake. Better put Pannal in brackets after his name. Save confusion ... Mr Pierce, if you have no objections I'd like to take Pc Blake back to town to make his statement for when DI Vellander arrives. We can get matron's statement later. That should be interesting.'

'Not a problem, Mr Robertson. Got your cuffs, Blake?

'Yes sir.'

'Go and get your helmet. Can't be seen outside indecently dressed.'

'I'll follow them down, sir,' said Sergeant Bell. 'Fetch Blake back when they've finished with him.

Fifty-Five

'What are you doing out of bed at this time?' was the comment from the desk clerk. 'Shouldn't you be tucked up all safe and sound.'

'Prisoner,' I said indicating Sergeant Palmer on my right. The desk clerk's face was a picture. 'Later.'

There was a strong smell of beer and stale piss. It must have been a busy night. Sergeant Palmer on one side of the desk. I stood with Sergeant Smith on the other. The only other person present was the gaoler. 'Blake, stand next to me and watch. Any questions later, all right?'

He took a very large pale blue form headed Detention Sheet from the drawer. 'There is a record of detention for every prisoner. It's standard throughout the Force.' He looked the Sergeant up and down. Filled in the top of the sheet with location, date and sequential number. 'You understand why you're here, on suspicion of murder?' The gaoler's eyebrows raised a few notches.

Sergeant Palmer nodded.

'Answer please.'

'Yes, I understand,' he gave me a filthy look.

'Good. Later today arrangements will be made for your civilian clothing to be brought here. Empty your pockets and remove your tunic.' He nodded to the gaoler. 'Search him.'

It was an interesting exercise. Entirely logical. There wasn't much property to enter. Sergeant Palmer was placed in a cell. It must have been a shock to his system when the cell door was slammed shut and double locked.

'Right, Blake, any questions?' he said and clipped Palmer's Detention Sheet next to Munday's.

'It's quite straight forward, so, no.'

The sergeant smiled. 'I've got one for you. Why do we search prisoners?'

I thought for a few seconds. 'It's not just curiosity. Anything relevant to why he's been arrested. He wasn't searched at Pannal, but I sat next to him on the way here and his hands were in full view all the time.'

'Nevertheless, always check any vehicle used in case something might have been hidden or slipped from a prisoner's pocket down the back of the seat. Anything else?'

'Offensive weapons?'

'Anything with which he can damage property or harm any person, including himself.'

'I hadn't thought of that.'

He had a warm smile. 'That's why you're at Pannal. The watchword is, *not on my watch*. Make sure that the things you are responsible for are straight. Your instructor will make sure your pocketbook is all right. 'One further question. Why are we arranging for civilian clothing?'

That was easy. 'So he can't walk out dressed as a police officer.'

'Have you learnt anything?' queried Inspector Robertson.

'Yes sir. Seeing it done for real is different from play acting, no matter how realistic that is.'

'Good. Now write out your statement, I'll have it typed and brought out to Pannal for signature.'

'If you have a typewriter, sir, I can type it myself.'

'You can touch-type?'

'Yes sir.' It was fortunate that I had a logical mind and good recall. It still took me forty minutes to type my statement. Signed and copy in my pocket I climbed into Sergeant Bell's car. It was almost daylight and not worth going back to bed.

'So, you slept in?'

'Yes Sergeant, and if I'd been up in time Mosley wouldn't have been injured.'

'You don't know that. But he is out of danger. They're keeping him in for observations ... You got an eyeful of Matron's tits?'

'Half an eyeful.'

'Very good,' he laughed. 'And Palmer was fastening his pants?'

'Yup.'

'I'll say one thing Blake, I've never heard of anyone's first arrest being for murder.'

'And they were in your class, Sergeant.'

His last question as we pulled into the Pannal Ash car park. 'How are you after the events of last Friday and the press conference.'

'Getting there, Sarge.' It seems that the chief constable had phoned the commandant and had asked the staff to keep an eye on me.

Fifty-Six

I can't imagine how long it had been since Chief Superintendent Andrews had been out of bed at this hour, but today he was. He lowered my statement before handing it to Sergeant Bell and turned to face me. 'You're absolutely sure about the voice?'

'Yes sir. There's no question in my mind whatsoever.'

He nodded, pausing for several seconds. 'This chokehold that you mention, do you teach it to your students?'

'No sir. It's far too advanced.'

The Commandant looked relieved. 'I'm pleased to hear it. However, your statement is very good, especially considering where you are in your career. Very well, Blake, I will let you go. No doubt your fellow students will require their curiosities slaking. A final word of advice,' his eyes narrowed as he smiled. 'Say as little as you can. Avoid any requests regarding Matron's state of dress. Tell them it is,' he paused and smiled. '*Sub judice*.' I'd just opened his door to leave. 'Blake,' he said. 'For your information, Sergeant Palmer did not leave any explanatory note.'

Following Walter Munday's arrest there had been precious little sleep in the dorm. Once I arrived there was none.

'How's Johnny Mosley?'

'As far as I know he's being kept in for observations.'

'Is it true you've arrested Sergeant Palmer?'

'Yes.'

'What for?'

'Suspicion of Julie's murder. He was doing a runner. It was the only way to keep him here.'

'Why didn't you report it earlier?'

'And say what?' said John Bradbury. 'Please sir, I've seen sergeant and one of the kitchen or domestic staff kissing. There are at least three from this course dating lasses from the kitchen. Why don't *you* report them?' There was a general rumbling of agreement.

'Was Palmer giving the matron one?'

'Not from what I saw.'

'You saw matron bollock naked.'

My lie was glib. 'No, I didn't.'

Eventually the questions dwindled. I got to go for my run. I would have preferred by myself but John Bradbury was waiting. He hadn't slept either. We chatted as we ran. I filled John in from my standpoint with the proviso that everything was, *sub judice.*

Fifty-Seven

I'd never needed a break as much.

There's nothing carved in stone or written in law that says a police officer in training won't have to fight for his life. It happens to people every day. Some win. Some lose.

One thing is certain. It brought me so much closer to my father when I pictured how he died, with the realisation that I was lucky to have been born, even luckier to still be alive.

I spent Friday night at Lucy's, for the most part talking things over with Lucy and Liz, taking care not to let the cat out of the bag. And some time with Lucy. She told me that it would have been the perfect opportunity for me to introduce her to sex had it not been for this mental picture of her father constantly looking over her shoulder. I'm not surprised she found that off-putting. As the Professor told us, it wouldn't do us any harm. That was a pleasure to look forward to.

Saturday morning we all went to the track. The gates secured. There was precious little to see. Yes, we knew where everything had happened but the only physical traces were the charred remains of the shed.

Lucy rode pillion across to Huddersfield. If she had squeezed any tighter there would have been two of me. Liz followed in the Bentley. Once again I had the camp bed in Clive's room. Lucy and Liz shared mine.

Sunday morning I went for a solo run. I needed the burn. Destination: follow the A640 which ran over the Pennines from Huddersfield to Rochdale. It was five miles to the Nont Sarah's pub, an isolated establishment in the middle of nowhere. A climb of 300 plus feet.

I had just passed the turn off to Bolster Moor when a Volvo saloon pulled in. No doubt someone wanting directions. It wouldn't be the first time. The front passenger window was wound down.

'Good morning, Brian.' Of all people it was Mr Syme. Inspector Thewlis at the wheel. 'Your sister, or one of them told us you were coming this way.'

I leaned forwards resting my hand on the roof. 'Good morning, sir. Yes, I'm just out for a burn after the last week.'

'Yes, you do like controversy. I've heard there's an isolated pub round here called Nont Sarah's, strange name. Why don't you hop in the back and direct us there?'

It might have been phrased as a question but his tone wasn't.

It was a five minute drive. The Volvo pulled onto a rough area on the left, thirty yards passed Nont Sarahs, where the footpath that runs alongside Cupwith Reservoir from the Colne Valley meets the A640.

'Shall we walk? Mr Thewlis will be quite happy minding his car.' The Inspector smiled as we got out.

Five yards in he stopped. Faced into the wind. Closed his eyes. Took a deep breath exhaling slowly. 'I've always loved these moors. In winter as well as summer.' He looked around. 'Desolate but beautiful,'

I knew what he meant. As far as the eye could see were grasses, reeds and sedge, whispering and waving as the wind decreed. Especially the bolls of the cotton grass.

'You know these moors, sir?'

'Yes, I was born just over the hill in Marsden,' he pointed and began walking again. 'The explanation we gave a week ago yesterday.'

'Yes sir?'

'Did the others buy it?'

'They did.'

'Good. And this conversation like the one you had with DS Mallory never took place. You understand?'

'Yes sir.'

'For some reason I was not made aware of your clash with Kuznetsov at university, otherwise we would have been more prepared.'

'The captain knew, sir.'

'Did he now?' he looked thoughtful.

'Yes, just before he shot Kuznetsov he told him it was because of that clash, my friendship with Lucy and, that I, as a policeman had been selected for the task.'

'Strange. Never mind... And he told you that secret documents were being smuggled out of the country having been pilfered from some government establishment.'

'Yes, he did.'

'It took a little while before we established the link between the thefts and the Spartan's continental tours. What we needed was someone like you. Someone who had every right to be there and who would not be questioned simply because they were.

'And if you were wondering, the documents, for which very large sums of money changed hands, were not in fact top secret. However they looked good and would have the soviets thinking that we were barking up the wrong trees. So no harm was done. Your arrest of Manville-Jones will have rattled the Soviets to some tune. If you watch the 6pm news this evening you will see the results of your efforts. For that the country will be grateful.'

'Can you shed any further light on the deaths of Bill Vernon and Lester Roberts?'

'In a word, Brian, no. According to our Dutch colleagues it was as reported. A simple road accident. And we have to accept that at face value. Although knowing who we were looking for was, how can I put it? bountiful.'

By now we were past the reservoir and the path was petering out.

'A couple of things and then you are free to run home or we can drop you off where we picked you up. The trial of Manville-Jones, and that is still secret, will be authorised by the Attorney General and held *in camera* at the Old Bailey within the next 12 weeks. The Judge will be Lord Justice Nevison. You and you alone will be required to attend. The others did not witness the shootings. You will attend in civilian clothes and the trial is scheduled to last for a maximum of five days. You can obtain a travel warrant from your station. I understand you will be posted to Westleigh.' Something I didn't know.

'Last, you will receive official recognition for what you have done. All of you. Confirmation will arrive in due course.'

And that was that. I could let Liz and Lucy know that it was an accident. Although to me the fact that the two people who had been contacted by Kuznetsov were the only ones to die was, in itself, suspicious. However, all doors were closed and secured. No further enquiries possible.

I could tell them about my pending court appearance and they were going to get an official *thank you* letter.

I always left home for Pannal at six. But today I waited for the six o'clock news. I wasn't disappointed:

Earlier today synchronised raids carried out by national police forces and security services across Europe broke up one of the largest espionage rings since the end of the second World War ...

'Do you think that's linked to our little adventure'; said Anne.

'I haven't a clue,' I lied. 'Who knows?'

Fifty-Eight

The Close, Westleigh, looked more like a corner terrace house than a police station. Nevertheless it was where I would be stationed.

I kicked the side-stand out removed my helmet and gauntlets, took a deep breath and entered.

Public desk on the right leading to an office. The sound of telephone conversation. A raised voice. 'Be with you in a sec.' Back to the telephone call. 'That's fine, Mr Simmonds come in any time to make your statement. Somebody will sort you out. Thanks. Bye.'

The sound of a handset being replaced and a chair being slid across the linoleum. The owner of the voice appeared.

'Come to produce your documents?'

'Not this time,' I said. 'I've been posted here.' I showed my warrant card and held my hand out, 'Brian Blake.'

'Jim Tyndall,' he said as he took my hand. He looked over my shoulder. 'Sergeant Meadowcroft, somebody to see you,' he said and winked.

A man with three stripes on his tunic sleeve appeared. 'What is it, Jim?'

He nodded towards me. 'Our new recruit, Sarge. Pc Blake.'

'Brian Blake?'

'Yes, Sergeant.'

He took a step back and smiled. 'Better come in and take a seat.'

He removed a buff coloured file from his desk drawer. 'I understand you've applied to take residence in a flat in Mirfield.'

'That's correct. I was informed there was a shortage in Westleigh.'

'Very much so. It has been approved so you can make your own arrangements.'

'Thank you.'

'You're not married.'

'Not yet, Sergeant,' I said and smiled.

'But?'

'I am engaged.'

'Fixed a date yet?'

'Not as yet.'

'That can wait then. You know you have to apply?'

'Yes, Sergeant.'

'Fair enough. Haven't decided which rota you'll be on. Probably Rota 2, in which case Jim Tyndall will be your tutor. That's all for now I'll give the thrupenny tour.'

There wasn't much to see. The mess room which doubled for report writing. A bank of personal lockers: 547 top right. Kitchen with its ancient gas cooker and fridge. Upstairs the Inspector's office, C.I.D. office and a large room with plenty of stacked chairs used for whatever. Outside, kennel for stray dogs, coal store and rubbish bins. Last the front office. I was handed over to Jim. Switchboard, table with typewriter, a large double-fronted cupboard stacked with folders, book and miscellaneous files. In the corner the sole cell.

'We used to have two cells but demand was so great they took one to use as a store.'

Two minutes to coffee time. Sergeant Bell surveyed the class. 'Your final exam is in two days, gentlemen. Any questions? Ask now, or, forever hold your peace ...'

The door opened. We all stood to attention as Chief Inspector Reynolds entered. 'Sorry to intrude, Sergeant, I'd like to borrow Blake.'

The sun was shining when we arrived at Harrogate police station. DI Vellander was all smiles. 'I've never done this before. Take note. You will be there to observe. You will stand behind me. No notes and no talking. Even if Palmer says something to you, which I doubt, you will ignore it. Understood?'

I *was* being given the opportunity to be present at Palmer's final interview before he was charged. 'Yes sir. I understand.'

'I will have a copy of the file prepared and sent to you at your posting. Westleigh?'

'Thank you sir. Yes, Westleigh.'

'You will find it useful in the future.'

DS Gough and DC Cope were no longer stationed at Harrogate. Both had received a severe reprimand from the chief constable. DS Gough was now a uniform sergeant in Castleford. DC Cope a uniform constable in Wombwell. DS MacFarlane accompanied DI Vellander. Chief Inspector Reynolds went for a cup of tea. Everyone in their place. Sergeant Palmer, as he still was, gave me a strange look but said nothing.

'Pc Blake is here as an observer,' said the DI. 'Shall we begin? Donald Palmer you are still under caution. Do you understand?'

'Yes sir. I understand.'

'You are a married man with three daughters. You have fifteen years in service with five as a sergeant. Your home force is Leicestershire. You have been an instructor at Pannal Ash for twelve months. Is that correct?'

'Yes sir.'

'How long have you been having a sexual relationship with the Pannal Ash matron, Valerie Johnson?'

'About four weeks.'

'She says, and I have her statement here, almost two months. Is she wrong?'

'I wouldn't have put it so long.'

'Hmm. Were you in love with her, or was she just something to fill the time in whilst you were away from home?'

'I wasn't in love with her.'

'She says she was in love with you. And, you did promise to write after you returned to your sick wife.'

'I wasn't in love with her. Stupid I know but I wouldn't have left my wife and daughters. And, I wouldn't have written.'

'So you say. Now, this illness of your wife's. What was she suffering from?'

'She developed a severe chest infection. I needed to be at home to look after my daughters.'

'And you left a note on the commandant's desk?'

'No. It was just something I said.'

'Why?'

'To placate Valerie.'

'When did you find out about your wife's illness?'

'When I called home at 6pm.'

'6pm? And yet you stayed behind to have sex with the Matron where Pc Blake interrupted you at 2.15am.'

There was no answer.

'Well, Palmer?' said Inspector Vellander when he refused to answer. 'It's strange, according to your wife she had what she described as a mild summer cold. Nothing more. More to the point she was wondering why you hadn't been home for a month. I would like to know as well? Where were you? Apparently you weren't at Pannal Ash from Friday night to Sunday evening for the previous four weeks.'

Palmer refused to answer.

'Well, who were you with, Valerie Johnson or was there someone else? ... If you refuse to give an explanation I will draw my own conclusions.'

'I've nothing to say.'

'Very well.' He nodded to DS MacFarlane.

'Do you recognise this woman?' DS MacFarlane slid a black and white 10x8 photograph across the table.

Palmer glanced at the photo. 'Yes, it's Julie Slater she worked in the kitchen at Pannal.'

'How well did you know her.'

'She's a nice kid. I chatted to her on the odd occasion'

DS MacFarlane removed a number of black and white 10x8 photographs from a folder. 'How about this?' he said pushing the first across. 'A photograph of Julie Slater's naked body as first discovered by Pc Bradbury. You have three daughters; how would you feel if this happened to any one of them?'

Palmer looked sick. 'That's terrible. Who would do such a thing.' He looked at me. 'But I thought it was Blake.'

'No, Pc Blake had stopped to re-tie his shoe lace. It was Pc Bradbury who first saw the fox with its bloodied muzzle.' He indicated the photo. 'Ring any bells?'

'What? You think I was responsible for this?'

'You are, aren't you?'

He shook his head. 'No. no, no. I wouldn't.'

'This is a close-up of Julie's face and throat. You will notice the bruising and scratches around Julie's windpipe and her swollen lips. 'Have you anything to say?'

Palmer was looking worse and shook his head again.

'This photograph,' he slid it across the table. 'is of Julie Slater's right eye. You can see these dots,' he pointed them out, 'are called petechiae, petechial haemorrhage's caused during manual strangulation. The same applies to this.' He slid the photograph of Julie slater's left eye across. 'You can see similar petechiae here ... have you anything to say?'

'No. Honestly, I didn't kill her.'

'This last photograph is of Julie, showing where the fox had begun to eat her body. It doesn't make good looking does it? Just imagine if some man had done this to one of your daughters. Go on. Look closely.'

This was brutal. So was Julie's murder.

The DI took over again. He picked a report up from the table. 'Palmer, I have here the post mortem report from the pathologist, Doctor Jackson. I'll paraphrase his conclusions. *The injuries to Julie Slater: The swollen lips, bruising to the throat, petechiae, fractured hyoid and haemorrhage of the laryngeal mucosa are classic features of death by manual strangulation.* The latter being something to do with the vocal cords. Furthermore, Julie Slater was three months pregnant. The foetus was also dead. Forensic examination shows that there was semen in her vagina. As a point of interest, Palmer, I believe that your blood group is 'O'. Is that correct?'

'Yes sir. But how did you know that?'

'All in good time. Julie Slater's blood group was also 'O'. At twelve weeks gestation it is possible to identify the blood group of a foetus. It and Julie Slater's baby's blood group were also 'O'. Telling don't you think?'

I had a quick recap on blood groups. Two type 'Os' can only produce a type 'O' baby. However type 'O' babies can be produced by five or six different combinations. At 48% of the population type 'O' is the most common blood group. It was still a good point to make.

'Sir, I did not kill Julie Slater.'

'Palmer, shall we go back to the start. It was the Thursday prior to the Annual Inspection. Pc Blake and some of his friends were in the bar when he realised he had left his money in the dormitory. He was about to descend the rear staircase when he heard voices. Both of which he had heard before but could not identify. One, a sergeant had dark hair going grey at the temples. He was supporting himself against the staff lockers. a signet ring clearly visible on the third finger of his left hand. Your hair is greying at the temples and you wear a signet ring on the third finger of your left hand. The other, a young woman with prominent breasts, hair cut into her neck. She was holding a necklace of butterflies across the sergeant's back. She thought it was beautiful. They were kissing passionately. He put his hand up her skirt. She grabbed his wrist and stopped him. Said not here and not now. They would meet in an hour at a location they both knew well.'

'Blake is mistaken, sir. That wasn't me.'

'Blake is mistaken about what? You weren't there, it was someone else. You weren't kissing Julie Slater? You didn't had your hand up her skirt? You didn't buy this necklace or give it to her?'

'Sir, all of it. I did not buy the necklace so I couldn't have given it to Julie. And, I wasn't in that corridor. So, no, I wasn't kissing her.'

'Did you ever kiss Julie or have sex with her?'

'No sir. I admit the relationship with Valerie but not with Julie.'

'Have you ever had a personal relationship, sexual or otherwise, with any member of the Pannal civilian staff other than Valerie Johnson?'

'No sir. Never.'

'Have you ever used the passage passed the lockers.'

'Well, yes. Often. Students are barred from using it but not instructors.'

'So no dalliances?'

'None sir. Honestly.'

'I take it then, Palmer, that your relationship with Valerie Johnson took place elsewhere. In that case where. We will check.'

Palmer sighed. 'The Bridge House Hotel in Malton and Heath Mount Hotel in Pickering. Valerie can confirm the dates. She did the booking.'

'Thank you. It's so much easier when you don't lie.'

'I'm sorry.'

DI Vellander nodded and turned to DS MacFarlane. 'The envelope.'

DS MacFarlane tipped the necklace onto the table. 'Sergeant, this is the butterfly necklace found by Pc Gardiner in the bush at the bottom of the sports field. You have never seen it before?

'Never. I've heard about it but I have never seen it.'

'A photograph of this necklace was circulated nationwide via Police Reports and the Police Gazette. Enquiries requested at all possible outlets. Two days ago I received a call from a Constable Dale in Northallerton. He had made enquiries at several premises including The Jewellery Box. A fancy goods come jewellers in Northallerton High Street. Mr Goodison, the owner, recognised the design. These are unique and made especially for them by a local artisan. They are not sold anywhere else. There is a reference number stamped on the back. In this case perhaps you would care to read it out.'

A very unhappy looking Sergeant Palmer turned the necklace over. DS MacFarlane pointed to the butterfly in question.

'B6472/7,' he read.

'Thank you. Yesterday I drove to Northallerton with the necklace and a photo ID folder of twelve members of the Pannal Ash training team. The eleven sergeants plus one inspector.' The DS took a blue manilla folder from the desk and opened it. Inside were twelve numbered but anonymous photographs of uniformed police officers. Mr Goodison identified you as the purchaser of this necklace and provided a copy of the bill.' He passed it over. 'You will see it refers to one butterfly necklace Ref: B6472/7. Price £3.10/-. It was paid for in cash.'

'There must be a mistake.'

'Oh, there is Sergeant. One point you are not aware of. Mr Goodison is a special constable and recognised the badge of the International Police Association you sport on your jacket. It stuck. Now will you reconsider your earlier comments about your possession of the necklace?'

'No, it's not true.'

'Very well. You asked a few minutes ago how we knew your blood group. Do you remember?'

'Yes.'

'You are a secretor. Which means that your blood group can be ascertained from body fluids other than blood. In your case from the semen gathered from Julie Slater during the post mortem examination. There is no mistake.'

Palmer sat there looking devastated.

'Sergeant. You stated that you were not the sergeant seen by Pc Blake engaged in a salacious encounter with Julie Slater or in fact with any other member of the civilian staff at Pannal. Do you remember?'

'I do sir. It wasn't me.'

'In that case, Sergeant can you explain how, following my conversation with Pc Blake, an officer from HQ Fingerprints retrieved your full left hand print from locker fourteen in the corridor and your full right hand print from locker sixteen, both at shoulder height. Just as Pc Blake described.

There was no reply.

'Palmer, I do not believe you. I believe that you had a salacious encounter with Julie Slater in the corridor as described by PC Blake. You met with Julie Slater at some point you where had met before and had sexual intercourse after which she told you she was pregnant. As a result of what followed you strangled her and later deposited her body on the periphery of the playing field where Pc Bradbury and Pc Blake found it. Where did you keep the body in the interim? And where are her clothes?

'I've told you; I didn't kill Julie. There was no body for me to hide.

DS MacFarlane flicked his head inviting me to stand by him.

'A lot of detectives would give their eye-teeth to be able to do this. You arrested him and the DI thinks you should charge him,' he grinned. 'I agreed, reluctantly. This is self-carbonating paper. Have you got a ballpoint pen.' I had. 'Read the name. The caution and charge. As it's written.

'Donald Palmer,' the DI said. 'Stand please.'

He looked an old man as he stood.

This I had not anticipated. My heart was thumping.

'Donald Palmer,' I said. 'Do you wish to say anything? You are not obliged to say anything unless you wish to do so but whatever you say will be taken down in writing and may be given in evidence.

You are charged that you did murder Julie Slater contrary to Common Law.

Palmer slumped onto his chair and said nothing.

I signed the form and entered 'No comment' in the response box.

Palmer refused to sign.

The interview room door closed behind Palmer. DI Vellander sighed, turned towards me and smiled. 'Ok?'

'Yes sir. That took me by surprise, but thank you.'

'Any observations?'

'Palmer must have been having eggs, bearing in mind that Evans and Allen were hanged last month.'

'Probably not. Remember that Palmer was an instructor.'

I thought for a moment. 'Ah. The automatic death penalty was removed by the Homicide Act of 1957. This was not one of the exceptions that would have meant that he could have been hanged.'

'Good. And the way that it's going we'll probably see the abolition in the not too distant future. What about the interview?'

'The way he kept denying everything, sir?'

'Exactly. Once that happens, for whatever reason and you have irrefutable evidence to contradict his version he's on thin ice. And when can you re-question a prisoner who had been charged?'

This was easier. 'to minimise harm or loss to any person or to the public or to clarify something previously asked.'

'Which means?'

'You can't re-question if you mean to introduce new evidence.'

'Well done. Get it right first time. There may not be a second.'

Fifty-Nine

Tomorrow was the final exam. Instead, John Bradbury and I would be giving evidence at the full inquest in regard to the death of Julie Slater.

But that was tomorrow. This was now. The notice suspended from the doorhandle read:

Silence
Examination in Progress

6.00pm. We stood outside the Instructor's office. My butterflies and I knocked. It was opened by Sergeant Faulkner. He smiled, stepped to one side and waved us in. 'The condemned men ate a hearty meal?'

'Yes, Sergeant,' We said together. The door closed behind us. The instructor's desk in front laid out with the question papers face down and work papers to one side. I sat.

'Name rank and number at the top of each sheet. Your time starts when you turn the question paper over. Good luck.'

I took a deep breath. John simply turned the paper over.

I put my pen down and raised my hand.'

'Finished?'

'Yes, Sergeant,' I said. John looked up and frowned. How much more he had to do I had no idea.

'You still have fifteen minutes left if you want to check again, Blake.'

'No, it's all right, Sergeant.'

'Very well. You can either leave or wait for Bradbury.'

''I'll wait.'

'Very well, sit by the window. Bradbury, you have thirteen minutes.'

John nodded and returned to the paper. From the look of it he was on his final question.

'All right gentlemen, you will find out on Friday. Until then?'

'Yes, Sergeant. We know nothing.'

9.30am. Chief Inspector Reynolds collected us from the library. 'Don't ask how you did in the exam, either of you. You will find out tomorrow.'

'Yes, sir.'

Harrogate Coroner's Court and once again the lugubrious Mr Waterton was in charge. It was a simple exercise of the Coroner going through the statements and asking questions. The jury's verdict – unlawful killing.

That was that.

Sixty

The formal passing out parade concluded without a hitch. Families and guests duly entertained.

I'd secured permission for Lucy and her mother to attend in addition to everyone else. We were now seated in the Hall waiting for the closing ceremony to start. The atmosphere was electric.

Our new Matron, a retired nursing sister with a no nonsense attitude was at the rear.

From the height of the podium the Commandant scanned his audience of students and families alike. After 45 years as a police officer he was retiring. That's some service.

First, the presentation of certificates. First aid – which everyone had obtained. Followed by the various grades of life saving qualifications, including one of Instructor. Nothing was missed out. I even received one for being Captain of the rugby team.

All the certificates handed out the room settled. 'I hope everyone has warm hands,' The Commandant smiled waiting for the laughter to fade. 'Ladies and gentlemen. At this point in the proceedings I would be getting ready to announce the officer who had come top of the course. However, in view of recent events, today's Review Officer, Mr Raymond Barton, Chief Constable of the West Riding Police, has asked if he might have a few minutes of your time. Mr Barton?'

To polite applause the chief constable took centre stage. He paused, looked around and smiled. 'They say that when policemen look younger, you are getting older. I'm beginning to feel very old.' He paused. The laughter subsided. 'It's always an honour to be invited back for the passing out parade, and, from what we have seen on the drill square, they are smart, agile and not without courage. As families I would ask you to compare what they were like just a few short weeks ago. This next point is specifically for the mothers amongst you. I am reliably informed by Sergeant Faulkner; they can now make their own beds. Fold and tidy their own clothes. Sweep the floor and press their own uniforms.' Another pause for laughter.

'We have seen their achievements celebrated by the number of certificates that have been awarded. And, they have been well earned. We don't give them out like Green Shield stamps just for being here. The public expect a great deal from the young men who leave these walls. But it is more than that. There is much more to being a police officer than being smart and knowledgeable. It is something that cannot be taught. Something inherent.' He paused and scanned us, then continued slowly. 'That is courage, both physical, and, moral.

Ladies and gentlemen, one of the great strengths of the British police service is that we come from the panoply of society. We no longer have chief constables appointed because they are ex-army officers and used to command. We bring with us all our strengths, and, all our weaknesses. The good, the bad and the downright ugly. The system operates on trust. We, as police offices trust that people will behave themselves and that that we can get home safely to our loved ones and enjoy our days off. Whilst you, the public, trust that we will respond to whatever threat presents itself. No-matter-what.

On the day that they join, every police officer swears an oath of allegiance. Not to any organisation. Not to a politician. But to the sovereign. We protect the Queen's Peace from whatever form a threat may take. And you never know just what is round the next corner or, behind the next door. That responsibility on the shoulders of these young men is onerous indeed. And,' he looked at the assembled officers, 'it matters not one jot how much service you have – you carry the uniform.

Just a few short weeks ago a series of events arose highlighting the worst that people have to offer. However, they do not detract from the reputation of this fine establishment. More importantly, how decisive action by two of the young men in this hall dealt with a young couple who had been assaulted. Unfortunately the young man died of his injuries. A colleague with a severe head injury, and, in a separate but simultaneous event, secured the arrest of a serving police officer who was responsible for the worst betrayal of the public's trust that I have encountered in many years.

Now,' he smiled as he continued. 'As they know they are always reprimanded should they step out of line. However, it is only fair that they should be commended if that is appropriate. I am going to call the names of the two officers in alphabetical order. If they will come onto the stage ... Constable 547 Blake and Constable 2134 Bradbury.'

John and I were sitting six chairs apart. We glanced at each other, eyes wide and exhaled. Sergeant Faulkner was there in seconds. 'Come on gentlemen take the praise. It might never happen again. Leave your certificates and take your helmets.'

'Sarge,' we both acknowledged, and stood as the applause began.

'At ease,' the Chief said. 'Relax. Take your helmets off ... That was outstanding, the pair of you. Well done.' The chief looked at me and smiled. 'Your initial action in the Valley Gardens in moving the young lady to safety, and, both your actions in applying cardio-pulmonary resuscitation in an attempt to preserve the life of the young man were exemplary. The fact that you did not succeed is irrelevant. You were present. You took responsibility and continued until the arrival of an ambulance crew.

Now, I understand that from your point of view, Blake, this latter incident started when you overslept.'

He had read the file or a comprehensive report, wanted to know everything. My first sighting in the corridor. Our finding Julie Slater's body. The necklace and details of the evening in question. Eventually.

'I think we've taken up enough of the Commandant's time.' He paused whilst we put our helmets on and shook hands with us in turn, handing us each framed commendations. They would be entered on our personnel records. We stood back and saluted. 'Oh, before you go. I have been informed that the Director of Public Prosecutions is quite happy, on the balance of your evidence, that there should be no difficulty in securing a conviction. So, you may get a day out at the Assize, both of you. It will be good experience. And, Blake, that other matter will receive due consideration in the fullness of time.'

Whilst the Chief and the Commandant were changing places there were plenty who were trying to cop a look at the Certificate.

The legends on mine were simple:

- *For exemplary action in attempting*

To save the life of an assault victim

- *For outstanding policemanship in*

Arresting a murder suspect

Sixty-One

The Commandant was once more centre stage. 'Ladies and gentlemen.' The chatter ceased. He cast his eyes round taking in all the family and friends. 'I have to state, the circumstances that gave rise to this presentation are few and far between. It is always gratifying to see excellent work duly rewarded. However, I do not intend to allow what happened to tarnish the memory of today. In my tenure as Commandant at Pannal Ash I have overseen 120 courses, in excess of 18,000 trainee officers passing through the centre.

Our job, to take from the rough clay and mould it into something resembling a police officer. The fine tuning to be completed in the field. Knocking the corners off, so to speak.' There was a slight pause as a ripple of applause crossed the auditorium. 'For me, this is a double valediction. It is not only my last course as Commandant of this fine establishment, but also my last day as a Police Officer,' he raised his hand, the applause died. 'I have to say that this course has been academically one of the better courses that it has been my privilege to run. I'm not saying where in the hierarchy it sits, just that it is one of the better courses,' he paused, the laughter subsided. 'The police service is a door that is open to everyone. It is however not a door through which everyone should pass. Not everyone stayed the course. That is not intended as a criticism of those who left; not everyone is suited to the police as a career. Make no mistake, gentlemen,' he paused and scanned our faces, 'it will not be a bed of roses.

Maurice Proctor, the retired police officer turned crime writer from Halifax, whom some of you will be familiar with wrote: The police force is like a body. The eyes are on the beat. The nose is in C.I.D. and, the bottom is in the Superintendent's chair,' he smiled and held up his hand again quietening the laughter and the applause. 'You gentlemen stayed the course. The real work begins next week once you have been thrust upon an unsuspecting public.' He raised his voice a notch. 'And let me assure you, confirming what Mr Barton said not many minutes ago, they will not care whether you have five minutes on the job or fifteen years, it is to *you* they will turn, or run away from. Some of you will be happy to spend your days on uniform patrol as the eyes on the beat, some road traffic or perhaps you have aspirations to join C.I.D. and develop your own nose. Or perhaps even one of the many specialised branches that we have nowadays. Exciting times lie ahead for all of you. Some of you will seek advancement. There may even be those amongst you who are carrying the proverbial Field Marshall's baton in your knapsack. Time will tell.

So far this afternoon you have seen numerous presentations made to the students who are about to leave us: first aid, lifesaving and sport. Now we come to the main event. Who has actually come top of the course, who will walk away with the P.M.A.S. Book Prize?'

'My final task ladies and gentlemen, and it is a task that I have looked forward to every month for the past ten years, but, on this occasion with a mixture of pleasure tinged with sadness, is to present the P.M.A.S. book prize to the student who had achieved the highest marks throughout the course. Under normal circumstances we have a clear winner. This course is different ... At the beginning of this week we had three students who were clear of the pack.' There was a bustle between the students as to who the winner might be. 'Those students were separated by just four marks. Those same students are the first three in the final exam.' He was enjoying this and paused to let the information sink in. 'It has been nip and tuck throughout. We do not have a tie for first place, we have a clear winner.' You could feel the tension building up. It could be me, John Masters from Sheffield City, or Graham Webb from Lincoln. 'However, we do have a tie for second place. By a single mark.' The tension was getting ridiculous and the Old Man was enjoying every second. 'We have a student who today has been on this podium more than I have. Awards for first aid, lifesaving and not least as Captain of the rug...'

I cringed as I heard the combined voices of Frankie, Jenny, Anne and Lucy shriek. 'He's done it!' and jump into the air as the place descended into laughter and applause in equal measure. I stood along with everyone else to see them sit down with their faces buried in their hands as everyone around them applauded, including Mum, Joe, Clive and Liz. I got slaps on the back from those within reach. The Old Man just laughed. It took almost a minute before everyone was seated again. 'I can see that someone has some fervent, and from where I'm standing, attractive supporters,' he added to more laughter and looked me straight in the eye. 'Where was I? Oh, and ladies,' he said directing his smile at the girls. 'That is permitted.' He paused again whilst the laughter subsided. The pressure was now off; I had come top by one mark! 'As I was saying,' the Old Man continued, 'and not least as Captain of the rugby team. The P.M.A.S. book prize for this course is awarded, as if we didn't know, to PC547 Brian Blake, well done Blake.'

This time there were no shrieks. A round of applause as I climbed the stairs for the last time and shook the Commandant's outstretched hand, 'Well done, Blake, a truly excellent result. I take it you'll be interested in C.I.D. as your father was?'

'Yes sir. That's what I'm aiming for.'

'Well, that particular door is open to those who earn it. The choice is yours and you've got a good start.' he smiled again. 'And before I forget I'd better give you this.' He handed over the Book Prize; as usual a Chambers dictionary. A weighty tome. Not expensive, but an acknowledgment of what I had achieved.

There was just one thing left to do. The drill instructor, Sergeant Faulkner, former drill instructor at the Guard's depot at Pirbright Barracks silenced everyone in his usual manner and ordered us all out onto the square in front of the Commandant's office. All we had to do was to be marched round to the rear of the building and formally dismissed.

As always, after each such event, light refreshments in the form of tea or coffee and cakes were provided in the dining room for those who didn't want to escape too quickly. Farewells, temporary and permanent were made. Married and single casting envious eyes at the girls who had taken possession of my commendations. I think they realised that Lucy was out of bounds. 'You should try living with these in front of you when you need a shave in a morning,' I called to John Masters, much to the amusement of the girls.

'Poor you,' said a doleful and playful Frankie as she patted my cheek, much to Lucy's amusement. 'So badly done to. It must be so difficult to have three admiring sisters to pander to your every whim.'

'Ha, ha,' I replied. The girls laughed again.

I took the opportunity to introduce John Bradbury and his wife, Christine, to everyone. He would be only a few miles away at Brighouse. Two-way visiting was on the cards.

The Old Man appeared shortly before we left, wished me well and told me that he expected great things. He would keep a close eye on my career and shook my hand again.

It was time to leave.

THE END

Nemesis

One

The trials, tribulations and success of my training were behind me. On the horizon and getting closer were the ensuing criminal proceedings. In the meantime, armed with my limited knowledge and experience I had to learn my trade as a police officer.

I took formal occupation of my Mirfield abode seven miles from Westleigh. A ground floor one-bedroomed flat. Rented and furnished courtesy of Joe. All I was waiting for was Lucy. The all-clear from the doctor and the insurance money from the accident she was now the proud owner of a new Benly.

I heard it well before it came into sight. With the throttle wound open it could produce an ear-splitting 10,500rpm and 15hp. It was a great bike.

After overnight rain the roads were drying. A weak sun attempting to make itself known. Standing on the footpath, helmet in hand, she stopped beside me. Her grin visible through the visor. Engine off. Bike on stand. She removed her helmet and threw her arms round my neck kissing me as hard as she could. The smell of her perfume, the patchouli and her skin were a heady mix. It was almost as if she were trying to leave an indelible impression – *This one is taken, hands off.* The moment accompanied by a fanfare from a couple of passing vans. An elderly lady added her contribution. 'Young people these days. Such wanton behaviour. No self-control. I don't know what parents are coming to.' To which Lucy responded in true Lucy style, 'You're only jealous.'

'Good morning,' I smiled. 'It's nice to see you too.'

'I've had to wait almost a week for that,' she said. 'I called your Mum and said we would be late. I want to see the flat. And, I've brought you a flat-warming present.'

'Come on then,' I said. She fished a ribbon wrapped parcel from the pannier and followed.

She had an appraising eye. 'This is nice,' she said in all seriousness. 'Is it carved in stone or am I allowed to make changes?'

I had to laugh. 'You mean you wouldn't anyway?'

There was an answering grin and few nods.

'Change what you like but go easy on the girly stuff.'

'Give me a bit of credit,' she said and wandered across to look in the bathroom, kitchen, and bedroom.

Here's your prezzie,' she handed me the parcel.

I slid the ribbons off, unwrapped it and smiled. 'Flat warming present? You meant bed-warming.'

There was an answering smile as she unzipped her jacket. 'Better pull the curtains.'

Two

Monday 5.30pm. I presented myself at the police station for my first shift as a police officer: Half nights: 6 – 2. Exhilarated and ready for the off. After the briefing I left the station in company with PC 'Jim' Tyndall. 'Just treat it like a training exercise, like those you did at Pannal, Brian,' he said. 'Keep it simple. Don't worry about comments of finding something useful to do instead of persecuting motorists. Most of the silly bastards never check their bloody cars anyway.' Two minutes later a 'cyclops' as Jim called them appeared. Just as Jim said. Keep it simple.

That was my first offence. If the driver had checked his car it wouldn't have happened.

It's as simple as that, kid,' he said. 'Think of it as a road safety lesson, teach 'em to think.'

There were a couple more minor offences before mealtime, or snap, as Jim called it. Return to the nick for sandwiches and a cuppa, accompanied by numerous questions. Oh boy. We took our meal at 10pm. With the 2-10 crew and Sergeants Meadowcroft and McGill there were ten grinning coppers in the office. On the rest room table was an open copy of the latest issue of the Police Review. I had my own copy at the flat. I knew what was coming.

Sergeant Meadowcroft, a sixteen year veteran, five ten, thinning dark hair and stocky, pointed to a column on the right-hand page: Those who had come top on the latest courses. 'I take it there was only one 547 Blake on that course?'

'Yes, sergeant,' I said.

'Well done,' there was a series of echoes.

The sergeant turned the page back. 'And this?'

He pointed to an article about Sergeant Palmer. 'Well?'

'Somebody put the kettle on and get Brian a cuppa, he'll be dying of thirst,' said Jim.

'Guilty, Sergeant,' my grin matched his. I almost disappeared under a welter of back-slaps.

'Locking a Sergeant up? That's a wet dream,' offered a north-eastern accent. Followed by howls of laughter.

'All right, Stan ... Now then young man,' said Sergeant Meadowcroft. 'The unexpurgated account, if you please.'

It didn't take long and I managed to start eating my sandwiches and swallow some tea. There were plenty of questions. A high percentage regarding whether I'd caught Sergeant Palmer and the Matron at it. And, had I clocked Matron's tits or anything else. Eventually, with a warning from both sergeants not to spill the beans to the Westleigh Chronicle the late turn crew departed. With me now working on their patch they were sure to try it on.

There were raised eyebrows when I asked if I should type the files before returning to patrol. Even more when I started typing. I'd finished in less than twenty minutes, all three files.

'Bloody Hell. You'll be handy typing like that, Brian,' offered Stan, the man with dreams of arresting a sergeant: big, raw-boned and happy-go-lucky from Sunderland. The detached beat officer from Midstones.

The voice of Sergeant Meadowcroft cut across the conversation, 'No he won't, you'll do your own files, Stan. If you start submitting files as neat as that I'll know, all right?' Stan grinned and nodded.

'Blake,' Sergeant Meadowcroft said. 'Don't let this load of idlers put on you, let them do their own files. Now, it's time you were out.'

Nothing had been mentioned about the incident at the Spartan's race track.

A steady walk into the town centre, Jim asking questions about where I'd learnt to type and why. I told him about university which he followed by an almost startled, 'And you've joined the bloody police?'

Without mentioning Dad, that would keep, I told him it was something that I'd wanted to do since childhood. Jim still thought I was mad.

The memories of that night drove me. Not just because I wanted to be a detective sergeant but I was fifty percent him. The more I achieved the more I was taking him with me.

'Every night we check vulnerable property, especially the rear;' Jim emphasised. 'You never know what you might find.' Across from the Post Office, in Lowside, there is a narrow covered passageway that Jim told me led to a cobbled delivery yard for the local shops. Vehicular access was direct from Bradford Road. The sound of voices and someone walking on broken glass met us half way. My heart rate picked up. Jim grabbed my tunic sleeve, put his finger to his lips and eased himself to the front. The yard was small, about twenty yards by thirty and illuminated, for want of a better word, by an ancient guttering gas lamp. There was enough light to see one lad struggling to get through a broken window without injuring himself on the glass still in the frame. Another youth walking backwards and forwards a yard or so away. 'Come on, bloody hurry up before the coppers find us,' he hissed at the other.

I'd slipped my handcuffs out of my pocket as we entered the yard. The one who was walking about looked up. 'Bloody Hell, run.' he shouted. Before he had chance to move more than a couple of yards I'd grabbed him and handcuffed him round the gas lamp. He was too shocked to react. I set off after the other. Jim was built more for comfort than speed. A trail of sweets spilling from the thief's coat pocket showed the way. I caught him by the bus station about a hundred yards down the road and marched him back through cheering pedestrians. Jim was sitting on a dustbin in tears of laughter. 'Welcome to Westleigh, Brian,' he said, wiping his eyes. My first prisoner protested volubly and glared at him, 'We've done nowt lerrus out.'

'Let me introduce the brothers Smith. That really is their name. The one keeping the lamp post company is Damian, and the one you've got hold of is Christopher.' I cautioned both of them and told them they were under arrest for shop breaking.

At the station Jim was still laughing, 'You've never seen owt like it Sarge,' he said, and shook his head. 'Brian was like a whippet. He 'ad Damian cuffed before I 'ad chance to breathe. Scared these two witless.'

Carl Beatty, the office PC, called the keyholder for *The Little Sweet Shop*. I presented my evidence to Sergeant McGill. 'And you handcuffed him round that gas lamp?' he queried, a broad smile across his face.

'Yes Sergeant,' I replied. 'Was that wrong?'

The Sergeant nodded. 'Different, Blake,' he said. 'Just different, but not wrong. Well done, it's a good arrest, these two are a nuisance.

I searched them both. Damian Smith had his pockets full of sweets. Twenty packets of cigarettes stuffed inside his shirt. Christopher Smith, the elder of the two, had a dozen packets of rolling tobacco, a box of bars of Cadbury's milk chocolate, £5.9/- in loose change inside his coat and, a screwdriver and a few loose sweets in his coat pocket. The remainder were scattered down Bradford Road.

Detention sheets completed. Prisoners in the cells. C.I.D. would interview them in the morning. A message was passed to Stan to inform the parents.

Whilst I was typing Jim was spreading the news amongst the night shift. Sergeant McGill left a short report for the information of Inspector Jeavons. Not exactly a break in at the Bank of England, but it had been a great first shift, just as I'd hoped.

Three

Thursday afternoon I called the Secretary to the Westleigh Rugby Club receiving an invite for the following Tuesday training session. So far so good. I missed the game. It would be good to get back on the field. According to the local rag I found in the office they were a good team. I might or might not get a game but it would be good to get back in action.

The evening similar to Wednesday, three minor traffic offences and a warning to a group of rowdy youths in the market place. After meal it was dead - it poured down. The only people enjoying the weather were us.

It might have been Friday Night is Music Night on the radio, but in Westleigh it was pay day and we were short staffed.

After meal I patrolled with Sergeant Meadowcroft. There were a few noisy groups who quietened down when we appeared. We were in Albion Street walking towards the Town Hall when we heard the shouting.

'Come on little chickens. Come to daddy. Come and be sliced.' It might have been funny had it not been for the broken bottle the man was waving about. 'Come on little ... Oh look, two big black turkeys just waiting to be sliced. Come on little turkeys. Come to daddy.'

'Put the bottle down, Fred. Before someone gets hurt.'

'Get back in your hutch Meadowcroft,' Fred replied waving the bottle in our direction. 'It's carving time.'

'Can I Sarge?'

'Don't get hurt, Blake.'

'I won't.' I began to walk towards the bottle waver.

'Look, the little turkey wants to be sliced.' He thrust the bottle towards me. I knocked his hand to one side and applied a chokehold. Took the bottle and cuffed him.

The sergeant gasped. 'Where on earth did you learn that? It wasn't at Pannal.'

'No Sarge,' I grinned. 'I'm a martial arts instructor.'

Malcolm Swinderby, the office PC on night duty, insisted he was placed in the cell furthest from the office so the sound of him banging on the door wasn't too loud. I typed my statement of arrest. He would be charged and bailed to court.

Saturday was different. I was on half-nights and back in company with Jim Tyndall. We were turned out early from the office, even before the briefing, to deal with a shoplifter at the local Buy Smart supermarket, recently opened in Broadway. Attracting the wrong type of customer.

Mike Preston the deputy manager greeted us. In his office, overwatched by a member of staff was a woman wearing a beige gaberdine raincoat and black shoes. She was holding onto a pushchair containing a baby that looked and smelled as if it needed a bath and a change.

'I was in my office looking through the window,' said Mr Preston. 'I observed this lady take these,' he indicated seven tins of baked beans on his desk. 'She looked around and slid them into the pushchair behind the baby. At the till she paid for these,' he indicated two further tins of baked beans. 'Tendering a £1 note. She made no attempt to pay for the seven tins of beans and left the store where I stopped her, told her what I had seen. She denied it and I called you.'

Jim nodded at me. 'Is what the manager said, true?' I said.

The woman nodded. 'Yes,' she said.

'I can add that she was given enough change from the purchase of the two tins of beans to pay for those she stole.'

I have to admit that I had felt sorry for her but she did have enough money to pay for them.

I checked with the divisional collator. Wendy Green, aged 27, had three previous convictions for shoplifting.

Stan did an address check. It was correct. However, her children were at home. The baby was her neighbour's. She was trying it on thinking that with a small baby she could get away with it.

We made our 8pm point at the telephone kiosk close to the fire station. We were told to come in and take an early meal, there'd been intelligence there was going to be some trouble between a couple of local gangs.

The first report was from a road traffic car. A known member of one of the gangs and three others in an old Comer van registered number PCX 74 had just driven past Oakenshaw church. They would be with us in less than five minutes. Leaving a couple of Special Constables to keep an eye on the town centre, Inspector Jeavons split what was left into two groups, one under his command and the other Sergeant Meadowcroft's.

The plan was simple. Most gang members have a sheep mentality and follow where others lead. Their views were that the best place to hide a tree was in a wood. The best place to be in a ruckus was in a middle of a large crowd.

'Blake,' said Sergeant Meadowcroft. 'Your job is to obtain full details of the drivers and issue an ticket to produce his documents. Check the registered number against the excise licence and report for any offences. If the excise licence has any alterations or is displayed on the wrong vehicle the driver will be arrested.'

'Yes Sergeant.'

We stopped every car as they approached Westleigh. I had two prisoners for theft of excise licences and three reports for no excise licence, plus forms issued to produce driving documents. Four passengers had to walk home.

Of the eight cars where there were no apparent offences the occupants were advised that if they entered the town and exited their vehicles they would be arrested and charged with the offence of 'conspiracy to cause affray'. There were one or two who complained that it was a free country and that they had the right to drive into Westleigh.

They were given the choice. Take the advice or appear before the Magistrates on Monday morning. In the end no-one drove into town. There were only the two Specials plus the six of us, and that included the Inspector and the Sergeant. That would have been an interesting evening.

I spent the remainder of the shift with Jim interviewing my prisoners. Sorting out the offences. Entering the details in the Offence Book and typing. I got off duty at 3.30am.

Four

2-10 Sunday was generally a quiet shift. At three o'clock Sergeant Meadowcroft picked me up from my point. There had been a report that Mrs Rose Baxter, aged 86, living on the Turnton Estate hadn't been seen since Friday. Her house curtains were still drawn. The chances were that she had died. Her son couldn't get in because the door was bolted. A small group of neighbours were discussing how the old lady would be missed. What sort of funeral she would have? Would it be a decent ham tea? They could have waited until we knew whether or not the old lady had died. Using the Sergeant's penknife, we managed to slide the window catch and open the living room window. Being the youngest and the most agile I was volunteered to climb through and unlock the door. Son Eric was reticent about investigating and finding her dead.

I was just about to unbolt the door when I spotted a prone bare leg through the kitchen door. An elderly lady in nightdress and dressing gown, right slipper missing. An injury to the left temple. She was still warm to the touch No reaction to light when I raised her eyelid but no carotid pulse. Mine was increasing.

The sound of someone walking in the first floor bedroom.

I motioned to Sergeant Meadowcroft and whispered what I found.

'Are you all right?'

'I'm fine, Sarge.'

'Upstairs. I'll follow.'

Half way up the staircase I stepped on a loose board. Sergeant Meadowcroft was close behind.

The footsteps stopped. I launched myself upstairs shouting. 'This is the police stay exactly where you are.'

I headed for the rear bedroom. The window was open. A young male was climbing out. 'Stay still,' I shouted and managed to grab the right sleeve of his anorak. He wriggled like hell to try and slide out of it and was succeeding. 'Sarge, I've got the sleeve of his anorak. Can you get round the back.'

'Will do.' Sergeant Meadowcroft turned and ran down stairs. Seconds later I heard the back door open.

I managed to grasp his shirt collar with my other hand as he tried to jump. He was in danger of hanging himself. Sergeant Meadowcroft appeared. 'Well done, Blake. You can let Taylor go now. I've got him.'

Andrew Taylor, 25 years, five six, had been out of prison for two weeks having served eighteen months of a two year sentence for factory breaking. I cautioned him. I'm arresting you for ...' and looked at Sergeant Meadowcroft.

'Suspicion of causing GBH.'

'I'm arresting you on suspicion of causing grievous bodily harm to Rose Baxter.'

'I didn't do it.' He protested. 'She were dead when I got in. I could see her through the kitchen window. Honest.'

'Blake, you will accompany the body to the mortuary. Some forces, like Leeds City, have dedicated coroner's officers. We don't. We are all coroner's officers. In view of the circumstances, until we know the result of the PM, this is a murder enquiry.' He went to the phone box fifty yards away. Within minutes a road traffic car arrived to act as a communications vehicle. Stan turned up to take over when I left.

Taylor was carted off to the station by a second traffic car.

Detective Constable Fred Smith arrived. I put him in the picture as to what I had observed and what Taylor had said.

He had a quick look at the body. Stood. 'Come on,' he motioned with his head. 'Let's have a look.'

Standing on tip toe you could see Rose Baxter, just not all of her.

'Could Taylor see her as he claimed?' said Fred.

'He's a climber so it's possible.'

'Agreed. Is that significant?'

'Perhaps. It doesn't exonerate him though. It depends on the timing. When did he gain access? When did the injury occur?'

'So far so good. You're doing well.'

Any further discussion kicked into touch by the arrival of Doctor O'Keefe, the Divisional Police surgeon. He felt for the carotid pulse and looked up from his crouch. 'Death certified at,' he checked his watch. '3.45pm. The head wound looks to have been caused when she fell against the table here,' he said pointing. There was congealing blood and hair adhering to the wood. 'The post mortem will answer the question as to why she fell. I'm afraid that is up to you gentlemen. She is flaccid and warm and rigor mortis has not yet begun. I estimate that death occurred ...'

'Less than two hours ago,' I said under my breath.

Doctor O'Keefe stopped and looked at me . 'What did you say?'

'I was just musing, Doctor,' I said.

'You said less than two hours ago, Pc?'

'Blake, Doctor.'

'How did you know that? Have you a medical qualification?'

I had to smile. And, as I explained the good Doctor did as well. 'I have a degree in exercise physiology, Doctor, with an added module of anatomy. The one covering post mortems.'

'Excellent. And, yes, I estimate within the last two hours.'

'But that is not necessarily when the injury was caused.'

'No, Mr Smith it isn't. The pathologist should be able to help you there,' he stood. 'If there is nothing else gentlemen.' He turned to leave. 'I shall follow your career with interest, Pc Blake. Good day.'

'So,' Fred said and turned to me and smiled. The doctor closed the door. 'Let's see what you're made of, Brian. Scenarios'?'

'Thanks, Fred. Is Taylor violent?'

'Nope. Soft as fluff. Good climber, but no violence.'

'No wonder he was rattled when Sergeant Meadowcroft said to arrest him on suspicion of GBH.'

'That would freak him out.'

'Ok, number one he's telling the truth. She tripped or had some form of catastrophic event: heart attack, stroke or an aneurysm, or maybe he broke in and startled her. Number two, he's an out and out liar and assaulted her in some way.'

'I agree. From what the doctor said death likely occurred between 1.30pm and 3.30pm. we shall have to wait for the PM. But you kept quiet about the additional module, Brian.'

'I've only been out of Pannal a few days, I didn't want people thinking I was bragging.'

'Fair point. Right walk me round the house. Have a looksee.'

It was a very small house, our tour completed as the photographer arrived followed minutes later by the fingerprint officer. Being present whilst Fred told them what he wanted was great. Last to arrive was the undertaker. Leading the hearse Fred stopped at the police station. 'Nip inside Brian, ask Sergeant Meadowcroft for the mortuary keys.'

I thought that a bit strange. However they were in the key safe in the sergeant's office. It was a five minute drive to the Council Yard. The mortuary was in the corner behind the gate backing against the outer wall.

The mortuary could only be described as functional. A couple of dissection slabs. A sink, water heater and not much else.

A tag tied round her right hallux bearing: the date, her name and my details We undressed her, bagged the clothes for her son and covered her with a sheet.

There were bobbies everywhere including Inspector Jeavons and Detective Inspector Greening. Five eight. Receding greying hair. Weather beaten lined face and well jowled.

'This is your first murder, is it lad?' Detective Inspector Greening smiled.

'Not exactly, sir,' said Sergeant Meadowcroft. 'Blake is the one who arrested an instructor at Pannal.'

DI Greening's eyes lit up. 'Are you indeed. So, locking up the likes of Taylor are just run of the mill?'

'I wouldn't put it like that, sir,' I said.

'Nor would I. Whether it's a murder or Taylor taking advantage of the old dear's death, well done.'

'Sergeant, you'll oversee Blake's pocket book and statement?'

'Next on the agenda, sir. The PM, could Blake ...?'

'By all means. Have you witnessed a PM before, Blake.'

'Yes, I have, sir. At university.'

The DI nodded. '10.00am tomorrow. You know where?'

'I accompanied the body to the mortuary, sir.'

'Good,' he turned to leave.

'Before you go, sir,' I said. 'Eric Baxter, Rose Baxter's son, was the one who notified us that his mother hadn't been seen. He only knows that she's dead. He hasn't seen her since ...'

The DI looked thoughtful. 'And you think we should let him view his mother's body before the pathologist gets to work?'

'Yes, sir.'

He was nodding slowly. 'The Westleigh mortuary isn't the most salubrious of places. If he really does want to visit tomorrow morning that's ok, providing he doesn't touch the body. It might be better to wait a little longer until she is in the hands of the undertaker. Sound him out.'

'He is quite timid, sir,' I said. 'I didn't think about that.'

'No problem. Check him out, Sergeant. Play it by ear.'

As I was leaving I spotted Fred Smith in a head-to-head with DI Greening. They glanced my way. 'Was he now?' I heard the DI say. 'One we'll have to watch.'

Eric Baxter decided to wait to see his mother. Probably a good idea.

Circumstances alter cases. I was now working Monday and taking Wednesday off instead.

10.30am Monday. The Home Office Pathologist, Professor Snodgrass's conclusion was that Rose Baxter had died of a ruptured aortic aneurysm and death would have been almost instantaneous.

Taylor was off the hook as far as murder was concerned. I spent the remainder of the day with Fred Smith. Taylor was interviewed. Almost in tears when he received the news. I charged him with house breaking with intent to steal.

Prosecution file completed; a Special Court was convened. In view of his recent release from prison and predilection for other people's property Taylor was remanded in custody to appear at the next Quarter Sessions in Wakefield.

Much to Lucy's chagrin I spent the night at the flat.

Don't miss out!

Visit the website below and you can sign up to receive emails whenever Jon Mason publishes a new book. There's no charge and no obligation.

https://books2read.com/r/B-A-ZRTW-CFVKC

BOOKS 2 READ

Connecting independent readers to independent writers.

Also by Jon Mason

Blake Detective Series
The Blooding of Brian Blake

Watch for more at www.jonmasonbooks.com.

About the Author

JON was born into post WW2 Yorkshire in England. His brother Stuart was born in 1938. His father, demobbed from the RAF where he had been a Dispatch Rider, returned to the tailoring industry. His mother had spent the war years x-raying wheels for battle tanks.

They lived in a small, inner two-bedroomed terrace house. There was no damp-proof course, double glazing, central heating or hot water on tap. The tin bath hung from a nail under the stairs and the lavatory was across the back yard..

Leaving school in 1962 he joined the West Riding Constabulary as a Cadet and as a Constable in 1965. His initial training carried out at No3 District Police Training Centre, Pannal Ash, Harrogate, in the then North Riding of Yorkshire.

Over the next three decades he gained experience across much of what the police service has to offer. 1965-70 on uniform beat patrol. From 1970-75 in the Road Traffic Division as an advanced driver and also where he was firearms trained. From 1975-77 Force Control where he learned his radio and computer skills before being promoted to the Western Area Control Room in January of 1977, Twelve months later he was seconded to the fledgling Computer Development Unit working with Ferranti International in the development of Stage 4 of a resource handling and incident recording system known as Command and Control (Not big Brother) and the setting up of the Communications Training Wing at the West Yorkshire Police training school. December 1983 saw him transferred to an inner city sub-division where he spent the last 10 years of his service as uniform patrol sergeant where he also worked closely with the Air Support Unit, Custody Officer and the last four years as the Station Sergeant.

In May of 1967 Jon and his fiancee married. A marraige which so far has lasted for over 56 years. He insists he has the scars ro prove it. They had two children, tragically Andrew, the elder, died of a heart attack in January 2018 - he was 48. Their daughter is still going strong.

Prior to retiement Jon qualified as a fitness instructor and subsequectly head-hunted to work in a new community based cardiac rehab programme where he had the opportunity to study cardiology at Leeds University Medical School and execise physiology at Carnegie. He also stuied bio-mechanics.

All that knowledge and experience Jon brings to his books.

Read more at www.jonmasonbooks.com.

About the Publisher

Milton Keynes UK
Ingram Content Group UK Ltd.
UKHW011807171023
430795UK00001B/36

9 781916 757059